I0690523

# I Broke the World

## A Rollicking Dystopian Comedy

### Allison McWood

Annelid Press

FIRST EDITION
Cover design and by: Graham Kennedy
ISBN: 978-1-990292-33-0

# A WORD FROM ALLISON:

Proceed with an open mind.

When the world suddenly ended in March 2020, I was inundated with messages from my readers, begging me to write a book about the lockdowns. I replied by saying, *'you know I write comedy, right?'* They persisted that the whole ordeal would make for a fabulous farce. To be honest, I was not okay at that time. Strange as it may sound, I struggled with the notion of the world abruptly shutting down with no notice. I was stunned, traumatized, confused, sad, disturbed, and isolated. I said to my readers, *'can you at least let me get through this first?'* I promised I'd write something as soon as I found out how it would all end.

But it didn't end.

And then it didn't end again.

Instead of ending, the situation continued to get weirder and weirder, so I finally just decided to take the plunge, write the damn thing, and make up my own ending.

I should begin by saying that this book is not about a virus. I am a comedian and in my professional opinion, there is nothing funny about viruses or people suffering from illness. This book is more complex than that, as I explore various human nuances, as well as the notions of empathy and community. This is a story about censorship, cancel culture, political elitism, and the *establishment*. The crisis in the story could be any global crisis, and the glaring question remains, *are political elitists qualified to lead us through a crisis?*

These are the things I laid awake all night pondering while the rest of the world was binge watching *Tiger King*.

Most importantly, I wrote this book because I felt strongly compelled to tell the stories that were not allowed to be told during the global crisis of 2020-2022. For some deranged reason, people who struggled and suffered collateral damage during this time because of public policy were shamed and even threatened into silence. I don't know about you, but as an ultra-sensitive person, I was deeply affected by this. It haunted me. My country is a kind country. When did we stop caring about one another's pain? Every story deserves to be told – even the inconvenient ones that make us uncomfortable. We cannot gain perspective otherwise.

I present to you a satirical farce, (or a farcical satire if you prefer) with nuances of surrealism. Nothing in this book is literal or realistic and will hopefully give you permission to enjoy a cathartic, comedic relief after nearly three years of proverbial Hell. Everything and everyone in the story are fictional. I took a more universal approach, writing politicians for example, who could be recognized as any world leader. After all, every global citizen was faced with the same challenges at the same time. We are all human, we all felt loss, isolation, despair. These are the things that polarized us when they ultimately should have connected us in a universal human experience.

Now for the fun stuff.

Apparently the angrier I am, the more hilarious my writing is. So when I get barking mad, I basically morph into John Cleese. I went through all kinds of wonky emotions during the lockdowns, from shock to grief to despair. But great news, guys! I'm mad now! In fact, I can honestly say I'm so mad that I accidentally wrote a grunge song. So enjoy my rage, everyone! You're in for a real treat!

FOR K

*"They fear love because it creates a world they can't control"*

*George Orwell*

# CHAPTER ONE

Her strawberry blond eyelashes fluttered. Clarity Trout blinked the dreamy delirium from her eyes, pulling herself out of a dark, sinking sleep. A weird feeling suddenly clamped her ribcage, causing a flutter of panic. Out slipped a mousy gasp.

*Am I awake?*

*What a weird dream.*

With her head still sunk into her pillow, Clarity's eyeballs lolled around the room. The concrete walls of her oppressively geometric bedroom intimidated her. The tiny, rectangular window offered little hope – in fact, it seemed to be squinting at her. Judgmentally.

"Fern?" Clarity said scratchily in an early morning octave. "Fern, I had a trippy dream."

With a weary groan, Clarity turned her foggy head to face a potted fern placed meticulously on a mismatched bedside table. She blinked hard, as she was prone to do, bungling on her notable stutter. "Of course, it wasn't real," she said to the plant. "How could it be? How could it... be?"

Another mousy gasp.

Scrambling from her squeaky mattress, fumbling, entwined in her threadbare, floral sheet, Clarity dashed to her rectangular window. Standing on her tippy toes she peered outside. Her eyeballs quivered.

A desolate, deserted street.

Not a single soul.

No one.

Anywhere.

A hauntingly red fug lingered in the sky.

A brownstone husk stood where the theatre used to be.

Outside, a flashing marquee was blinking the word *'NO'* largely and boldly.

The billboard across the street sported the same message. *'NO.'*

Spraypainted across the windows of random, vacated shops, *'NO.'*

Searchlights scoured the streets from seemingly nowhere. Possibly the sky.

An eerie silence loomed thickly in the air like a terrifying margarine.

Except...

*What's that sound?*

The throaty snarl of a... lion.

*Wait, lion?*

From the elusiveness of a dark alley, the indisputable figure of a sleek lion lurked around the corner and stalked the empty street. Each pad of his terrible paws composed the rhythm of a foreboding dirge. His ribs protruded hungrily, undulating through his amber fur with each step. Guttural threats emerged from deep in his throat as he lolled his mighty head back and forth as though patrolling the streets. For a split moment, Clarity thought she saw the ironic predator flash his unforgiving eyes in her direction.

"Fern?" Clarity quavered with a hard blink. "It... it wasn't a dream."

# CHAPTER TWO
## (SEVERAL MONTHS EARLIER)

Clarity burbled her lips as she gaped at her reflection in the mirror. Holding up a rather wholesome, floral frock, still on the hanger, a sinking feeling of self-conscious disappointment overwhelmed her. She looked practically translucent with her alabaster skin and stringy strawberry blond hair dangling limply over her face. Somehow the dress looked more worldly hanging on a rack at the thrift shop. But then, Clarity was not expecting to go anywhere important. She rarely left her compact apartment. The protective, concrete walls of the Brutalist residential tower block kept her safe.

Outside was too *people-y.*

The frock dress would have to do. She wasn't sure the whole Baptist church lady motif was the look she was going for but what other choice did she have? Her closet was lined with a perfectly symmetrical row of identical, white T-shirts. Up until now her only intention was to blend. To not draw attention to herself. But people are supposed to stand out in job interviews, right? Make an impression? Speak to an actual person? Make direct eye contact?

Clarity suddenly felt seasick.

The dress slipped onto Clarity's willowy body quite easily, fitting her like a potato sack. Clarity liked it that way. No need to draw attention to her hips or anything else that might suggest a womanish silhouette. She could not emotionally tolerate the feeling of people looking at her. She could sense people's opinions like a million, stinging tattoo needles pricking every nerve ending in her skin. What if they disapproved of her hair color? Her stutter? Her blinking compulsion? Her bony elbows? Her life choices? What if society *cancelled* her? What would happen to her blog?

Clarity winced as she bunched clumps of frock in her fists. Frumpy. Pathetic. Unprofessional. Why couldn't Daryl De Voort conduct a nice, anonymous phone interview like a normal person? It was too late to go shopping for a pant suit and even if that were a possibility, the situation would end calamitously. Pant suits gave Clarity stress hives. Pant suits and all that pant suits imply. Such attire is meant for women with poise and ultra-short, power haircuts. Not anemic, socially awkward bloggers who ugly cry whenever they have to order a coffee.

"Mmmfff!" Clarity whimpered, clutching her chest as her computer made a startling noise, alerting her of an incoming video call. Her heart gradually reduced tempo when she noticed her father's face on the screen. The jovial face of Torrence Trout, whose cheeks and button nose were perpetually pinkish, despite the lack of windchill or alcohol.

"Da," Clarity stuttered, sliding into an uncomfortable, wooden chair as it screeched across the cement floor.

"You're wearing color," Torrence said, his eyes bulging with wonder.

Clarity blinked hard. "Job interview. Today."

"In person?" Torrence asked, quirking a solemn eyebrow.

Clarity swallowed hard, hiding behind a fringe of wispy hair.

"You didn't tell me about this."

"Didn't want to disappoint you, Da," Clarity said, barely audible. "If things didn't work out. It's big, Da. The interview is with a major news outlet. Ever heard of *Verisimilitude Media?*"

Torrence grimaced.

"I... I suppose you wouldn't," Clarity blinked. "It's very urban. This could be my big breakout. I... I'm not the best at landing interviews and the other three I did were duds. This could be my chance."

Torrence groaned like a deflating helium balloon. "You've got your blog," he droned gingerly. "Why put yourself through..."

"I'm a..." Clarity stuttered with a hard blink. "I'm a journalist, Da. I did college by correspondence."

"Your blog is very good," Torrence nodded slowly and reassuringly. "You don't have to go out there, Clare Bear. You can stay in your cocoon. Or come home to the mushroom farm. This big, creaky house is so empty..."

"My blog is just a bunch of... I just... I write quality control reviews about refrigerators. I..." Clarity stuttered, "I want to write something important. I want to serve a purpose. I..." Clarity whispered confidentially, scoping the room for imaginary moles. "I reckon people think I'm... off."

"Refrid..."

"If you tell me refrigerators are important, I'm going to ralph all over myself on... on this here frock. Then what'll people think?"

Torrence bit his lower lip.

"I.. I'm a grown-up, Da. I have a... a diploma."

"I worry sometimes."

Clarity blinked hard.

"Why did you ever move to the city?"

"To... to be a journalist, Da. I... I want this so bad. Why else would I be torturing myself in this urban nightmare? With all these... all these people everywhere? People give me hives."

"All alone."

"I have a fern."

"You were so happy here on the mushroom farm."

"How are things?" Clarity stammered, trying desperately to change the subject. "On the mushroom farm?"

"Subsisting," Torrence dimpled. "But grateful. I'm particularly proud of the creminis this season. Got a deal with a local pizzeria down the hill. Giuseppe. From Naples, I think. Nice guy. He's gonna' source all his mushrooms locally. Doesn't get more local than us," Torrence chuckled, shaking his head fondly. "It's not the same around here without you though. I miss your ephemeral presence wafting down the stairs every morning, sniffing around for toast."

"I..." Clarity blinked. "I want to be a journalist. More than anything, Da. It's all I ever really wanted to do. I... I can't express... I express myself better in writing. I... need... expression. I want to be... heard."

"Your blog though..."

"The blog is just... just buying me time."

"We have a local newsletter here in the village."

"Da..."

"I just worry, is all."

"Please don't make this harder."

"Such a modest girl with such big goals."

"I need this, Da."

"Try to manage your expectations, okay? If it gets to be too much..."

"Da, I promised Ma."

Torrence whistled a slow exhale.

"Da?"

"You did?"

"All she wanted was for me to be..." Clarity stumbled, blinking hard. "...to be happy. She made me promise I'd give it all I had. Never give up until I made it... big. She knew I could. Even though I'm not always sure."

"S'pose you can't break a promise with your ma."

Clarity closed her eyes and exhaled softly through her nostrils.

"I do believe in you, Clarity."

"Yeah?"

"You've got the talent. It's just..."

Clarity squinted interrogatively at the screen.

"Eye contact and a firm handshake," Torrence advised. "Just as important as talent. Remember that, okay?"

Pearls of sweat formed on Clarity's forehead.

"Oh God..." she whimpered.

***

The hallway was empty. Clarity secretly thanked God for peepholes. She could slip discreetly out of her apartment and avoid human interaction on her way to the elevator. Once outside, she could disintegrate into the throng of people, anonymously walking like currents of fish through the city streets. She didn't realize she was holding her breath until she had a mild dizzy spell. Her face felt hot, and her eyes were stinging and reddening.

*All this for a measly job interview.*

*Dammit, Daryl De Voort.*

*This could have been a phone call.*

The empty hallway smelled like boiling marshmallow root as she brisked-walked towards the elevator, keeping her eyes on the cement floor. The twenty-third floor was perpetually quiet, which influenced Clarity's apartment choice. Apparently, the unit next door was haunted which would discourage any normal person from renting on the twenty-third floor. But Clarity didn't seem to mind. She figured the fewer neighbors she had, the fewer paper bags she would have to breathe into. Her only neighbors were a centenarian across the hall who had lived there since the tower block opened, and a doomsday prophet in apartment 2303 who ranted eschatologically on the street corner, wearing a sandwich sign. He was more concerned with apocalyptic horsemen than he was ghosts.

Taking refuge in the elevator, Clarity blew out the air she had been hoarding in her cheeks. Another perk to living on the twenty-third floor was that the elevator was usually empty by the time it reached the top level. The challenge was going down. Every time she heard the elevator beep as it reached the next floor, a wave of nausea would well up inside her. Nothing was more disturbing than being trapped in a confined space with another human. Small talk made Clarity chafe.

Beep.

One floor down.

Stop.

*Please, no.*

Gripping white-knuckled to the handrail, Clarity watched with recoiling anxiety as the elevator doors opened. She was greeted by a smile which happened to be on the face of Pax MacLeod, an amiable sort dressed with professionalism in an unpretentious suit. Despite there being literally nothing intimidating about Pax, Clarity instantly diverted eye contact and turned into a pickled beet. His genuinely compassionate glow was wasted on her.

*He's looking at me.*

*Why is he looking at me?*

*Do I have a bat in the cave?*

*Jaysus, Clarity. You know this guy.*

*Sort of.*

*You know him from the elevator.*

*And the internet?*

*Politics, maybe?*

*He's too glowy for a politician.*

*Politicians don't smile like that.*

*Seems harmless.*

*Breathe, Clarity.*

True, the man in the elevator was largely unoffensive, even to a train wreck like Clarity Trout. But Clarity knew from prior experience that elevator rides seem eons longer while trying to be invisible. Would she sweat through her ridiculous frock right before her life-altering job interview?

*Don't cry.*

*You'll smudge your mascara.*

*You never wear mascara.*

*Why did I wear mascara?*

*Why?*

"Twenty-third floor?" Pax said as though it was the most natural thing in the world to talk to another person in an elevator.

*Don't barf, don't barf, don't barf, don't barf.*

"Pax," said Pax, extending his hand. His eyes formed into crescents of friendliness.

"Wh..what does that mean?" Clarity stuttered with a hard blink.

"I've seen you in the elevator a few times," Pax explained, "but we haven't formally met."

No response from Clarity.

With lips pursed with concern, Pax shifted gears. "Do you know Norman?" he asked. "He's on the top floor too, isn't he? Norman is fantastic," he continued, smiling and shaking his head fondly. "He stops by my place a couple times a week to see how I'm doing. Sweetest guy. So much verve. Must be good times up on the top floor with Norman around."

Clarity blinked.

Biting his lower lip, Pax continued.

"Level with me," Pax said, jokingly confidential. "Is it true what they say about the unit upstairs being haunted?"

Clarity blinked hard.

"Back home in the Hebrides," Pax continued with a gleam of enthusiasm, "ghosts are kind of a big deal. Almost like they're part of the community. There was this one time in Stornoway…"

Clarity squeezed her eyes shut, hoping if she concentrated hard enough, she could teleport herself somewhere else. A place that lacked Paxes.

"Is everything okay?" Pax asked, cocking his head at Clarity who was now murmuring unintelligibly under her breath. "Are you in distress? Need assistance? Is there someone I should call?"

*Dammit, Clarity.*

*Pull it together.*

*The things he must be thinking.*

*About me.*

*Why can't I control…*

*Why does this have to happen to me EVERY time I'm in an elevator?*

*Maybe if I keep my eyes squeezed shut and focus hard enough, he'll dematerialize.*

Beep.

Ground floor.

*Sigh of relief.*

"See you around," Pax said in a way that did *not* make Clarity want to crawl in a hole and die. "Oh, and here's my..."

Clarity's eyes bulged when Pax pulled a business card out of his pocket and humbly handed it to her.

"You sure you're okay?" Pax asked, tilting his head quizzically.

Clarity nodded, but only in her imagination. In real life she was staring blankly, somewhat like a fainting goat in that brief moment before it buckles into a coma.

*He's clearly not a sociopath, please don't cry.*

*Don't cry, don't cry, don't cry, don't cry...*

*Damn tear ducts.*

"Call if there's anything I can do, okay?" Pax said, trying futilely to make eye contact with Clarity. "I'm around if there's something you need help with. I don't mind. It's kind of my thing."

By the time Clarity opened one eye to scope her surroundings, Pax had already unoffensively slipped out of the elevator like a normal person, waving at someone with a smile the moment he stepped outside.

"That went well," Clarity croaked hoarsely to herself.

# CHAPTER THREE
## (TRISTAN WINNINGS)

The fanfare of herald trumpets served no purpose, but Tristan Winnings requested them upon his arrival. He got the idea from a live performance of *Othello* he attended with an Eastern European supermodel a few years back. The dramatic effect, he decided, was exactly what he envisioned for his first day in office. He graced the floor of the conference room with a theatrical flourish and an artificially white smile. He felt quite sure of himself, although his political inferiors looked at each other bewildered and with quirked eyebrows.

"Tristan," mumbled his advisor, Hector Morosely, as he pulled Tristan aside by the suit sleeve, "stop that, please."

"I think I made an impression," Tristan said, adjusting his tie proudly.

"Mr. Prime Minister," Hector said confidentially, in that special, dry way of his, "can you perhaps not be quite so... *you?* It's bad for your image."

"But I went to Juilliard," Tristan said with a protruding lower lip, genuinely punctured.

"Smashing," Hector said with the same dryness. "But you have literally no political experience. You are going to have to try a little bit harder to be taken seriously."

"I'm trying really hard actually," Tristan pouted.

"Lovely," Hector sighed. "Now, you are about to make your very first media appearance as the Prime Minster of Umbravia."

"I've got this."

"Promise me you won't make jazz hands."

"I can't promise you that."

"Tristan..."

"What are you so worried about?" Tristan laughed, pretentiously flooping away the flaxen locks that were stylishly fringing his face. "I earned the popular vote. Everyone digs me."

"Everyone voted strategically," Hector said with even more dryness in his tone if that was even possible, "to defeat Prime Minister Enthwhistle after his unacceptable remarks which we've all agreed to never repeat. And you being a celebrity..."

"And here I thought you didn't recognize me," Tristan pretentiously jibed.

"It was a matter of voting for *the devil you know.*"

"You are so negative," Tristan said, playfully poking Hector deep in his upper arm. "Everyone loves famous people. That's why we're famous. And to think if my character hadn't been killed off in my soap opera..."

"For the love of... Tristan, try to understand. You are no longer an actor. You are the prime minister of a literal country."

"Not a problem," Tristan said, dimpling like an annoying twit. "There's a kind of theater to politics, no?"

"You are not playing the part of a political leader," Hector said sickly. "This is all actually happening."

"Don't worry, Hector," Tristan said, jiggling his arms in a weird pre-show warmup acting exercise. "I'm method."

"Tristan, do you want to be re-elected or..."

"Here goes nothing," Tristan said, rubbing his hands together and dashing to the platform in front of a room full of perplexed politicians and reporters.

"Oh dear God," Hector said evenly.

Tristan seemed to be able to sniff out every camera in the room, winking, pointing at himself, and making clicking noises with his tongue. Media reporters goggled for a moment before one of them eventually piped up.

"Mr. Prime Minister?" the first tentative reporter interjected.

"That's me!" Tristan said, stopping himself before he mistakenly made jazz hands.

"I'm confused, Sir," the reporter continued. "Aren't you a soap star?"

"Not anymore," Tristan said triumphantly. "I was killed off in Season 16."

"How though?"

"Unfortunate accident involving a sausage truck and military grade explosives," Tristan gleamed obliviously.

"No, I mean *how?*"

"Well," Tristan said, shuffling some papers at the podium. "The executive producer claimed I was high maintenance. But let's just call it... and I use air quotes... *creative differences.*"

Hector Morosely winced.

The reporter shook the confusion from his head. "No," he said. "I mean *how* did you go from being an unemployed actor to a leader of the free world?"

Tristan gaped.

"Mr. Prime Minister?"

Tristan's eyeballs instantly swerved towards Hector Morosely.

*"List your political talking points,"* Hector mouthed silently towards Tristan.

Tristan squinted at Hector's mouth, straining to decipher.

*"Foreign policy,"* Hector mouthed. *"FOREIGN POLICY."*

Still squinting at Hector, Tristan started making the sound of the letter F by biting repeatedly on his lower lip.

*"You're an idiot,"* Hector mouthed.

"I'm an idiot!" Tristan finally said with epiphany into the microphone. But the collective murmur from the crowd made him jolt and slap his hand over his mouth.

"Prime Minister Winnings," another reporter chimed in, "is it fair to say that your fame and above average attractiveness is what garnered votes?"

"No," Tristan said, squinting at the reporter. "No, I don't think that's fair at all."

"No?" the reporter said, writing something down. "So your charisma, money, celebrity, laser blue eyes, firm buttocks and *Malibu Ken* hair did not influence voters in any way?"

"That's insulting," Tristan said, pointing an accusing finger at the reporter. "Not insulting to me because everything you said about me just now is true. But rather insulting to the decent people of this magnificent country. Our citizens are quite intelligent, and they knew exactly how to vote without any promptings from mainstream media. Show some tact. Also, thank you."

"The question is quite simple, Prime Minister Winnings. What are your credentials?"

"I love this country," Tristan said solemnly, pounding his chest with a fervent fist. "And I love my people. I love every single one of you equally and for different reasons."

"What else?"

"I kind of feel like you guys are ganging up on me here," Tristan chortled nervously.

"I'm just trying to get an objective..."

"See, I'm the Prime Minister..."

"Should we be worried, Sir? About the next four years?"

"Of course not," Tristan smiled plastically. "I'm a worthy and compassionate leader with lots of clever ideas about my political objectives and other important things pertaining to this fine country. Also I'm very fiscal and I like the environment. A LOT."

Someone in the back cackled scornfully.

"Come on, you guys," Tristan implored. "You're not giving me a fair shake here. How can you just decide I'm going to be a failure before I even try? Let me prove this to you, okay? If my performance is suboptimal, I invite you all to give me a negative Yelp review."

"Excuse me," Hector said matter-of-factly as he dragged Tristan from the podium by the sleeve.

"What are you doing?" Tristan protested. "I was just starting to find my groove."

"I hate my job," mumbled Hector.

"Foreign policy!" Tristan shrieked before being dragged gracelessly from the room.

\*\*\*

"That was hard," Tristan said, rubbing his arm which still had Hector's finger marks in it.

"Calamitous." Hector complained.

"Did you see that?" Tristan squeaked. "Those journalistic tsetse flies were setting me up for failure. Not one of them asked me about my Emmy or my conditioning shampoo. *Not one.*"

"Try to understand," Hector exhaled. "The entire country is depending on you. Depending on you to not be a twat. Depending on you to not allow the nation to spiral into chaos."

"The media never treated me this way when I was a beloved, pop culture icon."

Hector pinched the bridge of his nose to stave off a migraine. "Tristan, you're an easy target for the media. You're famous enough to get everyone's attention but new enough to the political arena that the media feels compelled to put you on a sandwich. Also, you're a tool. You need to do something to improve your image."

"What's wrong with my image? I look astonishing."

"If you have any chance of being re-elected..."

"I have a significant, loyal fanbase."

"We've been over this, Tristan. They are called voters. Not fans."

"My fans voted for me, so I don't see the distinction."

"What about a wife?"

"What?"

"You don't have a wife, Tristan. That's political suicide."

"I don't think I'm emotionally ready for..."

"Don't you have like seven girlfriends?"

"Because I'm dishy," Tristan nodded, matter-of-factly.

"Then pick one and marry her," Hector said dryly. "It'll make you look wholesome. Voters lap that stuff up like a bunch of thirsty whippets."

Tristan pursed his lips.

"And you need a wedge issue," Hector added.

"Excuse me, what?" Tristan squinted.

"Something polarizing," Hector explained. "Something that will make people really angry, divide Umbravians and make them think voting for you is a matter of life and death."

"Divide... them?"

"You look like you ingested a ghost pepper."

"I thought I was supposed to please people."

"No."

"But I'm good at that."

"Dividing the nation will secure your power."

"I don't feel right about this," Tristan warbled. "I may have no idea what I'm doing but I'm also sort of... nice?"

"Nice," Hector repeated disapprovingly. "Do you seriously think anyone has ever achieved absolute power by being *liked*?"

"I like being liked. That's why God made me look like this."

"I can't let you spend the rest of your term in office floundering around like an utter moron," Hector scolded dryly. "What is that going to do for my reputation? You need to trust me, Tristan. I know what I'm doing. The military didn't make me the head psychological warfare for being a slouch."

"But..."

"I know politics, Winnings. You'd be prudent to heed my advice. You're coming across as someone who lacks maturity. Do you think that will garner respect? I need to rebrand you."

"You want people to dislike me?"

"*Fear* you. You need to assume dominance. Show them who's in control."

"I don't think I could..."

"Worry about that after you find a wife," Hector said, walking away with a *talk to the hand* gesture.

Tristan gaped.

# *CHAPTER FOUR*
## (PIPER AND OTTO)

Piper Oakley squinted at the chaos scrawled on the page. Sporadic, displaced lyrics were jotted everywhere. Music notes were squeezed into the limited blank spaces, crossed out and re-scribbled. Her scrawling was indecipherable to casual onlookers who couldn't help stealing a glance at the offbeat girl, sitting alone at the café with her conspicuous, intense focus and gentle, bohemian demeaner. There was something about her that drew people in, made them feel warm. Something intangible.

She was seated at her usual table by the window. Watching people bustling around outside in the city streets would feed her inspiration. There was no denying the creative vibe at *Otto's Cat Café* which made this Piper's favorite place to write songs. Her best friend Otto Zyker was the owner and mastermind behind this unique haunt which attracted an eclectic array of customers from posh executives to brooding poets.

Ever since Otto suggested that she do her work regularly at the café, Piper was able to harvest ideas at an alarming rate. Not bad for free office space. And it was much more stimulating than her bleak, Brutalist apartment at the tower block.

A familiar black cat swirled in a figure eight around Piper's legs. She instinctively nuzzled the top of his head with her knuckles without breaking her focus, humming a faint tune under her breath. The cats added an additional layer of creative energy to the café. Everything about the place stoked her imagination from the atypical artwork on the walls to the nifty cobbled effect of the floor tiles. Kitty perches were constructed artistically into the walls and there was just enough faux fur in the décor to create a mathematical balance between *cozy* and *weird*.

There was a distinct fruitiness in the air and the fervent chirp of cats watching birds through the windows sounded almost musical. Their tails swung like meticulous pendulums from the sills. Otto had a habit of mindlessly humming contagious, impromptu melodies while wiping down tables and preparing beverages. Occasionally Piper would quirk an eyebrow, trying to make sense of Otto's rhythm as he bopped playfully around the café, placing colorful frozen drinks in front of enamored customers who waited expectantly at their respective bistro tables. Otto gave Piper the bests ideas.

A watermelon smoothie suddenly appeared on the table in front of Piper. Agog, she looked up at the smirking face of Otto.

"How did you know what I was going to order?" Piper asked with one of her heart-meltingly shy smiles.

"I read your mind," Otto replied, playfully jouncing an ironic eyebrow.

"Weird," Piper said with pretend wonder as she maneuvered her lips around the straw.

Otto had already slipped into the seat next to Piper when he said, "Did you watch the vlog today?"

"No," Piper said, hurrying to swallow her sip of smoothie. "I was waiting to watch it with you. Your facial expressions enhance the experience."

"Same," Otto winked from behind his thick-rimmed hipster glasses as he scootched his chair next to Piper's and opened his laptop.

The black cat leaped like a ninja onto the table and nested on the laptop keyboard.

"Secret, you little nerd," Otto said affectionately, pulling the cat into his lap and kissing his head against the animal's will. "Strutting around here like you own the place."

"He does sort of," Piper pointed out.

"We're partners," Otto said in baby talk while cuddling the bejesus out of Secret until the cat's eyes bulged with revulsion.

"Otto, that cat is not consenting," Piper teased.

"You're not the boss of me," Otto said to Secret, again in baby talk, smooshing noses with his feline superior. "I hope Secret wasn't distracting you," Otto said, turning his head towards Piper. "He's quite attention seeking as far as cats go."

"He's my muse."

"I thought I was your muse," Otto said with impish jealously.

"Doofus," Piper laughed. "Sit down and watch the vlog with me."

Otto adjusted the laptop screen and clacked some keys until the garish visage of Willatrix Oleander appeared. Her haphazard shock of frizzy hair curled tightly as though she stuck a wet finger into an electrical socket. Her false eyelashes looked like spiders glued lopsidedly on her face. Her alien-green eyeshadow wandered all the way up to her penciled-on eyebrows. Her instinct to choose neon orange lipstick was questionable and someone really should have told her to lick the excess from her teeth before she livestreamed.

"Her face though," Otto said, leaning in confidentially towards Piper.

"You are so *bad,*" Piper snorted, playfully elbowing Otto in the ribs.

"Can you believe this is our neighbor?"

"She makes the twenty-second floor significantly more entertaining."

"Fair."

The orange lips on the screen morphed into an ethereal smile. Willatrix looked quite virginal in her ivory garb with the southern exposure sun spraying through her apartment window, illuminating her from behind. She placed her hands together like a praying angel and gleamed celestially at her viewers.

"Love and light," Willatrix said like a soothing zephyr. "I am here. Willatrix Oleander. Empath. Sage. Influencer. Spiritual guide."

Piper and Otto simultaneously sprayed out an explosive laugh before shushing themselves, re-nestling their butts into their seats and listening eagerly as though eating proverbial popcorn.

"I am here to assist you on your journey," Willatrix continued with a mystical flourish. "Poor souls. So lost. Befuddled. Wandering around aimlessly like a gaggle of erratic emus. I *feel* for you. Deep in my being. Put your hand on your computer screen. Can you feel my vibrations?" Willatrix cupped her hand to her ear as though waiting for an answer. "Good," she nodded slowly and deliberately. "Today I will be providing instructions on how to become an empath like me."

"*Become* an empath?" Piper whispered, leaning in towards Otto. "That's not something you can just randomly become. Besides, an actual *empathic intuitive...*"

"... probably wouldn't tell anybody," Otto finished with an  ironic wink.

Piper's lips parted.

"The day I decided to become an empath," Willatrix continued obliviously, "was the day I became enlightened. I marked the date on my calendar, actually. I observe it annually with a soothing, Neo-Druid bird ritual, a patchouli bubble bath, and a singular donut. Tangent. I was consulting with my spirit guide this morning."

Piper and Otto simultaneously gaped when Willatrix plunked a potato onto the desk in front of her.

"A potato?" Piper laugh-squeaked.

"This is tremendous," Otto said, rubbing his hands together in anticipation for more.

"What's that?" Willatrix said, putting the potato to her ear and listening intently. Then placing the spud gingerly back on the desk, she looked directly into the souls of her viewers. "Compassion," she nodded, deathly serious. "Compassion is the nucleus of the universe. Without which, our very lives will fall out of kilter. Everything is connected. Remember that, my precious co-humans. Compassion."

"I can't stop staring at this mess," Piper said, mesmerized. "I know I shouldn't but it's like watching…"

"… a car accident," Otto continued, nodding fervently at the screen.

Piper cocked her head inquisitively at Otto.

On the screen, Willatrix swooshed around for effect before saying, "Thank you for your attention. This has been Willatrix Oleander. Reminding you to be decent to one another. Just like me. Peace."

"*That* was rich," Otto said, slapping his laptop shut.

"Can you *even* with that girl?" Piper said, shaking her head.

"The sad thing is, I think she's serious."

"You think?" Piper said, squinching her nose analytically.

"What's with the squinchy nose, Pipes?"

"Nothing," Piper replied, scrambling awkwardly for her writing implements.

"I know that look," Otto continued.

"I had an itch."

"What's wrong with her?"

"Who?" Piper asked, standing, and instantly tripping over a cat.

"Willatrix Oleander," Otto enunciated playfully.

"It's just," Piper hiccupped, trying to avert eye contact, "you always want to see the best in people. You should be careful about that."

"Piper, it's me," Otto dimpled, pointing at himself for effect. "You don't have to hide…"

"I don't know what you're…"

"I know you can sense things about…"

"Thanks for the smoothie," Piper said hurriedly, stuffing things into her backpack.

"Going to work?" Otto asked. "Is it that time already?"

"I feel bad using up a table all morning," Piper said, relishing the weird feeling of Secret's tail curling like a candy cane around the ankle of her clunky combat boot. "You just opened this place a few months ago. I would hate to drive away customers who might want to sit here."

"You're not using up a table," Otto said, packaging up some surplus white chocolate biscotti and a stray muffin. "You've become part of the furniture. Part of my brand."

"What are you talking about?" Piper asked, her voice catching in mid-laugh.

"You attract business," Otto said, handing Piper a take-out bag containing some complimentary items.

"That's not a thing," Piper laughed, nervously fidgeting with the sleeve of her oversized, flannel shirt.

"People are weirdly drawn to you, Piper. They see you through the window and they come flocking in. It's uncanny. I do my best business the days you're here."

"Stop making things up," Piper said, playfully slapping the back of her hand on Otto's apron.

"Seriously, Piper," Otto insisted. "You breathe life into this place."

Piper's mouth wormed around for a few moments, trying to find words. "I should go," she finally said before darting out of the café, tripping over another cat on her way out.

# CHAPTER FIVE
## (CLARITY)

Sitting apprehensively in the office of Daryl De Voort, Clarity's leg twitched restlessly and compulsively. Her eyeballs lolled around the room, taking in the details like arbitrary photographs in her mind: A community college certificate hanging in a boring frame. A cigarette butt smoldering in an ashtray which was probably not supposed to be there. A very imperious Daryl De Voort leaning back sanctimoniously in a leather swivel chair. The sunburn on De Voort's bald spot. A dozen or so unsolicited manuscripts stacked on an outdated, metallic desk. An unfortunate smear of bird poop on the otherwise pristine window behind Daryl.

*This is a big mistake.*

*Look at him.*

*He's smirking at me like I'm some sort of punchline in a bad pun.*

*I'm out of my league.*

*Maybe Da was right.*

*The real world is no place for an agoraphobic country bumpkin.*

*With a stutter.*

"Why are you here?" asked Daryl De Voort, leaning in on his elbows and steepling his fingers.

*Why AM I here?*

*Only bad things happen when I leave my apartment.*

*Bad, bad things.*

"So you think you're a journalist?" De Voort asked with a farty exhale.

*Well, that was rude.*

*I AM a journalist.*

*I just haven't... done any journalism.*

*Yet.*

"You don't say much for a wordsmith," De Voort observed.

"I..." Clarity stuttered with a hard blink. "I am very eloquent. In written form."

"Have you written anything other than refrigerator reviews?" De Voort challenged.

Clarity gagged on the silence that followed.

"Experience please," De Voort exhaled through his nose.

"I... write online greeting cards," Clarity gulped. "To... supplement my income. Sometimes eblasts for alternative businesses..."

"Journalism experience."

"Oh... I..."

"Is this your way of saying you have no journalism experience?"

"I was the editor for... for my college's online newspaper."

Daryl De Voort burbled his lips with exasperation.

"I did college online for... for journalism. I was at the top of my class. Highest grade point average. My... my teachers said I had a bright future ahead."

De Voort buried his face in his hands.

"For school I wrote six mock articles on topical issues." Clarity blurted quickly. "Urban raccoons. Community gardens. Rice..."

"You wrote an article about rice?"

"My teacher said it... it was surprisingly insightful."

"I'm going to be frank with you, Clarity Trout. This isn't going well. In fact, the only reason I called you in is because your name is fun to say, and I think it could entice people into clicking your links."

Clarity blinked.

"*Verisimilitude Media* is one of the most influential news outlets in the country. Over nine hundred and fifty-seven million followers, globally. We dominate nearly every social media platform and search engine. Last year alone we garnered sixty-one billion clicks. Give me one reason why I should hire *you*," De Voort said, leaning imposingly into Clarity's personal space.

"I want..." Clarity stammered. "I want this so bad."

"A lot of people want to be journalists, Clarity Trout," De Voort said, very pleased with himself for finding an opportunity to say her name again. "That doesn't make you special."

"There's... there's no one like me. Anywhere."

De Voort sniggered.

*I'm flubbing this.*

*So bad.*

*I was an ignoramus thinking I could pull this off.*

*I'll never be a journalist now.*

*Everything I've worked for.*

*My whole life.*

*The only thing I've ever truly wanted.*

*Gone.*

"There's something about you, Clarity Trout."

"I... What?"

"You're an earnest little bird, aren't you."

Clarity nodded earnestly.

"I can see you are in literal, physical pain you want this so badly," De Voort nodded in agreement with himself. "That intrigues me."

"I'll... I'll do whatever you tell me to do," Clarity said quickly. "Literally anything. No matter what it takes, I'll do it. Long hours. Unrealistic deadlines, you name it! I am your doting draft horse."

Clarity winced at her own stupidity.

"Do you have any samples?"

"You mean like a drug test or..."

"*Writing* samples."

"Have... you read my blog?"

"I'm not interested in purchasing a Maytag side-by-side, you little twit. I want to see if you've got chops. Grit. Moxie."

"I... I have journalistic integrity?"

"Cute," De Voort said dismissively. "But that doesn't draw people in. It doesn't drive people into a mad rage. You need to make people feel things. Big things."

"I... I can do that," Clarity tried to convince herself.

"Yeah?"

Clarity nodded.

"You're sure about that?" De Voort said, furrowing his unibrow. "You can drum up controversy? With your sadistic allure?"

*What in flaming heck is sadistic allure?*

*I am a lot of things.*

*Weird.*

*Timid.*

*Doughy.*

*Rural.*

*Agoraphobic.*

*But gritty I am not.*

*This sure is different from my college newspaper.*

"Clarity Trout?" De Voort interrupted.

Clarity startled out of her stupor. "I... I..."

"You can get a sample on my desk by tomorrow?"

"Tomorrow?" Clarity blinked.

"Unless you're too busy writing about refrigerators. And rice."

"I... can," Clarity nodded circularly. "I can do that. I'm a journalist."

Daryl De Voort pinched Clarity's shoulder blade challengingly. "Prove it."

# CHAPTER SIX
## (MALLY AND FELIX)

Grunt.

Her arms hugged tightly around the bulging, paper grocery bag as Mally Rue approached the main entrance of the tower block. She grimaced when she heard a rip and the subsequent sound of cans clanking all over the sidewalk.

"Got it!" Felix Clover piped up as he appeared from seemingly nowhere.

Pleasant endorphins crackled in Mally's brain as she looked down to find Felix on his hands and knees, collecting cans of navy beans, cream corn, tomato soup and spaghetti O's. She watched him a bit too long, pondering his fondness of corduroy. His brown pants, fedora and even his bow tie were corduroy. As far as Mally was concerned, Felix was the only man on earth who could pull off this dweeby style. He was absolutely perfect with his auburn soul patch, espresso breath and indecipherable accent. She sighed as Felix looked up at her, humbly offering a parsnip.

"I couldn't save the beefsteak tomato," Felix said woefully.

"This is such a pain in the arse," Mally quavered. "I was almost home."

"You can put some things in my bicycle basket, and I'll bring it all inside for you."

"Thank you, Felix," Mally twittered, trying not to twitter.

"Let me get that for you," Felix said, dashing ahead of Mally and holding the door open for her.

Mally blushed as the pair sauntered inside and stepped into the elevator.

"You're fond of navy beans," Felix finally observed after a hormonally charged silence in the elevator.

"I have an iron deficiency," Mally said, feeling the blood rush to her face.

"Really," Felix said as though iron deficiency was the most fascinating notion on earth.

"It's no big deal, really."

"What do navy beans taste like?"

"You know. Beans."

"Cool," Felix nodded, genuinely engaged.

Beep.

When the elevator doors opened, Mally and Felix were too preoccupied with looking at each other to notice when the elevator doors started to close again.

"Woop," Felix yipped, using his front bicycle tire to activate door-opening censors.

Mally pursed her lips girlishly as Felix escorted her down the bleak, cement hallway to her apartment door. They stopped for a moment, chuckling nervously under the light of the dim hall sconce, looking down as though eye contact would be sinful.

"There you go," Felix said, sneaking a shy peak at Mally's adorable freckles. "Home safe and sound."

"Okay."

They hesitated before Felix quickly quipped, "You do a really good job styling your hair."

Mally gaped. "It's just a braid. With bangs."

"It looks good," he concluded before putting his hand on the door handle of the apartment next to Mally's.

He paused.

Mally paused.

"I mean you could come in if you want," Mally said quickly before she had a chance to change her mind.

"Really?"

"If you don't want to, that's totally fine too. Your call."

"I've never seen the inside of your place before."

"You must have at some point," Mally said, twiddling her braid. "You've lived next door for what, like three years?"

"Three years, nine months, two weeks and six days," Felix said instinctively. "Approximately."

"Okay."

"Okay."

"Yeah."

"Yeah."

"So..."

Mally shouldered the door open, and Felix entered behind her with his bicycle. Felix looked all around at the ceiling to floor bookcases along every wall, shelved with hardcover novels. A wingback chair was nestled in the corner next to an Ikea floor lamp.

"Very literary," Felix nodded, turning his whole body around to behold the bookish spectacle. "So you read?"

Mally blinked.

"I mean..." Felix stammered.

"I'm a purveyor of fiction," Mally admitted, still twiddling her braid. "English Literature degree."

"Nifty," Felix said, wide eyed, still trying to take everything in. "I mean I know you work at an independent bookstore, but I had no idea... I mean this level of commitment. Like. Wow!"

"I want to show you something," Mally said giddily.

Felix perked up expectantly.

With a flick of a remote control, Mally activated a mechanism that opened up an entire wall, revealing a hidden alcove with... wait for it... more books.

"That is epic."

"I don't show this to people," Mally admitted bashfully. "You're the first."

"What's the big secret back there?"

"That's where I keep my first editions," Mally beamed proudly. "Kind of like a panic room for fictitious characters."

"Pure genius," Felix said, unable to unlock his ogle from Mally's amber-flecked eyes.

"Can I offer you anything?" Mally asked. "Vitamin water? Funyuns?"

Mally squeaked with surprise when Felix grabbed her by the shoulders and passionately smushed his lips against hers. They melted into each other's smooch for an eternity. Or you know. Three solid seconds.

"Does this mean you'll be staying for dinner?" Mally asked, discreetly wiping the sin from her mouth. "Hope you like fettuccini."

"Mally?"

"Huh?"

"You want to get married?"

Mally blinked. "Yeah, sure."

"Yeah?"

"Okay."

"You don't think it's.."

"No, no. It's cool. I'm totally in love with you."

"Oh my god. Same."

"Yeah?"

"It's not like we're strangers."

"We've been neighbors forever."

"Friends."

"Elevator friends."

"I feel as though our souls..."

"... vibrate at the same frequency."

"This all makes total sense."

"Do you suppose we could keep our respective apartments?"

"Oh... I sort of thought we'd..."

"It's just I have all these books and..."

"You know what? Sure. We can work something out."

"Felix, you are tremendous. I've always thought so."

"Maybe we could tear out a wall here and have kind of a conjoined..."

"Brilliant!"

"Brilliant."

Mally and Felix looked awkwardly at each other before tumbling urgently to the floor in the form of a human pretzel.

## CHAPTER SEVEN
## (GIRARD AND FLOSSIE)

It was mostly the rhythmic thumping and pterodactyl shrieks coming from 2201 that caught the attention of Professor Girard Gosh and his wife Flossie as they were just about to unlock their door across the hall from Mally's.

"What are they doing in there?" asked Flossie. "Sacrificing a goat?"

"Sounds like," Girard smirked as they entered their apartment.

Girard dropped a stack of textbooks onto his mahogany desk which took up about one-third of the room, positioned near the windowed balcony door. Flossie flumped on the chocolaty leather couch, skimming her emails. The pair had met, courted, and even wed at the university where Girard was a professor of moral philosophy and Flossie was a researcher in the faculty of human psychology.

"Mind if I join you?" Girard asked, sliding in next to Flossie who molded snugly into the crook of his arm. He whipped out his cell phone and clicked on to a press conference video.

"What do you think of the new prime minister?" Flossie asked, nudging her head towards Girard's phone. Smirking.

"It would be morally wrong for me to form an opinion prematurely," Girard winked.

"You nutter," Flossie teased, bopping Girard with a fluffy throw cushion. "You must have formed an opinion after the first media appearance. Herald trumpets? *Really?*"

"Flossie, you know I'm apolitical," Girard said, affectionately playing with strands of her sleek, perfectly straight black hair. "Otherwise, how can I remain objective? I can't form a moral or philosophical analysis with political bias impairing my judgment."

"Oh my God, what is he *wearing?*" Flossie asked, craning her head to get a better look at Girard's phone screen.

"And furthermore," Tristan Winnings said in the press conference, wearing what looked like a Victorian cape, "I intend to use my maturity and political prowess to..."

"Prime Minister Winnings?" a reporter interrupted from off camera.

"You interrupted," Tristan said like a stern schoolteacher. "But go on."

"It seems you have your first scandal," the reporter continued.

"Perhaps you are confusing me with my soap character," Tristan said with a gameshow host smile, directly at the camera. *"Roderick Von Trapezoid.* Beguiling estate master and love addict." Tristan finished with a suggestive eyebrow gesture.

"Is this your way of dodging the accusation of your involvement in the *Sordid Squirrel Scandal of Engledorf?"*

Tristan gaped.

"Any idea how squirrels entirely disappeared from the region of Engledorf, *your* place of residence during the time in question, for no apparent reason?"

"I am a very powerful man," Tristan said indignantly, "but I have no authority over squirrels. A species that notably does whatever it pleases."

"You were quoted in The Post as saying, *"Nobody likes squirrels."*

Tristan's mouth moved around silently for a few moments before pointing authoritatively and saying, "No."

"So you didn't use your wealth, fame and influence to have the squirrels inhumanely disposed of? You realize if proven, this could infuriate the animal rights activists. They dominate social media and could ultimately destroy you. Comments?"

Tristan's eyeballs swerved off-screen for a moment before lolling back towards the camera.

"Foreign policy," Tristan stated matter-of-factly. "Employment equity. Tax adjustments. Subsidized housing. Human rights..."

The room suddenly erupted with applause.

Tristan jolted with surprise but then bowed with feigned modesty and gratitude.

Girard shut off his phone. "Psych eval?" he asked, lolling his head towards Flossie.

"Certifiable," Flossie confirmed.

# CHAPTER EIGHT
## (TRISTAN WINNINGS)

"Better," Hector said unimpressed as Tristan removed his cape in a nondescript room. "But depressingly suboptimal."

"Hey," Tristan objected. "I stayed in control of the dialogue, assumed dominance. And I dodged the squirrel curveball."

"Was there merit to the squirrel accusation? Hector deflated. "Because if so, I'm going to punch myself in the face right now."

"That was just the media being *the media.*"

"So you didn't cause all of the squirrels in Engledorf to mysteriously disappear?"

"Oh I did," Tristan nodded earnestly. "But it was taken totally out of context."

"How does one take the vanquishing of squirrels out of context?"

"It was done humanely."

"Humanely?"

"Of course, I'm not a psychopath."

"Tristan, how did this happen and also, please kill me."

"I had them humanely relocated to Wyoming and my reasons for doing so were valid."

"Understand this," Hector said, still surprisingly dry. "Squirrels are furry with large, expressive eyes. Such characteristics evoke maternal feelings in people. Do you see what you've just done here? If anyone gets dirt on this, regardless of your intentions or humane methods, you will lose the entire women's vote."

"Didn't I do a good job diverting to political talking points?"

Hector was nonplussed.

"Oh!" Tristan said with a clap of epiphany. "Wait until you see what I did. You'll be so proud of me. Hey Gloria!" he called. "Come on in and bring the little muffins!"

"The little…" Hector said, his lip curled with repulsion. "Oh. My. God."

A delightfully blond, petite woman with big blue eyes and glossy lips walked demurely into the room wearing a 1950's style, polka-dot dress, along with two equally blond children.

"Hector," Tristan said, dimpling proudly, putting his arm around the stunning lady, "This is Gloria. My wife."

"Your…"

"And these little muffins are Simon and Angelica," Tristan said, patting both tots on their perfectly symmetrical heads.

"How though?" Hector squinted.

"You said I should have a wholesome family," Tristan said, deflating with disappointment. "You know. For my brand."

"How did you get married and have two school-aged children in less than six hours?"

"It wasn't hard," Tristan bragged. "I paid extra for the blondness. And a premium for a male child who resembles me."

"You," Hector squinted, "purchased them?"

"No, no, no," Tristan chuckled. "No, it's all good. Gloria is Equity. She'll be compensated according to industry standards."

"So you…"

"Hired them."

"Tristan…"

"I know Gloria from a T.V. miniseries I filmed a few years ago. She owes me a favor."

"It's a pleasure, Mr. Morosely," Gloria said demurely, extending a dainty hand for Hector to shake.

"She's good, right?" Tristan said, elbowing Hector. "She's method."

"I need a drink," Hector droned.

# CHAPTER NINE
## (CLARITY)

*Focus on the sidewalk cracks.*

*Focus.*

*Focus.*

*Avoid eye contact.*

*Breathe.*

*You're almost home.*

"THE END IS NIGH!" a familiar voice screeched. "DOOMED! WE ARE ALL DOOMED! IT'S COMING FOR YOU! PREPARE FOR THE END!"

*Ignore him, Clarity.*

*It's just Ezekiel.*

*He's attention seeking.*

*He wants you to look.*

*Don't look.*

*Don't engage.*

Clarity yipped when she was grabbed by the arm by Ezekiel Mortimer, a bedraggled mad prophet. As per usual, he was wearing a sandwich sign, upon which were doomsday scrawlings, judgement and warnings of humanity's impending demise.

"Sinner!" Ezekiel warbled, looking directly into Clarity's eyes.

"Let go," Clarity pleaded, trying to wriggle from his grasp. "I just want to go home."

"Doom!" Ezekiel persisted. "Its arrival is pending! Nobody is safe!"

"Y... you're making no sense."

"You think I'm mad?" Ezekiel said, his eyes widening existentially. "The truth is glaring in your face like a black mamba! Acknowledge the truth or you will be swallowed up like all the rest of them!"

"I... I said LET GO!"

A scornful scowl formed on Ezekiel's jowls as he loosened his grip, watching Clarity flail into the tower block. He squinted intensely at her.

"Karma has teeth," Ezekiel seethed.

***

Breathless, Clarity flattened herself against her door, now safe inside her apartment. She squeezed her eyes shut, giving herself permission to finally release tears, sobbing freely.

"Fern," Clarity quavered to her botanical, potted friend, "I'm never leaving this apartment again. Ever. It's not worth it. It's just not."

"Ello?" came an endearingly scratchy voice from the other side of the door.

*Not now, Norman.*

"Young lady?" Norman tried again. He had the kind of voice that sounded like he needed a lozenge and he whistled whenever he pronounced the letter S. "Are ye in there, sweetheart?"

*Please go away.*

*Please.*

*Just please.*

"I brought ye some marshmallows," Norman persisted. "I made them me-self. Doesn't get fresher than this."

Clarity chewed her bottom lip. As far as neighbors go, Norman Lovelorn was a gem. At the age one hundred and six, he was just as nimble and sprightly as a man seventy years his junior. And she had to admit, Norman's marshmallows were pretty special. After a traumatic day, sinking her teeth into a warm, gooey, homemade marshmallow would be heaven. But that would require opening the door. And Clarity was just not emotionally prepared for that.

"How's about I leave the marshmallows out here in the hall for ye?" Norman suggested compassionately. "That way, ye can grab them whenever you're ready."

Clarity exhaled slowly. After a few brief moments she put her ear to the door. She could hear the shuffle of Norman's loafers walking further down the hall, followed by the sound of the elevator doors opening. She squinted through the peephole. No Norman. She slowly creaked the door open and found a Melmac plate on the floor, upon which were three, generously sized marshmallows, lopsided from warm freshness. Clarity quickly snatched the plate and slammed the door shut.

# CHAPTER TEN
## (NORMAN)

The weathered hand of Norman Lovelorn rapped on the door. When opened, Mally's face lit up with a delighted smile, although her braid was askew, and her pale pink lipstick was almost entirely smeared off her mouth.

"Norman!" she said, her eyes gleaming with affection.

"Marshmallows here!" Norman said proudly, presenting a plate of marshmallows he retrieved from a clunky catering cart. "Made a new batch this morning. With love. Started on the top floor and I'm working me way down."

"Norman, you really are something," Mally marveled, graciously accepting the plate.

"Wouldn't want to leave anyone out," Norman said earnestly. "Just delivered a plate to that quiet girl upstairs. Poor soul. Do ye happen to know her name? I never quite know what to call her."

"Bless you, Norman," Mally said, putting her hand over his. "Seems you're always on the go. Always up to something. On the move. Always thinking of every single one of us in this building."

"I'm one hundred and six years old," Norman whistled. "I want to do as much as I can with me life before I have to start slowing down in about thirty or so years."

"These smell glorious, Norman," Mally said, her face softening into a smile. "I'll leave the plate outside your door tomorrow with a nice novel you can borrow. Do you like Aldous Huxley?"

"Is that Norman?" Felix asked, popping his head out from around the corner. He was zipping his corduroy trousers and there was more pale pink lipstick smeared on his face than on Mally's. "My man Norman!" he continued, giving Norman some kind of secret handshake involving a few hand slaps, a finger gun and a fist bump explosion.

"Didn't realize ye had company, Miss Mally," Norman said with a sideways expression.

"The most wonderful thing has happened," Mally gushed.

"Ye two finally getting hitched?" Norman asked, his shaggy eyebrows rising with hope.

"How could you possibly know that?" Mally asked. "Felix and I didn't even know until about twenty minutes ago."

"The sexual tension between ye has be excruciating to watch," Norman cackled gleefully. "It's about time ye did something about it. Quite obvious the two of ye's are meant to be together. I tell folks, I tell 'em, *'find ye a man who looks at ye the way young Felix looks at Miss Mally.'* I say that to folks, don't ye know."

"Are those fresh marshmallows I smell?" asked Girard as he emerged from his apartment, following the aroma into the hallway.

"Every Tuesday!" Norman chimed, offering Girard a plate.

"I don't know how you do it," Girard said, shaking his head in sheer wonder. "At one hundred and six no less."

"Good genes," Norman nodded. "Sense of humor. Fresh air. Take the stairs thrice a week. Them's a lot of stairs! Crossword puzzles and good folks are what keep me going. So many good folks in this building. Quite a tight community we've got here. And I've been here since the place was built"

"Astonishing," Girard smiled.

"Obliged, Professor."

"Norman, please," Girard said, placing a gentle hand on Norman's shoulder. "I keep telling you. Call me Girard."

"That wouldn't be proper," Norman said, taking a humble bow. "Ye worked hard to get where ye are now, and ye deserve to be recognized for your efforts. You're a clever lad, Professor Gosh. A clever, clever lad. I feel smarter just standing here next to ye."

"When's your new book coming out, Girard?" Mally asked, eyes wide with intrigue.

"Getting close," Girard smiled giddily. "It'll be on shelves in a few months."

"What's it about again?" Mally asked fan-girlishly. "I was trying to tell the concept to Felix in the elevator, but I didn't explain it well."

"It's about my theory of *Tribunal Compassion*," Girard answered, trying his hardest to hide his swelling pride with a bashful smile. "The concept of society deciding who deserves compassion and who doesn't."

"And it's based on the notion of people having this mental block, where they're seemingly incapable of feeling compassion for more than one person or group at a time, correct?" Mally said, feeling quite proud of herself for remembering something so cerebral.

"You get an A plus," Girard beamed, pointing directly at Mally. "Take note that compassion is not technically something you can run out of. Yet it's become entrenched in our subconscious that empathy is something that needs to be rationed. There's no logic in that. Empathy is exhausting and time-consuming, but also an inherent instinct that is critical to our survival as a species. But what concerns me is how the masses avoid empathizing with those who *don't make the cut* by gaslighting them into feeling unworthy of compassion. That's where the danger lies. Persecuting people for suffering is the ultimate immorality."

"Wait, wait, wait," Felix said, creating a letter T with his hands. "Who decides who's deserving of compassion and who isn't? Like, who has the authority to do that?"

"The system," Girard explained, the word tasting like curdled milk in his mouth. "Elitists. It's rather ambiguous where the pyramid begins, but thanks to groupthink, nobody really questions where the rules come from. People just sort of mindlessly fall in line. It's sad."

Norman dabbed the emotion from his eyes with a checkered handkerchief.

"I don't get it," Felix persisted. "How does *the system…*"

Girard winced at the word.

"Just read the book," Mally teased Felix when she noticed his brow becoming crooked with confusion. "Won't you come in and help Felix and I celebrate our engagement, Norman?" Mally asked. "You and Flossie are welcome too, Girard."

"Engaged?" Girard gleamed. "Well damn! Ha! It's about time. Flossie and I were placing bets. I'll go get her."

"Norman?"

"Love to, Miss Mally," Norman said regretfully, maneuvering the wheels on his squeaky catering cart. "But I've got twenty-one more floors to do. Wouldn't want to disappoint anyone. They're all counting on me."

Mally and Felix watched adoringly at Norman as he pushed the creaky cart down the hall.

"I totally love that guy," Mally sighed.

"We all do, Mal," Felix said, putting his hand on the small of her back. "Every one of us."

# CHAPTER ELEVEN
## (WILLATRIX)

"I love every single one of you, my darling merino lambs. My heart bubbles with love for all persons." Willatrix said, looking ethereally into her computer screen, livestreaming from her apartment. "I am here. Willatrix Oleander. Empath. Sage. Influencer. Spiritual guide. Today we rejoice. For I have reached two hundred followers. Gratitude, my gentle lemmings," she said, making humble praying hands. "Two hundred souls I have reached. Two hundred lives I have touched. Two hundred more empaths cultivated, who will ultimately make the world radiate with compassion. Remember, compassion is a supernatural power bestowed upon many, but utilized by few."

There was a knock at the door, which Willatrix grudgingly tried to ignore.

"Speaking of compassion," Willatrix continued. "I offered a sandwich to a vagrant this morning. I asked for nothing in return. My reward was merely the look of utter amazement on the vagrant's gaunt, cocaine-powdered face. I couldn't wait to share this with all of you, my trusted ones. I just know it will inspire you to do likewise. I want to challenge every one of you to follow my example and do something kind for a stranger today, without expectations of anything in return. It need not be a vagrant. Simply find a stranger and feel his agony. Hug a janitor. Sponsor a nice alcoholic. Stand outside the main entrance of a mental health care facility and offer a word of affirmation to the first person who walks out the door. Mental health," Willatrix said emotionally, placing her palm over her heart. "So important. Remember, I am a safe place if you ever need to confide in someone about being mentally fragile. I have a safety pin. You can always trust a person with a safety pin."

Another knock at the door.

Willatrix squinted with annoyance, but persevered.

"As I was saying," Willatrix continued, "I am eager to see how my altruism has influenced you all, so please direct your selfies to my Instagram handle and use my special hashtag so you can be an example to others. Tangent. My boycott of the day is *Arvo's Finnish Fusion Bistro,* where the assistant manager allegedly mansplained something to a waitress. Friends, to support this business would be misogynistic. My soul screams in revulsion at the thought of patronizing this den of iniquity. We must collectively agree to boycott *Arvo's* to ensure this injustice is never played out again. Please don't wait for the reports to be confirmed. There's no time for that. We must drive the business into the ground. Because compassion. Thank you, my beloved. And please tell your friends."

Another knock.

Willatrix took a very long, deep breath and exhaled loudly and slowly.

"This is Willatrix Oleander," she said with a plastic smile. "Reminding you to be decent to one another, just like me. Thank you for your attention."

Knock, knock, knock.

Angrily, Willatrix *Jerry Lee Lewis-ed* her chair backwards and stormed towards the door, opening it aggressively. She found a plate of marshmallows placed lovingly by the door and she could hear the squeaky wheels of Norman's catering cart as he meandered down the hall.

"Feck off, Methuseleh!" Willatrix barked at Norman.

Perhaps it was the hair in his ears. But whatever the reason, Norman did not hear Willatrix. He simply whistled a Gershwin melody as he pushed his cart of marshmallows down the hall.

# CHAPTER TWELVE
## (CLARITY)

Smushing an entire marshmallow into her mouth, Clarity stared hopelessly at a blank computer screen. Blank screens, as far as Clarity was concerned, felt like driving at high speed down a steep hill. With shoddy brakes. Clarity winced when her cell phone beeped with a text from her dad.

*"How did the interview go? Call me."*

The text was heartwarmingly sweet, but Clarity pretended to ignore it. She was still trying to unravel and process the overwhelming events of the day. Now, she faced the impossible task of writing a mind-blowing piece of sample writing that could possibly forge her entire future. With an addled brain. By the following morning. How could she articulate any of this to her dad? She could barely make sense of the marshmallow.

"I'm toast," Clarity admitted to her fern. "I'm too flustered to have something ready for Daryl De Voort by tomorrow morning. And if I call Da, he's... he's going to try to convince me to come home to the mushroom farm. Don't... don't tell Da, but I secretly hate mushrooms. They're shaped like atomic warfare and taste like anguish. I don't have the heart to tell him, Fern. He's so passionate about his mushrooms. He'll keel over if I told him. Plus, there's just so many memories there of my ma."

Clarity blinked hard.

"I don't know if I'll get..." Clarity stammered. "... get another opportunity like this again. I can't get past the interviews. I... I just fall apart. I can't even help it. Fern, what if I botch this? The stress might kill me before morning. My entire future depends on me coming up with something..." hard blink. "... something brilliant. Something gritty? In less than eight hours. What am I even going to write about? My brain is full of London fog."

The fern did not reply.

# CHAPTER THIRTEEN
## (PIPER AND OTTO)

"Sushi in the hall?" Otto asked when Piper opened her apartment door. "My turn to pay."

A smile of relief formed on Piper's face as she took a seat in the hallway with Otto, under a flickering sconce that made the cement hallway look almost Gothic. She looked somewhat bedraggled after an afternoon of dull data entry, but her funky bucket hat adequately covered her frazzled, dirty blond hair. Secret meandered out of Otto's apartment, sniffing the fishy air, then sat pertly and expectantly next to Otto.

"You always seem to know exactly when I need you to show up with sushi," Piper observed as Otto popped open a Styrofoam takeout container. She crossed her legs on the cold floor. As she did so, her shredded jeans ripped a little more at the knees.

"You're easy to read," Otto winked, handing Piper chopsticks.

"Most people think I'm an enigma," Piper said, popping a wad of perfectly pinkish salmon sashimi in her mouth.

"What's the point of best friends if we can't sense each other's need for sushi?" Otto jibed. "How was your day?"

"I thought you could read my mind."

"I can," Otto shrugged with his mouth full of maki. "But you're clearly dying to vent on someone. Go ahead. Lay it on me."

"I hate Tuesdays," sighed Piper. "Data entry is a slow form of torture. And the people at work, they're all just so... mechanical? The same? They don't even look at each other. It's freaky. Yet they give off this vibe like I'm the weirdo."

"I like weirdos."

"My boss had a word with me today about my bucket hats."

"Who has a word with someone about bucket hats? That's just bent."

"He said my hats are making people uncomfortable."

"Are you going to stop wearing them?"

"Hell no. He can eat me."

"My girl," Otto grinned proudly. "Did you tell him that?"

"Of course not," Piper sighed. "I care too much about people's feelings."

"You have a ginormous heart, Pipes."

"Which has its detriment on occasion."

"You're a mesmerizing juxtaposition of sugar-sweet gentleness and edge."

"That's subjective," Piper dimpled shyly.

"This job is beneath you," Otto said, nosing around for a spider roll. "You should consider working in a less standardized environment, where they'd appreciate your brand of genius. I'd hire you but I'm not at a place financially where I can support a staff."

"The whole world is standardized, Otto. Imagine seeing things differently, feeling things differently and perceiving things differently than other people — no fault of your own — and then being born into a world where everyone is forced to conform. If you don't, you're basically punished for the rest of your life. It's a total mind-feck."

Otto swallowed some eel with a hard gulp. "Don't ever do that. Conforming is for mortals."

"Why is the word *normal* even in the English language?" Piper asked. "I'd rather be a colony of fecal bacteria than to be normal."

Otto suddenly sprayed lemon San Pellegrino from his mouth in a sudden burst of laughter. "I freaking love you, Oakley. Can I please adopt you?"

"Why the heck not?" Piper shrugged. "I'm sure the parental units would be happy to leave me in a basket on your front doorstep."

"Whuuuut?"

"I had to choose between using my college fund to pay for university or to buy a vintage Fender Mustang with decent sound equipment. Yep. My parents were mad."

"They'll come around," Otto said. "Once you find a job that showcases your awesomeness. Once they hear you sing…"

"Without a formal education," Piper continued, "my employment options are limited. I mean, you basically need a degree to sell hotdogs outside Bentley Stadium these days. So I'm stuck mindlessly entering millions of eleven digit numbers into an obsolete computer which is probably sucking the juice from my eyeballs every single day."

"Only three more afternoons until the weekend."

"Weekends are draining," Piper moaned. "I spend the whole time dreading Monday."

"Maybe you could pick up a few gigs on the weekends," Otto suggested.

"That was the plan," Piper sighed. "But in order to do that I need visibility. Working full-time makes that challenging. I'm utterly exhausted juggling work and songwriting, I just haven't had the energy to market myself. It's a vicious cycle of subsistence. Besides, who's going to hire a data entry clerk for gigs?"

"Alt rock musician," Otto corrected her while dipping some eel into a plastic container of soy sauce.

"Maybe someday," Piper said faintly.

Otto suddenly dropped his chopsticks with revelation. "You can perform at the cat café."

"What?"

"You have the mornings off," Otto said eagerly. "And weekends. You've got the sound equipment. A portable amp..."

"Otto, that is so incredibly kind but..."

"I could make an ad for my social media platforms," Otto continued, counting ideas on his fingers.

"Can you even do that?"

"I can do whatever I want, my beautiful, flannelled friend," Otto said, practically bouncing. "It's my café."

Piper watched Otto as he animatedly described his vision with a series of hand flourishes and wide-eyed expressions. His energy was so sunshiny. Vibrant. It was impossible to be sad when Otto was in the room. He connected so easily with his customers, who clearly graced the café to feed off his crackling essence. He was the heartbeat of the place and just being in his café gave everyone a sense of belonging and community. He truly had a gift of being able to bring people together.

There he was, offering his shiny, new cat café as a free music venue for Piper. Taking a chance on an unknown. He had worked so hard to build his charming little business from quite literally nothing. He left a secure job as a veterinarian to pursue his dream of bringing his cat café to life. His vision was to create a gathering place where everyone, regardless of their opinion of cats, would feel welcome and appreciated. It also gave him the opportunity to bring Secret to work with him. He risked everything. Piper winced, imagining how one sour performance could prompt a negative Yelp review. This early on, one negative comment could undo all the hard work Otto poured into this business venture.

"But you've been working so hard to build your brand," Piper grasped."

"So I'll change my brand."

"But what if your cliental isn't into my kind of…"

"This is such a delicious idea," Otto beamed. "I can't believe I didn't think of this before."

"You've already done so much for me," Piper implored. "Letting me occupy a table every morning. Free biscotti…"

"Piper, why are you trying so hard to find reasons not to do this? You have an amazing sound. This is perfect."

"When have you ever heard me sing?"

"You sing all the time in your apartment," Otto shrugged. "I can hear you through the air vents."

Piper blushed, biting her lower lip.

"Don't look so embarrassed," Otto said, playfully fisting Piper's shoulder. "You're basically a cranberry." Otto curled his lip. "Or a pixie? A fighter of foo? A pumpkin in the process of smashing…" Otto smacked his hands together in a confident clap. "You're Joey Ramone!"

Piper unexpectedly exploded with laughter. But the gleam of pride and giddy exuberance in Otto's eyes made her stomach tangle into a Palomar knot. She would be a fool to pass up this opportunity. Piper only wished she could be as sure of herself as Otto was.

# CHAPTER FOURTEEN
## (CLARITY)

Still goggling at a blank screen, Clarity became acutely aware of night creeping into the sky outside. The notion of time was taunting her as she struggled to breathe. The fact that Ezekiel was screaming **'REPENT!'** from his apartment did not help matters.

She blinked.

An hour went by.

And another.

And another.

One hour bled into the next as she felt a growing urgency to type something. She had never worked under this level of duress before. In college, it never would have occurred to her to wait until the night before to complete an assignment. To quell anxiety, she would do assignments at least a month in advance, giving her a buffer of time to bungle over ideas. Proofread. Revise. Revise again. Her nerves would never have forgiven her otherwise.

*How did I ever get like this?*

*Why can't I just be normal?*

*A normal person could pull this off.*

*Do a job interview.*

*Leave her apartment even.*

*Without having an episode.*

Clarity's computer startled her when Torrence Trout rang her with a video call from the mushroom farm.

The mushroom farm.

Why did the very idea of mushrooms make Clarity feel queasy? Perhaps she associated them with her isolated childhood. As a child, Clarity was homeschooled since the nearest school was a three-hour drive from the farm. She became quite used to her independence, spending most of her time in her very yellow bedroom. She was not unhappy per se. She took comfort in her own little version of *normal*. Doing her worksheets without any worries in the world. Warm meals to look forward to. Nice things to look at through the window. She did not really feel lonely because she was not entirely sure what the word meant. There was a period of time up until around the age of six, when she was unaware that other children actually existed.

Torrence and Theresa Trout did not consider themselves to be negligent parents. They simply mistook Clarity's lack of complaints as contentment. As Clarity was their only child, they were unaware that children are not essentially mute. They thought it was normal that Clarity only communicated in written form, even at the age of eight or nine. They didn't have many friends themselves. Gasoline was expensive and farm life can be all-consuming.

It wasn't until some cousins visited from Belfast when reality sunk in. Clarity's cousin Liam was nine years old, same as Clarity. Imagine the Trouts' astonishment when Liam was speaking in complete sentences and even competing in regional speech meets. Ashamed, Torrence and Theresa realized that Clarity needed socialization. They had never felt the need to compare her to other children and had assumed she was just shy. They decided they needed to rectify the situation for Clarity's sake.

Theresa was a trembling gelatin of emotion when she put Clarity on a school bus for the first time at the age of nine. Kissing Clarity's forehead, she told her little girl that she was going to change the world – but first, she needed to make some friends. Clarity's eyes bulged with fear as the bus pulled away. She glared imploringly at her parents with her palms pressed against the back window as the bus disappeared down the dusty street. Torrence comforted his wife by reminding her that children are resilient.

Clarity was agog seeing more children at the school than she ever dreamed existed. The sounds of sneakers squeaking on the floor, a traffic jam of sweaty, verbose students, all the voices echoing throughout the halls and the alarming bell that made Clarity cover her ears... It was all just too much. Several kids conspicuously plugged their noses and complained with loud whispers that Clarity smelled like a barn. Like manure. She was snagged by a teacher who seemed annoyed that Clarity had not yet found her way to class.

She survived most of the day simply by saying nothing, which was apparently considered good behavior in a school setting. It wasn't until third period when the children, one by one, were asked to stand in front of the class and talk about their favorite breakfast cereal. When it was Clarity's turn, she stood in front of her thirty-seven classmates and gaped silently for a few too many excruciating moments with her mouth moving around wordlessly. The taunting giggles and nose plugging made Clarity feel like she was immersed in water.

The teacher, having not been informed of Clarity's nonconformity due to an administrative oversight, chastised Clarity for not listening to the instructions. Stiff as a corpse, Clarity peed her pants in front of everyone, feeling the horrible, warm liquid trickle down her leotard, and realizing all too late why the kids were pointing and howling with laughter. While the teacher smacked her meter stick against her desk, demanding order, Clarity darted from the room and ran flailing out of the school, tears streaming down her face.

Once outside, Clarity breathlessly looked around, having no idea how to get home. Never having been to a city before, where would she have acquired the instinct *not* to run directly into oncoming traffic? Alas, as the honking Toyota approached her, it could not screech to a halt fast enough as Clarity stared bug-eyed at the impending headlights.

KABUMP!

As she lay in the street, sobbing and clutching her broken arm, an irate driver loomed above, berating her for leaping mindlessly in front of his vehicle. The string of profanities and names involving Clarity's stupidity would echo through the caverns of her brain into adulthood.

She survived her first ride in an ambulance and when she finally made it home to the mushroom farm, Theresa swore at herself for subjecting her baby to such horror. She honestly believed that the experience would be good for Clarity. While Clarity was balled up on her bed, hidden under a quilt that night, Theresa promised her daughter that she would never be forced to leave the farm ever again.

"The people out there are cruel," Theresa said, stroking the ball of Clarity under the blanket. "But you're safe now, Clare Bear. Safe in your cocoon. Ma won't let anything bad happen to you. From now on, you can stay in here where it's safe."

# CHAPTER FIFTEEN
## (LOLA)

"Shhh," Lola hissed at a toddler who was pulling on her baggy mom jeans. "Everyone's sleeping."

Lola Brunt, wearing a newborn in a sling, was pushing a double stroller down the dark, cement hallway with one hand, using the other to tote a large, rolling suitcase. Two little girls followed closely behind. Looking around apprehensively at her surroundings, she squinted at the number on a door and fidgeted with a key in the dark.

"Why won't this key..." Lola said through clenched teeth, wriggling the key futilely in the keyhole.

"Mummy, I'm hungry," came a little voice in the dark.

"Just let Mummy do... this," Lola said, still struggling.

The door opened and Lola gasped when Pax answered, yawning.

"Oh my god," Lola shrieked. "I'm so sorry. Isn't this 2206?"

"That's next door," Pax said, unperturbed and softening with sympathy when he spotted Lola's entourage of littles. "Are you just moving in?"

"I'm sorry," Lola repeated, flustered. "Sorry. I just… it was kind of an emergency, so I had to do this at night. Sorry."

"Hey, hey, there's no need to apologize," Pax assured her. "Let me give you a hand. I'm Pax, by the way."

"Lola," Lola grunted. "Garthie and Enzo are in the stroller here. The girls are Izzy and Sara-Sue. Bobby is the one I'm wearing. You've probably guessed he's brand new. I'd offer you my hand to shake but I have a million babies and luggage."

"MUMMY!" Enzo wailed while Lola frantically tried to shush him.

"Sorry, they don't really have any filters," Lola apologized. "They can get loud."

"I really don't mind," Pax smiled.

"You might mind now that we're neighbors," Lola said, opening the door next to Pax's. "They could go at this all night. We've been on a bus all day. It's been… stressful."

"Is everything okay?"

"You don't need to hear my problems," Lola said, bouncing a screaming Enzo on her hip. Her eyes were puffy and weary.

Pax's forehead creased with concern. "Are you okay?" he repeated.

Lola relaxed a little when she noticed Pax's genuinely kind eyes. "I…" she hesitated. "I had to leave in a hurry. The kids and I just couldn't take it anymore, you know? We finally decided to just up and leave… him."

"Oh Lola," Pax said, his face melting with sympathy.

"Oh he didn't hit me or anything," Lola said, shaking her head earnestly. "It was all head games. Gaslighting."

"You shouldn't downplay that, Lola. You did the right thing leaving. Protecting your babies."

"I don't know what the right thing is anymore," Lola said, flustered. "I just knew I couldn't take it anymore. I'm sure people will have their opinions about me."

"I'm not one of those people," Pax said flatly. "In fact, we have a great community of people here at the block. This building may look like a Medieval asylum for the criminally insane, but there's some great folks living here."

"SHUT THE FECK UP!" Willatrix screamed from inside her apartment.

"Except maybe her," Pax said, pointing at Willatrix's apartment with his thumbs.

Lola found a tentative smile and tried it out.

"If there's anything you need…" Pax began.

"My church will be sending me some things tomorrow. Furniture. Stuff. Food and the like. The church arranged this apartment, actually. Taking up a collection every Sunday to try and help with the rent until I get started. And the appliances are already included so... We'll be fine," Lola said, uncertain.

"What about tonight?" Pax worried. "Where will the babies sleep?"

"We'll manage," Lola said, her eyes bulging with fear.

"I'll get some blankets," Pax decided definitively. "And milk. I just bought some. Wait here."

"Pax, no. You don't have to do that."

"We're neighbors," Pax said, already in his apartment, rummaging for extra pillows. "We all look out for each other around here. Wait 'til you taste Norman's marshmallows."

Lola swallowed awkwardly, mentally counting the tops of her children's heads.

Pax returned with armloads of provisions.

"Pax..." Lola said humbly. "This is just too much."

Ignoring Lola, Pax brought the supplies into her empty apartment. Lola wandered in behind him.

"That should help you get settled in," Pax said with his hands on his hips, nodding as he surveyed the stash of essentials. "And listen, if you need any support..."

"You've already been too kind."

"I'm right next door," Pax reassured her. "And I can suggest government resources…"

"Government resources?"

"I'm a member of provincial parliament," Pax smiled. "I'd be happy to advocate for you if there's any way the government can help."

"The government has never helped me," Lola said, clenching her jaw.

"Right," Pax deflated. "The government can be a bit of a twat, can't it. But that's why I got into politics. I was hoping I could…"

"What's going on in here?" Flossie asked, poking her head into Lola's apartment, pulling her bathrobe closed. "I thought I heard babies."

"We have a new neighbor," Pax announced.

"Sorry, I'm Lola," Lola apologized. "Sorry about all this…"

"Flossie," Flossie smiled kindly.

"Say Flossie," Pax asked, "any chance you have some extra toilet paper? A cot, maybe? Lola's things won't be arriving until tomorrow."

"Sorry, it's just that I had to flee in the night with my kids…"

"Oh, Honey," Flossie hummed sympathetically.

"It's fine," Lola lied. "I'm fine. We. We're fine."

"That expression on Flossie's face?" Pax said wryly. "That's what she looks like when she's analyzing someone. She's from the faculty of psychology at the university."

"Crap," Lola swore under her breath.

"You apologize a lot," Flossie observed.

"Sorry about that... I mean..."

"He was a narcissist, wasn't he?" Flossie asked, folding her arms and cocking an eyebrow.

"I don't know," Lola shrugged. "I guess."

"Gaslighting?" Flossie guessed. "Never did anything wrong? Everything was always YOUR fault?"

"It's creepy how accurate you are," Lola said. "But hey," she continued sarcastically, "he apologized sometimes." Lola counted her children to make a point. "Exactly five times."

"I'm glad you're here, Lola," Flossie said, squinting at her analytically. "I'll get some toilet paper."

Lola smiled with limp uncertainty. "Sure."

# CHAPTER SIXTEEN
## (CLARITY)

Clarity jolted awake the following morning to the sound of a text on her cell phone. With her hair tangled in a staticky mess, Clarity blinked around the room, trying to make sense of the sunshine squeezing like a slit through the window.

"No," she moaned. "No, Daryl, no."

The text from Daryl De Voort glared at Clarity from her phone.

*"Where is the sample, Clarity Trout?"*

Wincing, Clarity impulsively thumbed *"It's coming"* into her phone. Then she rammed her head repeatedly against her desk, cursing herself. When a reply suddenly chimed on Clarity's phone, she sat in her chair, erect with surprise and dread when she read.

*"We need to talk. My office. 10:00."*

# CHAPTER SEVENTEEN
## (MALLY AND FELIX)

"Mayonnaise," Mally said after swinging a sledgehammer through the wall. "Fascinating!"

"It pays the rent," Felix said, wiping drywall dust from his corduroy pants."

"All this time and I had no idea you worked in a mayonnaise plant," Mally said, taking another swing of the sledgehammer. "I always imagined you being a mumblecore filmmaker."

"Why mumblecore?"

Mally shrugged. "Maybe it's the soul patch. Or the corduroy."

"You're cute," Felix said, his mouth curling into an amorous smirk.

"You have an artist's hands," Mally said, taking Felix's hands in hers and thumbing the powdery debris from his slender fingers.

"I used to play the harpsichord," Felix admitted bashfully.

"Really?" Mally said, her eyes widening with wonder. "Why did you stop?"

"I had planned to continue my musical studies in college, but as it happens, there's no such thing as a harpsichord scholarship," Felix replied while taking a turn with the sledgehammer. "I had no money saved for college, so I chose a trade." One more swing of the sledgehammer. "Mayonnaise."

"You keep surprising me, Felix. I love that about you."

"You're not disappointed?" Felix asked, musing on his artist hands, and subtly playing invisible harpsichord keys. "About the mayonnaise?"

"I happen to be very fond of mayonnaise," Mally assured Felix. "It's my favorite garnish. And so versatile."

"It's like our souls knew each other from the moment we first met," Felix said thoughtfully.

"I love how we can finally talk so openly like this," Mally said, marveling at the enormous, gaping hole where the wall used to be. "No more awkwardness. Being hormonally tongue-tied. Worrying that Morgan Freeman's voice might be literally narrating our impure thoughts out loud for the whole world to hear. Crushes are the absolute worst."

"I've wanted this for a very long time."

"Me too."

"And the best part is," Felix said, raising an index finger, "we can skip the whole cumbersome dating thing and go straight to the good stuff."

"Ugh! Dating is gauche."

"It's more of a ritual than anything."

"We did the groundwork beforehand."

"Friendship."

"Respect."

"I've looked up to you since the day I met you, Mally."

Mally's eyes glowed with surprise and adoration. "Really?"

"Your devotion to literature," Felix relished. "The way your face lights up when you talk about whatever book you happen to be reading. Your mind intrigues me. You perceive the world differently than anyone I've ever met."

"You gathered all that from our encounters in the elevator?"

"You can learn a lot about people in elevators," Felix nodded intently. "And we had an awful lot of elevator rides together."

"Knock, knock?" Pax said, popping his head through the open door. "What are the two of you up to?"

"Smashing out the wall," Felix said, demonstrating.

"We're combining our apartments," Mally beamed.

"Cool," Pax nodded. "That's impressive that the super gave you permission. He's usually such a hardhead."

Felix and Mally slowly looked at each other, ashen.

"Sorry to interrupt," Pax continued. "We have a new neighbor — Lola - who moved in last night with five young children. She just escaped a very bad relationship, and she could use our help."

"Oooh," Mally said empathically, hand on heart.

"Lola's looking for work," Pax continued. "Any leads at the mayonnaise plant, Felix?"

"Sorry, man," Felix apologized. "There's been a hiring freeze."

"Oh, that's a shame," Pax deflated. "I'll keep asking around. Do either of you have any childcare solutions for her?"

"Betty Agnew," Mally suggested. "She's a retired schoolteacher looking for some income. Eleventh floor."

"Perfect," Pax said, writing something down. "I'll go knock on her door. Flossie's setting Lola up with some counselling," Pax said, reading down a checklist, "Otto set up a crowd funding campaign, Piper offered to babysit, Girard offered to run some errands for Lola, Willatrix... said she'd consult with the potato?... And Norman is making a fresh batch of marshmallows for the kids. If you guys can think of any employment leads, that would be amazing."

"Sure thing, Pax," Felix said as Pax waved a brief good-bye.

"He's so nice," Mally observed. "When Pax sets his mind to something, he really knows how to get things done."

"Absolutely," Felix said, adjusting his bow tie. "Hard to believe he's a politician."

# CHAPTER EIGHTEEN
## (BIFF CHESTERFIELD)

"Oh gosh, this in an honor Sir," said Biff Chesterfield, shaking Tristan's hand with exuberant, nervous fervor. "A real honor. I was hooked on your soap. Totally bummed when Roderick Von Trapezoid exploded like that. What a shame. You were the best part of the show and I'm not just saying that. I mean it, Mr. Prime Minster."

Tristan cackled pretentiously while shaking Biff's beefy hand. "I know, Biff. I know." Then turning to his well-rehearsed wife, he said, "Gloria, I'd like you to meet Biff Chesterfield. The premier of Scatopia."

"Charmed," Gloria said in a Shakespearean way, elegantly extending her perfectly manicured hand to Biff.

"She sure is pretty, Mr. Prime Minister," Biff said with verve.

"Biff," Tristan said with a pompous smile, "for God's sake just call me Tristan. We're basically colleagues, except I'm much more powerful than you are. But that's a minor detail."

"Golly, that's swell, Sir," Biff said, beaming like a buffoon. "I really appreciate that. Maybe us and the wives can go get a pop sometime."

"Maybe Biff," Tristan said, still smiling stiffly, slapping Biff on the back. "Maybe we can do that. I'd like to introduce you to my newly appointed Chief Situational Officer." Tristan gestured towards an awkward woman, slightly cross-eyed who donned a perpetual look that suggested she had no idea where she was or how she got there. "This is Dr. Beepy Deerlight."

"Um… my name is not Beepy," the woman said with her usual, stunned monotone.

"It's an extreme pleasure to meet you, Beepy," Biff said, his face reddening even more than normal.

"It's B.P. actually," the woman said with the same stunned, monotonic inflection. "Like the initials?"

"Beepy comes to us with a background in quantum physics," Tristan continued obliviously. "I felt that up until now, quantum physicists have been sorely underrepresented in politics."

"I couldn't agree with you more," Biff said, loosening his collar to relieve his sweaty, ape-like neck. "You are a fair and equitable man, Tristan. I fully endorse your decision to appoint Beepy."

"Brenda Penelope," B.P. tried again. Her voice was not nearly imposing enough.

"I pride myself in achieving parity on my team," Tristan gloated. "Women. Science. Two things I fervently respect."

"You kidnapped me from the lab actually," B.P. pointed out dryly.

"So admirable," Biff said, humbly shaking his head.

"Strong women are my inspiration," Tristan said, squeezing Gloria's hand. "When I saw the opportunity to work alongside Beepy, I just grabbed it."

"Literally," B.P. blinked.

"I'm so proud of you, my darling," Gloria doted.

"I know," Tristan said, booping Gloria's nose.

"That's so beautiful, you guys," Biff said, wiping away a single tear with his sausage thumb.

"Why am I here even?" B.P. asked monotonically.

"Beepy, do you mind?" Tristan said condescendingly. "We're talking here."

"Tristan," Biff said, running his fingers nervously through his thinning hair, "I hope this isn't inappropriate, but could I please have your autograph? Sorry, it's just that *Lust Triangle* is my favorite soap."

"Biff," Tristan smirked arrogantly, "never feel as though asking such a thing is inappropriate." He scribbled his signature on a piece of paper which Gloria had provided on cue. "I am more than happy to oblige."

"What's a Chief Situational Officer?" B.P. blinked.

# CHAPTER NINETEEN
## (CLARITY)

"I didn't think you had it in you, Clarity Trout," said Daryl De Voort, spinning around in his swivel chair with uncharacteristic verve.

"I... I don't get it," Clarity blinked.

"A cowering little mouse like you?" marveled De Voort. "Who knew you could be so gritty?"

"What are you talking about? I haven't..."

"Got it in just under the wire, but damn!"

Clarity gaped.

"Do you think you can crank out more articles like this one?" De Voort beamed. "If so, I think you have a bright future here at *Verisimilitude Media.*"

"I think there must be some kind of…" Clarity blinked hard. "…mistake."

"What, you don't want to be a permanent member of my writing team?"

"I… I do, but…"

"Good," De Voort nodded affirmatively. "Because I have already added you to the payroll."

Clarity's lips parted.

"Send me your banking information," De Voort said, slapping a palm loudly on his desk. "Your article will be live within the hour. We've been doing an emergency print run so hard copies will be available at the same time. Start thinking about a follow-up article."

Clarity goggled.

\*\*\*

"Fern, there's been a terrible mistake," Clarity said to her fern. "I think Daryl De Voort has me confused with someone else. He's publishing my article, but… but *I didn't write an article.* I missed the deadline this morning. I thought he was calling me in to yell at me for wasting his time. But he said I'm gritty and I'm on the payroll now. I tried to come clean but he… he just wouldn't listen. What do I…do? I don't want to be dishonest, but how in the heck am I supposed to get another opportunity like this?"

The fern did not reply.

"I'd..." Clarity blinked hard. "I'd be taking this opportunity away from someone else. The person who actually wrote the gritty article. But... but come on. If the writer is that gritty, chances are they'd find other opportunities. Most people aren't like... me. They could do other interviews. And it wouldn't be a big deal for them. But for me... I'm a good writer. I know I am. All I need is for someone to give me a... chance."

The fern seemed to wilt with disapproval.

Clarity flopped backwards on her bed.

"I guess..." Clarity stammered. "I guess I should just go with it."

# CHAPTER TWENTY
## (PIPER AND OTTO)

"Excited?" Otto gushed while setting up a portable amp at the front of the cat café.

"I might throw up," Piper replied, squeezing the neck of her fiesta red Fender Mustang. She scanned the room which was already peppered with a smattering of people. A dusty fellow wearing orange industrial overalls. A churchy woman waiting to order a guava nectar smoothie and a raisin scone. A studious individual, enthralled with his glowing laptop screen. A gaggle of twittering teenage girls who were most likely ditching school. Norman, giving Piper a thumbs-up from a table in the corner.

"This is the best possible place to make your debut," Otto assured Piper. "No critics. No snobs. Just a few nice people who have gathered here for a fruity drink and some socialization. Cats. And maybe a scout if we're lucky."

"No pressure," Piper said tremulously.

"Everybody loves you," Otto said cheerfully, mussing Piper's bucket hat – a purple one today. "You literally make the sun shine. We can all sense it. I wish you could..."

"I've never performed in front of people before."

"Knowingly," Otto winked. "You've serenaded me several times through the air vents."

Piper pursed her lips as she eyeballed more customers meandering into the café.

"Piper," Otto said sincerely. "I am so proud of you."

Piper's eyes welled with tears. "Nobody's ever..." she whimpered. "You realize I'm going to have to hug you now."

"Come at me, Bruh," Otto said animatedly, assuming the hug position with arms stretched out like elastic bands.

Piper hugged Otto tightly and felt his crackling energy zap through her. She tingled with inspiration, motivation, confidence, glee. Otto's hugs made Piper feel like she could do anything.

"I really believe in you, Pipes," he said in mid-hug as Piper held on just a bit too long. "You are going to do great things. You just need to take this first step, okay? I'm here. Norman's here. How can anything bad happen with Norman around?"

"Young Otto?" Norman beckoned from his seat.

Otto swerved around to find Norman reading a newspaper.

"Did ye read this?" Norman asked, pointing at an article on the front page.

Otto and Piper read over Norman's shoulder.

*"It's coming?"* Otto read, perplexed.

"What's coming?" Piper asked.

"That's all it says," Otto said, scratching his head.

"Anyone heard of Clarity Trout?" Norman asked. "Seems she's the journalist who covered the story."

"There must be a mistake," Piper said, consulting the newsfeed on her cellphone. "There must be more to it... Oh my God."

"What?" Otto asked.

"It's everywhere," Piper answered, scrolling. "It's breaking news. Every news outlet is reporting it."

"What do you mean, Miss Piper?" Norman asked.

*"It's coming."*

## CHAPTER TWENTY-ONE
### (GIRARD AND FLOSSIE)

"*What's* coming?" Girard asked as he pulled on a pair of argyle socks in preparation for his midday lecture.

"*It,*" Flossie replied with her mouth full of toothbrush and paste. "It's all over the news. Nobody can make any sense of it."

"Did they check their sources?" Girard asked in a professor-ly way.

"It's the media," Flossie said after spitting in the bathroom sink. "Of course not."

\*\*\*

When Girard and Flossie entered the elevator, they found Lola holding the door open for them.

"Lola," Flossie said kindly. "Girard, this is Lola, who I was telling you about."

"Nice to finally meet you," Girard nodded cordially.

"I'm just headed to a job interview," Lola said self-consciously. "Pax found a guy on the third floor with a lead on a job. Hair salon. Answering phones, taking appointments and stuff. Betty's minding the kids. She seems nice."

"I'm so happy to hear that, Lola."

"We'll see how it goes," Lola shrugged.

Flossie pursed her lips sympathetically, academically reading Lola's submissive body language.

"Lola," Flossie hesitated. "I don't want to overstep, but can I tell you something? The people in this building, we really care about what you've been through. I know it's hard to trust..."

"I'm good," Lola said bluntly as she stepped out of the elevator with her nose in her phone. "But thanks."

As Lola walked through the hollow foyer of the block tower, her brow furrowed with worry. *"It's coming?"* she muttered, reading a headline. "Oh crap, what now?"

# CHAPTER TWENTY-TWO
## (WILLATRIX)

"Love and light," Willatrix livestreamed, on the verge of faux tears. "I am here. Willatrix Oleander. Empath. Sage. Influencer. Spiritual guide."

Then pointing at her tears, she continued, "See these? I'm crying right now because of the fear and uncertainty you must all be feeling. Oh, my heart. You may have heard the breaking news. *'It's coming.'* I wish I could quell your fears. I wish I could cradle you all in my arms. Lull you into a peaceful slumber. Cover you with my feathers. We need compassion more than ever, my absorbent, little sponges. So please urge your friends to follow my vlog. I may not be able to stop it from coming, but here's what I can do. I'll generate millions of peace particles and make them waft right through the screen. And with the help of my spirit potato, I will guide you through the confusing times ahead. Thank you for your attention."

# CHAPTER TWENTY-THREE
## (PIPER AND OTTO)

The news ticker scrolled quickly across the bottom of the screen, saying *'It's coming'* over and over again. Piper, Otto, Norman and all the customers huddled together by the flat screen T.V. mounted on the café wall.

"*It's coming,*" Tristan Winnings said from a press conference in a voice that sounded like the narrator of a movie trailer. "We have no idea what that means," Tristan said with a seriousness that he only could have learned at Juilliard, "but we do know that it is on its way. And until we evaluate the threat of this thing which we know not of, we must do whatever we can to secure the nation. Thankfully, I had the foresight to appoint a Chief Situational Officer. Because as you can see, we have a situation."

B.P.'s eyes bulged when the camera briefly panned over to her.

"With her expertise in quantum physics," Tristan continued with theatrical somberness, "Dr. Beepy Deerlight will be my consultant throughout this unprecedented crisis."

B.P. raised a finger but chickened out of saying something.

"As we evaluate the threat," Tristan said stoically, "I am putting forth a federal decree that every citizen of Umbravia must go home immediately and remain confined to your home until we navigate through this matter."

There was a collective gasp throughout the café.

"All businesses, institutions, gathering places, event venues, sporting facilities, theaters, and literally anything else must be shut down immediately."

"Your café," Piper said in a strangled voice, squeezing Otto's arm.

"The borders are officially closed," Tristan said, glaring at the camera. "And you all have exactly one hour to get your affairs in order and to retreat to your homes."

Commotion began to swell in the cat café as reporters inundated Tristan on television with rapid-fire questions.

"How will people get food?" one reporter called out.

"We haven't figured that out yet," Tristan replied.

"Sir, what about the homeless?"

"That's not really my problem."

"Expatriated citizens stranded outside the borders?"

"Borders closed. I said what I said."

"How long will people be confined, Sir?"

"There's no way of knowing that at this time."

"Do you think you might be overreacting?"

"Security," Tristan said, squinting at the reporter's name badge. "Take this one away. Fred. He's causing problems here."

Reporters stormed the prime minister with more questions as he descended from the podium.

"What in the hell is going on here?" screamed a customer who was getting lost in the commotion.

"I'm sorry everyone," Otto said, trying to be heard above the frantic din. "Please grab your cats and run. We don't have much time to close up shop."

"I'll help you close," Piper said, already stowing bistro chairs in the kitchen.

"What can I do?" Norman asked earnestly, with chaos all around him.

"Run," Otto advised, his eyes brimming with concern. "Please Norman. Just run."

# CHAPTER TWENTY-FOUR
## (BACK AT THE BLOCK)

"What's going on out there?" Mally asked, looking out the window of her apartment.

Felix joined her at the window, watching in stunned silence as a massive stampede of people outside jostled, shoved, trampled, and screamed, *'It's coming!'* They spotted Lola, trapped in the throng, being jounced around in a jungle of hysterical humans.

"Oh my God," Felix said, blanched.

\*\*\*

"My babies!" Lola shrieked, getting swallowed in the street crowd.

"Lola!" a voice could be heard somewhere in the mob.

Lola scoped around, until a hand came out from seemingly nowhere and yanked her.

"Don't let go of my hand," the voice said.

Swallowing hard, Lola obeyed. All around her was a sea of elbows, screaming faces, hair, hands, and fear. She could feel bruises forming all over her body and her heart raced at a dangerous speed. She thought she tasted blood on her lip. When she eventually realized she had made it into the foyer of the block tower, Lola discovered Girard's face securing eye contact with her, looking distressed behind his spectacles.

"Are you okay?" Girard said, mentally inspecting Lola's face for injuries.

"What just happened?"

"The entire city has collectively lost its mind," Girard said, trying to remain calm.

"Hurry," Flossie said, poking her finger into the elevator button hundreds of times, as though that would make the doors open faster. "Apparently they've deployed the military."

"Seriously, what's going on?" Lola squeaked.

"It's hard to explain," Girard said. "But you're going to be fine, Lola. Once the hysteria dies down. In the meantime, just go back to your apartment and try to stay calm."

"Stay calm?" Lola shrieked. "Perhaps you didn't see the apocalyptic riot outside. Is the world ending or something?"

"No," Girard said, locking eyes with Lola. "It's just... Everyone read a soundbite."

"The best thing to do," Flossie said when they finally made it into the elevator, "is to lay low until the hype dies down. In the meantime, just try not to be confronted by the military."

"But what about my kids?" Lola yelped.

***

When Lola arrived at her apartment, her children were not there.

"Izzy!" Lola shrieked hysterically. "Sara-Sue! Garthie! En..."

"They're here!" Pax called urgently, peeping his head out of his apartment.

"What the..." Lola panicked. "Where the hell is Betty?"

"It wasn't her fault, Lola," Pax said, handing Bobby to Lola and escorting the rest of the tots into the apartment next door. "It was mayhem after the press conference. The halls and elevators were clogged. Everyone screaming. Betty had to get back to her apartment before the military..."

"Oh my God!"

"They're okay, Lola," Pax assured her. "I promise. I gave them a snack. Bobby's diaper still smells okay."

"You gave them a snack?" Lola hyperventilated. "You didn't give them tree nuts... they're allergic..."

"Apple slices and juice," Pax said, snagging a toddler escapee by the shirt and guiding him into the apartment. "It's all good."

"All good," Lola muttered ironically through the white noise of slamming doors, crashes, and blood curdling screams.

"Please be safe," Pax urged before retreating to his flat. "And if there's anything you need, please call."

With a sleeping newborn sagging in her arms and hyper children jumping on a springy cot, Lola gawked with disbelief out the window.

"I didn't even make it to my job interview," she said faintly to herself.

\*\*\*

When Piper and Otto returned, breathless to the tower block, a soldier decked in camo, wielding an inappropriately sized weapon was manning the front entrance.

"There's a soldier now?" Otto pointed in disbelief. "Are you freaking kidding me?"

"Your hour is up," the soldier said in a dead voice. "Explain yourself."

"My cat café was shut down with no notice," Otto said breathlessly. "I got out of there as fast as I could but keep it real. It takes more than one hour to shut down and secure a business and then shoulder your way through a literal H.G. Wells novel to get home."

"Don't make him mad," Piper stage whispered.

"We were following orders," Otto said to the soldier. "We're only six minutes after curfew."

"I've been given orders to discipline you," the soldier said, emotionless.

Piper burst into tears. "My music debut was supposed to be today."

Otto used one arm to shelter Piper in a half-hug while using the other to gesture his protest to the soldier. "You have been given orders to discipline us *how?*"

The soldier gaped. "Shut up and get in the building."

\*\*\*

Clarity squeezed her pillow until feathers burst everywhere. What she saw out her rectangular window reminded her of the first and only Sci-Fi horror movie she watched when she was twelve. It gave her nightmares about aliens and escaped lunatics, and she had to sleep with the lights on for seven solid weeks. But the film paled in comparison to what was happening in that moment. This was real. This was out of control. This was a veritable catastrophe. And all because of a hasty text she sent while she was half-asleep. The marquee across the street flashed *'IT'S COMING'* threateningly in garish, red lights.

"Fern," Clarity warbled. "What... have I done?"

# CHAPTER TWENTY-FIVE
## (TRISTAN WINNINGS)

"That went well I think," Tristan said after the cameras were turned off and the reporters fled in terror to their homes.

"What just happened?" B.P. said monotonically.

"Tristan, I think you're finally getting it," Hector said aridly. "You assumed dominance by inciting fear. You can't tell by looking at me right now, but I am moved."

"I gave some thought to what you said before, Hector," Tristan said, taking a swig of water from a bottle made of single-use plastic. "About being re-elected. I did some soul searching, Hector and I realized just how much it means to me to have a private jet. All of a sudden, I have a whole bunch of special friends who offer me free vacays and obscene amounts of money in exchange for little favors. And after enjoying the obscene square footage of my special, prime minister mansion, it really made me never want to leave, should I be voted out in the next election. And I think I felt my id tingle when you were talking about world domination. That sounds like fun."

B.P's eyes bulged.

"I do have one question though," Tristan mused.

"Hmm?"

"Now what?" Tristan asked.

"Keep them scared," Hector said flatly.

"You mean I have to do all that again?" Tristan asked with widening eyes.

"This media blitz is the best thing that's ever happened to you," Hector explained. People are more pliant when they are paralyzed with fear. They'll do literally anything you say. Just keep acting like you're concerned for the fate of the nation."

"I," Tristan interjected tentatively, "am. Concerned for the fate of the nation."

Hector was nonplussed.

"It's freaky," Tristan said, shaking his fingers as though he just picked up something gross. "Make no mistake, I'm glad I've finally managed to garner respect..."

"Fear."

"... but what IS coming, exactly?"

"Nobody knows, Tristan."

"What if it's something horrific?"

"The article was two words long, Tristan. Calm down."

"What if the journalist who wrote the article only had time to write two words because something grotesque was chasing her?"

"Tristan..."

"If the world ends, that may affect my popularity in the polls."

"Look," Hector seethed dryly. "Maybe this nebulous scourge is plotting out the demise of mankind or maybe it's just another soundbite being used to sell something. The fact is, we do not know either way. And it is this uncertainty you need to take by the underpants and yank."

"But..."

"The public clings to their leader during times of uncertainty," Hector continued. "Those who would otherwise be distrusting of the government will beg you to take control if they believe you are their only hope."

"How in the world am I supposed to navigate through all this with literally no idea what I'm doing?"

"That's what the Chief Situational Officer is for," Hector said, pointing at a very perplexed B.P. Deerlight.

"Shit..." B.P. said, slightly more cross-eyed than usual.

# CHAPTER TWENTY-SIX
## (CLARITY)

The following morning, Clarity woke up and for a split moment she thought the whole thing was a dream. When she heard nothing but silence outside and Ezekiel screaming *'told ya'* from his apartment, Clarity suddenly felt like she swallowed a live hummingbird. She lay catatonic in her bed, too stunned to feel fear, guilt or even confusion. She simply existed, and even that was a challenge.

When she noticed an incoming video call from her dad, she scrambled to answer. If Torrence was hurdled into the basement of despair, it was certainly her fault. Her poor father was all alone and this whole ordeal must have been shocking and traumatic for him.

"Da..." Clarity said quickly to the screen.

"How are you doing, baby girl?" Torrence asked with worry creased into his pinkish forehead.

"I..." Clarity said, shaking the fuzz from her brain. "I don't know."

"You all alone with your fern?"

"I don't mind," Clarity shrugged. "I... I prefer being confined to my apartment."

"Oh Clarity..."

"Weirdly," Clarity stammered, "I feel safer now than I have since I first arrived in the city. How're you doing, Da?"

"I'll manage," Torrence said, stretching like a cat. "Not allowed to harvest mushrooms seeing as how I'm housebound. But nobody ever became a farmer because they wanted to take the easy route. The government will figure things out and I'll be back out in the field before you know it."

Clarity blinked.

"You never told me how the job interview went," Torrence reminded Clarity.

Clarity shrugged. "Fine."

"Does that mean you got the job, or you didn't?"

Clarity's eyeballs wandered around the room, focusing on anything but Torrence. "I guess."

"Well damn!" Torrence said, slapping his knee. "That's my little girl right there! When will you be published?"

"I mean no!" Clarity said quickly, squeezing her eyes shut. "I didn't get it. I mean."

"Oh," Torrence deflated. "You'll get 'em next time, Clare Bear."

"Da, are you sure you're okay?" Clarity asked again. "I worry about you."

"I'm a little stir-crazy but I'm quite used to being alone," Torrence chuckled. "But you need to stop making yourself so scarce, so I know you haven't been swallowed into a supernova. If I don't check up on you, it's possible you could lose yourself in... yourself."

"I thrive in this kind of environment," Clarity mumbled.

"Solitude is not an environment," Torrence said, pointing a finger at the screen. "Remember what happened to you when you were nine?"

White-knuckled, Clarity clutched the sides of her chair, sweating and feeling the hummingbird she allegedly swallowed trying to peck its way out of her stomach.

"Promise you'll call," Torrence said, looking directly into the screen.

Clarity nodded.

# CHAPTER TWENTY-SEVEN
## (GIRARD AND FLOSSIE)

"Well," Flossie said, sitting pertly on the couch. "This is different."

Girard plunked next to her, removing his spectacles, shaking his head, and just stared. "I've never seen anything like that, pretty much ever." Then he cocked his head at Flossie, who was pursing her lips in pensive thought. "You're worried about the psychological fallout of all this, aren't you."

"I can't help it, Girard," Flossie said, grimacing. "The thought of all those people. Like literally everyone. Going through a collective trauma. It's just too much."

Girard placed his arm around Flossie and rested his head against her shoulder. "It's natural to worry about them, Floss. The establishment has pulled off some rather egregious things. But this..."

"Lola didn't even make it to her job interview, today," Flossie said, shaking her head in disbelief. "What about those kids? How are they all going to manage? And what about Norman? If anything happened to him..."

"Let's hope this will all blow over soon."

"What if it doesn't?" Flossie said, standing and pacing like a listless tiger. "The messaging concerns me. Winnings has veritably traumatized the entire country and we don't even know what's going on yet. You can't easily reverse shock and trauma, Girard. Even when this is over, people are going to be too freaked out to leave their homes. They could all end up like that poor girl upstairs."

"Flossie..."

"What if this drags on indefinitely?" Flossie said with a liberal use of hand gestures. "Everyone experiences isolation differently. We are social creatures. You can't just..."

"The government has a moral obligation to us," Girard said, the words prickling his lips as he said them. He was well-aware of how morally bankrupt the system can be. But Flossie looked so helpless. He couldn't bring himself to tell her about his own grave concerns. "They can't just coop us up indefinitely."

"But the messaging strongly implies..." Flossie squeaked. "Winnings wouldn't shut down the country if he was planning on springing us tomorrow."

"I... know."

"Do you even know what isolation can do to people?" Flossie asked, her voice catching emotionally. "It can cause depression. Anxiety.

Hallucinations, both visual and auditory. It can cause brain degeneration. Paranoia. Aggression. Antisocial tendencies. Inflammation, immune deficiency, cytokine storms and a plethora of other health problems. Isolation can literally cause your entire mind and body to deteriorate. Make you forget how to be human."

"I've got you," Girard said, coaxing Flossie back to the couch. "Please don't worry. Please, Love."

Flossie cocked her head at Girard. She could almost see an academic cog circulating in his brain. "You're doing it too."

"Trying not to."

"It's hard not to consider the moral implications of this," Flossie said, stroking Girard's arm.

A beat.

"Want to play Boggle?" Girard shrugged.

# CHAPTER TWENTY-EIGHT
## (LOLA)

"Squeeee!" squealed four of Lola's five children as they pounced on a feeble air mattress, on loan from some guy named Maurice on the twelfth floor.

Lola's church did not get a chance to deliver furniture and provisions, but the flat was sparsely speckled with a mishmash of odds and ends, provided the previous night by various residents of the tower block. The air mattress would serve as a bed for the children and Lola would sleep on the cot. There was an ottoman, a faded set of lawn chairs, a card table, an ancient rabbit-eared television set, ugly lamp, five mismatched throw cushions, a pile of blankets, and a Rubbermaid bin filled with random items.

Her bleary eyes glassed over like empty windows as Lola sat, stunned on the ottoman.

*I was finally free.*

*I was so close.*

*Steps away from a real job.*

*Independence.*

*How long will this drag on?*

*What will happen to my children?*

*Can I do this by myself?*

*What if I'm useless like Shane said?*

*Was he right?*

*Stop it, Lola.*

*You did the right thing.*

*You can... do this.*

*Dammit.*

*All these nice people in the building...*

*Now they're all out of reach.*

*This is my life now.*

*For God knows how long.*

*I don't think I have it in me...*

"Is something wrong, Mummy?" asked little Izzy who looked at Lola, wide-eyed with apprehension.

Lola instantly snapped out of her stupor. "Of course not, Honeybear," Lola said, conjuring a smile.

"What's going on?" Izzy asked, blinking away tears and wincing when she heard a blood curdling scream coming from outside.

"We," Lola said with forced enthusiasm, "are about to have an epic adventure!"

# CHAPTER TWENTY-NINE
## (PIPER AND OTTO)

The agony was unbearable. Cocooned in her blankets, Piper curled into a ball in her bed, crying a thousand different varieties of tears. The heaviness she felt made it virtually impossible to get out of bed. A tsunami of emotions crashed over her, making her head throb with crushing pain. Every nerve ending in her body screamed with fear, shock, confusion, loss, horror, loneliness, dread, anger, hopelessness, and despair. All the feelings. All *their* feelings.

A million soundbites swirled through her mind as she curled more tightly like a snail into a shell. Images of every person she knew. Every person she didn't know. The sound of their cries. Screams. Frantic questions. The fear in their eyes. The darkness. The numbness. The ache. The bleak thoughts. It was all just too much.

Normally Otto would be the first person Piper would go to when she was going through something. He was her ride or die. And his presence had the same effect on Piper's neurotransmitters as lavender aromatherapy. His words, energy, hugs, and mere existence soothed her stress. He was like human dopamine. Piper's brain knew that she and Otto were not actually related, but her heart insisted they were brother and sister. Piper was unable to convince her heart otherwise. And now it was legally impossible to be in the same room with him. Was this even real?

Piper needed a hug.

She REALLY needed a hug.

"Otto," Piper whimpered faintly.

As if on cue, Piper's cellphone lit up with a text message from Otto. *'You okay?'*

Piper burst into tears.

Her cellphone suddenly rang.

"Hi," Piper said weakly, answering the phone.

"Something's wrong," Otto said on the phone.

"It's too hard to explain," Piper moaned.

"You can tell me anything, Pipes. You know that."

"I want to. It's just…"

"You absorb people's emotions," Otto said matter-of-factly.

"You… you know about that?"

"I figured it out a long time ago."

"You did?"

"I understand, Piper."

"How?" Piper sniffled. "I don't even understand."

"This must be so hard for you," Otto sighed. "There's so much pain out there right now. And you're feeling it all? Ouch."

"I'm feeling all these things," Piper tried to explain.

"But the feelings aren't yours," Otto finished.

"You don't think I'm crazy?"

"It's beautiful," Otto assured her. "I don't know anyone else like you."

"This feels wrong," Piper whimpered. "You're just next door and yet you feel so far away."

"I know," Otto agreed. "We used to see each other every day. You've become part of my mental wallpaper."

"Can you stay on the phone with me?" Piper quavered. "Until my battery runs out?"

"Anything you need," Otto swallowed.

An excruciating silence followed while Piper's face wrenched with emotional agony and rivulets of tears formed on her cheeks. Otto somehow knew. He mashed tears back into his eyes with the palms of his hands, sympathy tingling in his ribcage.

"How long is this going to last?" Piper finally squeaked.

"I... I don't know."

# CHAPTER THIRTY
## (WILLATRIX)

"Love and light," Willatrixed vlogged. "I am here. Willatrix Oleander. Empath. Sage. Influencer. Spiritual guide. You may have noticed that the world suddenly ended. Thank goodness I'm an empath," she said, fanning her hand over her heart with gratitude. "I have the emotional utensils to tell you all how to feel during this utterly perplexing time. Please don't try to make sense of your thoughts and emotions right now. There is no frame of reference for what we are collectively experiencing. Allow me to prompt your emotional responses. That's what I'm here for. And remember, my little miracles. We are all hurting together."

Willatrix fluttered her fingers mystically.

"My heart is throbbing with humility and joy. For I have acquired five hundred new followers since last time. Thank you, earth angels.

Thank you for inviting your friends to follow me on my quest to enlighten mankind. My heart gives thanks. The universe is blowing you kisses. A gentle reminder that we are one."

After a brief, meditative chant Willatrix continued.

"Tangent. At the moment there are no businesses to boycott. Since there isn't much to do right now other than look at screens, my boycott of the day is an ultra-low budget film called *Born in My Heart* by independent filmmaker, Celeste Bobkins. Don't let the theme of adopting underprivileged orphans deceive you. The film contains child actors, which is repulsive and unforgivable. There is no justifiable reason to exploit actual children when Bobkins could have easily used CGI. Friends, I urge you to not only militantly avoid this film, but please inundate every internet thread and comment section with your ire. Put pressure on every streaming service to cancel this horrid filmmaker. We must take punitive measures to ensure Bobkins never makes another film as long as she lives."

Then she concluded with praying hands, "This has been Willatrix Oleander, reminding you to be decent to one another, just like me. Thank you for your attention."

# CHAPTER THIRTY-ONE
## (FELIX AND MALLY)

Taking refuge in Mally's quilty bed, Felix and Mally held each other protectively. They had barricaded the bedroom door with a knotty pine armoire and stockpiled copious amounts of canned tuna fish in the closet. The window was blanked out with masking tape.

"Do you think it's an asteroid?" Mally asked, safe in the haven of Felix's auburn-haired arms. "It's an asteroid, isn't it."

"I've got you," Felix breathed, "I think I just pissed myself, but I've got you."

"It's not fair," Mally sniffled. "I finally have you after years of pining and now we may only get a few hours to love each other."

"I know," Felix said, kissing Mally's freckled forehead. "I don't want to die this way. This is so typical."

"This kind of thing happens to you often?"

"Typical in the sense that we're all just set up for failure," Felix snuffed. "Regardless of all the sensible decisions I've made, nothing works out for me."

"That's not true," Mally said, rolling over and smudging a tear from Felix's cheek with her thumb. "We're together now. This would have been so much worse if we were both still alone."

"And just when my life started to suck less, the universe murders me."

"Felix..."

"I did everything I was supposed to do. Things are supposed to work out for people who do sensible things. Regardless of..."

"You're regretting your decision to give up on the harpsichord."

"How would I have made a living?" Felix squeaked. "Playing at Renaissance festivals? Providing ambient noise at the *Haunted House of Wax?*"

"It would have made you happy," Mally said, stroking Felix's hair.

"Happy," Felix muttered.

"Don't you think being happy for a little while is better than not at all?"

"Squeeze me tighter," Felix swallowed.

"I feel like there's so much I still don't know about you," Mally said, clutching Felix tightly.

"I enjoy a good macchiato," Felix said soothingly, twiddling with Mally's braid. "I was bullied a lot in middle school because of my milky-smooth girl hands. Always wanted a giraffe. Never got one though. My favorite memory is the time I saw a real moose on a camping trip with some buddies of mine. Don't remember their names now. I think one of them was Phil. I enjoy muffins. Bran. I can't cook to save my life. In fact, I accidentally set my sleeve on fire once when I attempted to roast a capon. I tried weed once. Threw up. I'm allergic to pollen and I met Lin-Manuel Miranda one time. Nice guy. We compared scarves and talked about the health benefits of avocados. My lifelong dream has always been to visit Kathmandu. I guess that's never going to happen now."

Felix nudged Mally.

"My favorite author is George Orwell," Mally quavered, nestling deeper into Felix's embrace. "PG Wodehouse is a very close second. I grew up with horses. I miss riding sometimes. My parents are divorced but they're still good friends. When I was a kid, I would go to the butterfly conservatory on *Dad Weekends.* Afterwards he would take me to the retro diner for a cola ice-cream float. It was the absolute best. I've never had a boyfriend. Except maybe Wilbert Fudge from summer camp but he doesn't really count. I love to roller skate. Bake chocolate chip cookies. Go for long walks in the city. Pigeons make me laugh. The subway kind of freaks me out though. I don't know why. My secret weakness is spray cheese. And sometimes I dream that I'm a character in someone else's work of fiction. Weird, right?"

"I don't think so."

"I'm so glad you're here, Felix."

"Same."

# CHAPTER THIRTY-TWO
## (TRISTAN WINNINGS)

Tristan wrote, *Very Important Meeting* on a white board and underlined it three times.

"This is a very important meeting," Tristan said with a pin-straight mouth. "We need to navigate the national threat of... whatever it is that's coming. Beepy, do your thing."

B.P. blinked. "What's my thing?"

"You are the expert," Tristan nodded. "I'm consulting you."

"I'm a quantum physicist," B.P. pointed out monotonously with a stunned gape.

"And your life's work involves the study of parallel dimensions, no?"

"I guess," B.P. said blandly, totally lost.

"So you're saying we are dealing with an entity from another dimension."

"That's really more of a theory?" B.P. said blankly.

"Can you prove this thing is NOT an invisible enemy from another nefarious space-time continuum?"

"Um... no?"

"That doesn't give me peace of mind, Beepy," Tristan said, urging a secretary to write something down. "The situation is bleaker than I initially thought. Without proof that this is not the case, we can only assume that it is."

"I mean," B.P. said, "the whole multi-dimension thing is mainly a bunch of math? I've never found a portal or anything."

"Larry," Tristan said, snapping his fingers at a guy at the table whose name probably was not Larry, "make a note of that. There's currently no evidence to refute the existence of portals and be sure to defund any peer reviewed study that suggests otherwise."

"Can I interrupt for just one minute?" Biff Chesterfield interjected.

"Yes, Biff," Tristan said smugly. "Thank you for attending, by the way."

"I just wanted to say," Biff continued earnestly, "that the province of Scatopia is in a state of sheer chaos."

"Understandable," Tristan nodded.

"Now maybe this is just me," Biff said, raising his palms as a disclaimer, "but I feel like your decree could potentially dismantle human civilization as we know it. Again, just throwing that out there."

"Biff, it's not my decree that's causing the country to descend into chaos. It's the thing that came out of the portal."

"My bad," Biff said, raising his palms again. "Sorry to interrupt. You're doing great, by the way."

"Level with me, Beepy," Tristan said, freaking B.P. out with his immediate eye contact, "what is this thing called?"

"What?"

"The thing that's coming."

"I don't know what you..."

"Give it a name."

"I don't know..." B.P. said in bewilderment. "Bruce?"

Tristan smacked his palm against a conference table. "Bruce."

"I have to go to the bathroom," B.P. lied.

"I should have known," Tristan said with a weird seriousness. "Bruce. It all makes sense now."

"Okay."

"What a fiend," Tristan said. "Assuming a human name. Feigning humanity. Bruce must be stopped."

"I don't really know what you're talking about?"

"Beepy," Tristan said with a determined, fiery glare. "Tell me everything you know about Bruce."

B.P's lips parted.

# CHAPTER THIRTY-THREE
## (NORMAN)

Norman shuffled across the room with his microwaved Salisbury steak — the rations which were left outside his door by a soldier. He sat on an autumnal-colored velour sofa which was most likely older than Norman. He placed his plastic tray on the coffee table next to a can of cola, removed the cellophane and waited for the hot steam to dissipate. The news was already on the television, and he watched while chewing on a piping-hot forkful.

"Bruce," Tristan said, deathly serious in a press conference. "Our Chief Situational Officer has identified the scourge that is hectoring our nation."

Norman's eyes bulged in mid-chew.

"Bruce emerged into the human population through a portal," Tristan said in his austere soap opera voice, "from another dimension of which we still have very little understanding. I would like to invite Chief Situational Officer, Dr. Beepy Deerlight to the podium to explain this lack of understanding. Beepy?"

B.P. awkwardly approached the microphone and looked at it cross-eyed for a moment before speaking monotonically into it. "Certainly, the laws of quantum mechanics would imply that Bruce consists of an atypical molecular composition that differs greatly from beings in our dimension, rendering it invisible. And certainly, we can hypothesize that such a being could be sucked in a vacuum through a quantum physical wormhole or portal, if you prefer, which is yet to be peer reviewed, but certainly this is the case. And the mathematics seem consistent with the notion that Bruce is lurking in the human population, preying on our very humanity, which could be disputed in public, scientific debate, or not, depending on government policies. In the worst-case scenario, we should certainly err on the side of caution and hide."

The news ticker scrolling across the bottom of Norman's television screen read the following in a loop: *"Invisible entity (Bruce) has emerged into the human population from another dimension. Preys on humans. Experts advise us to hide."*

"Mercy me," Norman said with his mouth still full of simulated mashed potatoes. He turned up the volume.

"Dr. Deerlight," a reporter called from the midst of a restless sea of reporters all shouting at the same time. "May I ask you a question?"

"Certainly," B.P. blinked blankly.

"You say that Bruce is preying on humanity. In your professional opinion, what does that mean, exactly? What is Bruce capable of doing to us?"

"Certainly, I have no idea," B.P. blinked.

"Does the Prime Minister have intentions of mitigating our humanity in some way?" another reporter asked, aggressively sticking a microphone in B.P.'s face."

"I have no idea what the Prime Minister's intentions are at this time."

"Where is this wormhole?"

"How long will the citizens be confined?"

"Should we redeploy the military to target Bruce instead of holding our citizens hostage?"

"Is Bruce inherently male?"

"Can you show us the mathematics you used to come to these conclusions?"

"What does it feel like to have your humanity sucked out? How can we tell when it's happening?"

"Could this be the end of mankind as we know it?"

"Are we all at the same individual risk or does Bruce target certain demographics more so than others?"

"What are the implications for children?"

"What resources do we have to prevent Bruce?"

"Does Bruce affect other countries or only ours?"

"What purpose do you serve in the government? I'm genuinely curious."

"Could we potentially coexist peacefully with Bruce?"

"Can we sense when Bruce is approaching us, or does it wait in ambush?"

"Do we have the budget to deal with this?"

"I'll let the Prime Minister take things from here," B.P. said with her eyeballs googling in different directions.

"Thank you, Beepy," Tristan nodded seriously as he returned to the podium. "As you can see, Dr. Deerlight has made it quite clear. We are in imminent danger and every citizen of this country must remain confined to their homes until I say so. The only exceptions are politicians and military personnel because we are important and because we are committed to taking care of you. Rations will continue to be delivered to your household, while supplies last. Under no circumstances are you to leave your homes. Like at all. Dissenters will be disciplined."

Norman's jaw quivered and his eyes glassed over with shock.

"The teleprompter is alerting me that alarms have been sounded in countries around the world," Tristan continued. "Bruce has become a matter of global concern. Humanity is under attack. I repeat. Humanity is under attack. But please, don't panic and enjoy your Salisbury steak."

Norman quickly and nervously grabbed his telephone. "Young Pax?" Norman quavered. "I'm watching the news. What's going on?"

"Hey Norman," Pax said on the phone. "Just trying to figure that out myself."

"Is it true what they say about Bruce?"

"I'm not exactly sure," Pax admitted. "I've got Premier Chesterfield on the other line right now."

"The Prime Minister told me to enjoy my Salisbury steak," Norman warbled. "How am I supposed to enjoy my Salisbury steak when humanity is under attack by an invisible Bruce?"

"I'm going to get to the bottom of this, Norman," Pax promised. "I'll call you back as soon as I can.  Please, Norman. Take care of yourself."

# CHAPTER THIRTY-FOUR
## (PAX)

"I need answers, Biff," Pax said to Premier Biff Chesterfield on the phone. "I've got a backlog of calls from my constituents, and they are all utterly confused."

"Nobody's as clueless as I am," Biff answered, shaking his head in perplexity. "One minute I'm cutting a ribbon with giant scissors at a mall opening, and the next minute I'm put in charge of vanquishing an invisible monster that's trying to decimate my province."

"Wait," Pax squinted. "You've been put in charge?"

"I'm afraid so."

"What does that even mean?"

"Tristan delegated to the premiers."

"What is Prime Minister Winnings doing then?"

"Press conferences," Biff nodded.

"But you have no idea what's going on," Pax pointed out.

"I have advisors?"

"But how are they going to advise you?" Pax asked, massaging his temples. "It's an emerging situation and nobody understands what's happening."

"Buddy, listen," Biff said. "I didn't ask for any of this. When I signed up for this job, all I thought I'd do is make empty promises about taxes and decide which trees are allowed to get chopped down. I never guessed that I'd be expected to save mankind from their imminent demise. That's a little extra."

"You seriously think you can do this?"

"Well shucks. I don't want to let Tristan down. That would just about break me. He's a good guy, Tristan. Fine actor too."

"Okay whatever," Pax said, flustered. "Listen, there's people in my building who have some concerns. A single mom of five young children informed me that her ration included only one microwavable Salisbury steak dinner."

"Yeah," Biff said, scratching his sparse hair. "I was advised to only include adults in the rations. Figured the kids could pick off the parents' plates, you know?"

"That's inadequate," Pax said firmly. "Children need to eat. My constituent was forced to divide her one meal into four portions for her children. But she's breastfeeding so her infant will be undernourished if she doesn't eat anything."

"See, that's unfortunate," Biff said, hanging his head. "Very sorry to hear about that. But think of it this way. Kids waste a lot of food, you know? They kind of pick at it and throw the rest on the floor. If we give them each their own meal, it's like throwing the provincial budget in the garbage, get me? I knew you'd understand, Pax. You're a good guy. I don't tell you that nearly enough."

"The elderly in my building are telling me they've all received a letter slipped under their door that they won't be receiving their pension checks until the crisis is over," Pax said, doing his best not to yell.

"About that," Biff exhaled through his nose while scratching the bunchy seat of his pants. "We need to reallocate funds towards our Bruce efforts. We had to cut corners somewhere and the expert figured since the elderly seldom use the internet, they're less likely to complain on Twitter about government policies. I don't like it either Pax, but it is what it is."

"A neighbor of mine, a researcher of human psychology at the university downtown, says she's concerned about the mental health of our citizens," Pax persisted. "What resources will we be providing for them..."

"I'm going to stop you right there, Pax," Biff said, subtly sniffing his armpit. "The Minister of Catastrophic Events suggested we rebrand the term *mental health* to *attention seeking*. A little progressive for my taste, but dagnabbit, she's a smart lady and I think we should give it a whirl."

"That's obscene."

"These are unprecedented times, you know? Gotta' adapt. Or at least that's what the expert said."

"What expert?"

"You know the expert, Pax."

"I don't."

"Sure you do. You know, the guy? The one who knows more than me about stuff?"

"There's only one?"

"We only need one expert, Pax. Saves a lot of time bickering. I'm a guy who likes to get things done."

Pax blinked.

# CHAPTER THIRTY-FIVE
## (CLARITY)

That night, Clarity planked in her bed, stiff with insomnia. Every hour or so, she could hear the clunk of military boots stalking the hallways as soldiers patrolled. There was no road noise outside. Like at all. The silence reminded her of nights at the mushroom farm. The only exception now was the lack of nocturnal wildlife hooting, howling, or scuttling outside her window.

Just dense, eerie silence.

Clarity jolted and yipped mousily when she heard a disturbing, long creaking noise coming from next door. Ominous sounds followed which Clarity could not decipher. Feeling suddenly cold, she clenched her blanket up to her jaw.

"Fern?" she stage-whispered. "Did you hear that?"

A ghostly moan echoed through the wall.

"The ghost?" Clarity choked. "Seriously? Like I don't have enough problems."

\*\*\*

"Clarity Trout?" the voice of Daryl De Voort said shrilly in Clarity's ear.

"S'me," Clarity slurred into the phone, barely awake.

"Were you asleep? It's like 6:30 a.m."

"Yes," Clarity said, shaking her head with her eyes still closed.

"Splash some water on your face and listen," De Voort said in an authoritative staccato. "We need to talk about your follow-up article."

"Already?" Clarity accidentally asked.

"Be serious," De Voort snorted. "Surely you can see what an impact your first article made. You made the world essentially end in only two words."

Clarity bit her lower lip.

*Should I say something?*

*I should say something.*

*This is bad.*

*Like REALLY bad.*

*Everything has spiraled out of control with freakish speed.*

*Because of a stupid text.*

"Let's recap the success of your first article," De Voort said, licking his lips avariciously. "Your brilliant hook has been re-shared and paraphrased by over twenty million news outlets, globally."

*How do you paraphrase two words?*

"In less than twenty-four hours, you managed to influence the government of every country except Lithuania, to declare a state of emergency. When Prime Minister Winnings closed the borders, it inspired every country to close theirs. Peer pressure and all that. The world has essentially ended and society as we know it has spiraled into chaos. Way to go, kiddo!"

"Okay," Clarity said sickly.

"We need to keep this going."

"We... we need to do what now?"

"That sharp, pointy article of yours resulted in over eighty billion clicks in the first day. That's a personal best for us. Our advertisers basically peed their pants."

Clarity turned a curdling shade of green.

"People are freeeeaking out!" De Voort said, unable to hide his enthusiasm.

"Sorry?"

"Why the hell are you sorry?" De Voort practically squeaked. "You are the unofficial Queen of Doom Bait. People want more now. They're glued to their screens. And now that they are indefinitely confined to their homes, they'll have nothing better to do than gape mindlessly at their phones."

Clarity gurgled a fluish attempt at a laugh.

"The world is desperate to see what happens," De Voort continued. "Think of the clicks, Clarity Trout. Consider the money. Billions, potentially. If you keep this up, you could become a very powerful journalist. You'll be set for life. Did you not say you wanted this more than anything? It's happening. Come on, Clarity. Show the world nobody can push you around."

Clarity cocked her head like an inquisitive spaniel.

"To boot," Daryl continued, "we've received a massive boost in federal government funding. I was told that the funds will flow copiously so long as we continue to generate panic."

"What if..."

"...you don't?" Daryl said sharply. "Then the federal funds will be cut off. You don't want that on your conscience, do you?"

Clarity gaped.

"Follow up," De Voort clapped. "Keep it suspenseful. Keep the clicks coming."

"I..." Clarity stammered. "I have reservations."

"Cancel them," De Voort said obliviously. "Everything's closed now anyway. Because of you, my bright, shiny garnet! Get your next masterpiece ready by the end of the day."

# CHAPTER THIRTY-SIX
## (PAX)

"Norman?" Pax called, rapping on Norman's door with his index knuckle. "Everything okay in there?"

"That you, Pax?" Norman asked, pressing his ear to the other side of his closed door.

"I was worried about you after our phone call last night," Pax said, tilting his head and eyeballing the hallway for potential soldiers. "I thought I'd check up on you on my way to Parliament."

"What are ye doing outside of your apartment?" Norman squeaked. "With them soldiers thumping around in the halls?"

"I've been granted a pistachio," Pax explained in a voice that was much less ironic than you would expect.

"Eh?"

"A pistachio," Pax repeated, turning a green nut between his thumb and index finger. "Politicians and military personnel have been deemed *Imperative* and have therefore been issued pistachio nuts as a kind of ticket to leave our homes."

"That seems a little random, don't ye think?"

"It makes about as much sense as anything else these days," Pax sighed. "Look Norman, is there anything I can get you while I'm out?"

"Answers," the old man whistled through his teeth.

"I'll try, Norman. I really will," Pax said, his shoulders heaving with a sigh. "How are you otherwise? Did you sleep?"

"Tried," Norman shrugged. "Not much sleeping going on with that ghost across the hall. He was up to his antics again last night."

"So there IS a ghost? I knew it!"

"I'd imagine that's where all the moaning, spectral echoes, muffled, staticky voices and eerie Halloween sounds were coming from," Norman nodded. "They say ye can smell phantom cigars when there's a ghost around. Smelled me a big, fat Arturo Fuente."

"Jeez," Pax winced. "That must have been weird for you."

"Meh," Norman shrugged. "He's a little noisy but the ghost don't scare me. Lived here so long, I probably know him."

Pax chuckled. "Glad you're relatively okay, all things considered."

"Do ye know when they're planning on springing me?"

"That I do not know."

"Tell those stuffed shirts I don't want to spend the last half of me life watching daytime gameshows. I've got magical bosh to do."

"Okay, Norman," Pax said, placing his palm on the door, laughing and blinking away stinging tears simultaneously. "I'll see what I can do."

"Don't ye go and lose your pistachio!"

\*\*\*

"My question is for the Minister of Catastrophic Events," Pax said to the Speaker of the House as he rose from his seat in Parliament. "Minister Spiderly, my constituents are scared. Confused. Hysterical. Desperate. My concern is that the government's response to the Bruce crisis may be rash and short-sighted."

Pax paused, biting the side of his cheek while being heckled by his pistachio-wielding cohorts.

"I'm getting flooded with emails and phone calls from my constituents. *'My dog swallowed my phone charger, and the vet won't see him. Also I can't charge my phone.' 'I'm stranded in Helsinki and can't get home to my wife.' 'Have you ever been confined to the house indefinitely with three toddlers? How is this not child abuse?' 'My gran needs assistance, and I can't get to her.' 'I'm barely subsisting and can't afford to miss work.' 'Today my cat scratched me and I kind of enjoyed it, please help.'* Minister, can we please have a constructive dialogue about this? While I appreciate you are trying to protect our people, this whole thing is a logistical nightmare. Is it necessary to essentially close the world and dismantle human civilization as we know it?"

"Honorable Minister of Catastrophic Events?" said the regally-robed Speaker of the House.

"Thank you, Speaker," rasped Eva Spiderly as she stood, penetrating Pax with her perpetual, steely squint. "The short answer is yes. It is quite necessary to dismantle human civilization. What we have here is a catastrophic event, the very reason I have been summoned. From Day One, which was essentially yesterday, we have dutifully consulted with the expert, who advised us to block Bruce's access to Scatopians. This is consistent with the federal decree. The Chief Situational Officer of Umbravia has sounded the alarm that Bruce feasts on humanity. While we have no idea what that means, the expert agrees, with himself I suppose, that the best course of action is to hide Scatopians until we analyze which human nuances need to be banned."

"Honorable Member for Agora East?" the Speaker of the House said, quirking an eyebrow at Pax whose jaw had dropped conspicuously in a WTF kind of way. "You have a supplementary question?"

"What do you mean *ban* human nuances?" Pax practically squeaked. "Are you saying you plan to deny Scatopians the inherent right to be human? Minister, if you would just..."

"Who let this guy in?" cackled an anonymous heckler in the back of the room.

"Disgraceful!" another heckler spat.

"Let me finish my..." Pax tried.

"He's dissenting! We were told not to do that!"

"Consider the collateral damage if we..." Pax shouted over the din of heckles.

"Hogwash!"

"I have a responsibility to my constituents..." Pax said louder.

"He doesn't care about Scatopians!"

"How can you be so confident of your tactics," Pax hollered, "if you don't even understand what the hell's going on? It's an emerging situation. Not even the scientists understand Bruce yet, so how can YOU be so sure..."

"He's not a team player, Mr. Speaker!"

"People matter, Mr. Speaker!" Pax insisted.

"Agora East is talking out his..."

"I'm going to put my fingers in my ears and say 'neener, neener, neener, I can't hear you!'"

"Jerk!"

"Because of the volume of the hecklers," the Speaker of the House exhaled, "I can't hear the member for Agora East."

"Forsooth, he's a *member*," snorted a heckler.

"*Forsooth?*"

"Shuhshuhshuh," shushed the Speaker of the House. "Member for Agora East, continue."

"Thank you, Mr. Speaker," Pax continued. "Minister Spiderly, honorable members of the House, might I suggest we have a public dialogue between a variety of different experts in varying fields? My neighbor is a professor of moral philosophy..."

"Irrelevant!" barked a heckler.

"There has to be a better way!" Pax insisted. "Please do not misunderstand. The fact that I am questioning the government's response to the crisis does not in any way mean that I am *denying* there is a veritable crisis occurring. God only knows what Bruce is capable of. But Mr. Speaker, *friends*, this is no time to demoralize our citizens. We need our humanity more than ever now in the face of Bruce. Either we do this together or not at all!"

"Minister of Catastrophic Events?"

"Thank you, Mr. Speaker," Eva said superiorly as she rose to her feet. "I'm not sure why the member is being so melodramatic. We are doing what we have to do to protect our citizens. End stop. According to Dr. Beepy Deerlight, it is impossible to decipher who among us has been dehumanized as the process is painless and there are no noticeable signs of dehumanization. And since the scourge is invisible, there is no way to detect its presence in our community. We must only assume that everyone is unhuman until proven otherwise. Quite the dumpster fire, you understand. Therefore, the government's response to the crisis is quite rational. If Scatopians can't handle this minor inconvenience..."

"*Minor* inconvenience?" Pax intercepted.

"Order," droned the Speaker of the House.

"Yes, *Agora East*," Eva seethed. "A minor inconvenience compared to the damnable fate of any poor wretch who encounters Bruce. Do you wish to have your humanity sucked out to be potentially used as alternative gasoline in a parallel dimension? I for one, would prefer not. We are all vulnerable. And steps will be taken in the coming weeks and months to determine how we can dupe Bruce into thinking that Scatopians are not, and I use air quotes, *human*. It's the only logical solution."

"How is this logical?" Pax spoke out of turn. "We do have the option of targeting Bruce instead of turning on our own people..."

"Clearly the member has never seen *'Invasion of the Body Snatchers'* or the satisfactory remake staring Nicole Kidman," Eva said in her predictable staccato. "All Scatopians must pretend they are not human so as not to be recognized by Bruce. The anecdotal evidence makes it quite clear. Humanity is a liability and must be suppressed. While other countries may interpret this data differently, that is the way science works in Umbravia. Anyone who grieves for their lost humanity is a science denier. Perhaps the situation is too complex for the member to intellectualize."

"Oh come ON!" Pax lashed back. "Even a spotted toadstool can see how bent..."

"Withdraw?" the Speaker of the House said warningly.

"Withdrawn," Pax exhaled, slumping into his chair.

## CHAPTER THIRTY-SEVEN
### (EVA SPIDERLY)

"We are so screwed," Biff Chesterfield exhaled as though he just finished competing in a triathlon that he was grossly unqualified to participate in.

"Don't you think I know that?" spat Eva Spiderly as she shook her aluminum-colored hair free from her much-too-tight ponytail. After doing so, her steely squint was slightly less squinty. And as it happens, her severe lipstick was the same aluminum color as her hair. And pantsuit. And complexion. And eyes. Basically, she looked like foil.

"I've bitten off more than I can chew," Biff breathed heavily, shaking his head.

"D'ya think?" Eva said, squinting severely at the premier.

"I think maybe Pax is right."

"Are you on glue?" snapped Eva. "You can't pivot your response now! Not after you deployed the military."

"That was the Feds."

*"That was the Feds,"* Eva mimicked snarkily. "That is so like you. Always blaming the Feds for your ineptitude."

"Hey, there's a federal decree…"

"And Winnings delegated to the premiers. This is on you, Chesterfield."

"I didn't want to let Tristan down," Biff said earnestly. "He's a real cracker, that one. And a worthy leader. I have a poster of him taped to the ceiling above my bed."

Eva tried to shake the image out of her mind. "If you change your stance now, you'll look weak."

"For what it's worth, my approval ratings are already at a historic low," Biff said, raising an index finger. "I reckon folks already think I'm weak. So I might as well just…"

"What did the expert say?" Eva hissed, pinching the bridge of her nose.

"He said I should do something to improve my approval ratings," Biff said dolefully. "Which is why he suggested I try being more ham-fisted. Which makes sense because that's what Tristan's doing. I wish I was more like him," Biff added in a sad, faraway voice.

"About *Bruce?*"

"He said Bruce is my best chance at being re-elected."

"Focus, Biff," Eva said through clenched teeth. "You bought us tickets for this runaway train. Now be a leader and tell us how to crash it."

"I... really don't know what I'm doing."

"If you lose the next election, I'm out of a job too," Eva snarled. "Changing policies in the middle of a crisis is going to make us both look like goobers. And I assure you, Chesterfield. I am no goober. In fact, a crisis is just the thing I need to propel my career."

"How so?"

"I'm the Minister of Catastrophic Events, you potato. Before now, most people didn't even realize Scatopia had a Minister of Catastrophic Events."

"We've never really had a catastrophic event before."

"Exactly," Eva nodded sternly. "So don't screw this up for me."

"The thing is," Biff snuffed, "we have a literal crisis here and neither of us are qualified to confront a malevolent energy coming at us through a wormhole."

"I resent your claim that I am unqualified," Eva said, wedging an angry fist into her hip like an indignant, evil robot from the future. "I happen to have a diploma in air ticketing from Flemblatt Vocational School."

"Aren't you even a little bit skittish about Bruce?" warbled Biff. "By the sounds of it, Bruce is pretty darned dastardly. You said yourself we're all vulnerable..."

"Biff..."

"I've never encountered a fiend from a parallel dimension before," Biff shuddered. "Makes me want to turn in my pistachio sort of."

"Politicians and military personnel have been deemed *Imperative*," Eva repeated from muscle memory.

"But isn't it kind of a double standard that we get pistachios while the rest of the world is confined to their homes?"

"Of course not."

"Really?" Biff said, scratching the stubble on the back of his sweaty neck. "Because I feel like Bruce is an opportunistic predator and..."

"They wouldn't give us pistachios if there was any threat to our safety."

"Sure, that's what the expert said," Biff nodded. "But it seems to me that if this thing is preying on humanity..."

"Military personnel have been trained to suppress their humanity to protect them from enemies just like this one," Eva exhaled as though it was the most obvious thing in the world. "And politicians are not entirely human. Trust me, Biff. We're good."

Biff burbled exasperated air from his bulbous lips.

"Guidance, Biff," Eva said, snapping her fingers impatiently. How she did so is anyone's guess, given her three-inch, aluminum-polished nails. "What are the next steps according to the expert?"

"He's hatching a plan," Biff said, his eyes bulging with eager wonder. "He'll be in his *thinking room* for the next few days, musing on ways we can conceal the various human nuances that Bruce may be sniffing around for. He reckons we'll need to bend the law a bit and fritter around with the whole notion of human rights, but he'll figure it out. He's awful smart, Eva. The expert knows all kinds of things. What it must be like to spend a day inside that guy's brain," Biff said, shaking his head in amazement.

"Curious," Eva said, pacing like a thoughtful, Amur tiger. "Where do you suppose the expert acquires such knowledge?"

# CHAPTER THIRTY-EIGHT
## (WILLATRIX)

"Who's ready to acquire some knowledge?" Willatrix said, wide-eyed to her virtual followers, who now added up to a stunning number of nearly eleven million. "Today I will bestow on you all a sense of virtue and decency. I can see from the sudden accrual of followers that my wisdom is not only a rare, spiritual gift, but also consistent with popular opinion. I pray you therefore take heed."

Revealing a pair of binoculars, Willatrix swerved her swivel chair around to face the window and beckoned her viewers to follow her gaze.

"In times of global emergency, we must all do the honorable thing, and unite in our collective sense of righteousness. There is very little we can count on in these uncertain times. Except morality. Cling to morality. It is our only hope. Our only constant. Security blanket.

Morality will lead us unscathed through this crisis. If your moral compass is a little blurry or cracked, take comfort. That's normal when you experience shock or trauma. Be assured, I will be your moral compass. I will instill in you the precepts of morality, as outlined by our sage political elitists."

Willatrix randomly did an impersonation of *the dove of peace.*

"While it makes my heart hurt to say this, we must identify the immoral ones before they divide and endanger us." Willatrix pressed the binoculars against her eyes and glared out the window. "Name and shame."

A subtle, guttural snarl emerged from Willatrix's throat as she spotted someone outside the tower block through her binoculars. The snarl sounded like the word *Jennifer*, perhaps played backwards and on the wrong speed.

"I see a miscreant sneaking her schnauzer out for a discreet pee," Willatrix informed her viewers. "I recognize her as Jennifer Flarton. A resident of my tower block. She lives on the ground floor, as if that gives her a right to flout one of the tenets of our survival. Beloved, you will find the number for the Scatopia Narc Hotline at the bottom of your screen. Call it. Don't let Jennifer Flarton get away with... Oh look at that," Willatrix said, firming the binoculars more snugly around her ocular cavities. "She's darting back inside like a guilty puma. *She knows*," Willatrix said, slitting her eyes with ire.

Then swerving back to face her computer screen, Willatrix suddenly morphed into the literal personage of Jophiel.

"This has been Willatrix Oleander, reminding you to be decent to one another just like me. Thank you for your attention."

# CHAPTER THIRTY-NINE
## (CLARITY)

"She knows."

Clarity whelped as she watched Willatrix on her computer screen.

"This has been Willatrix Oleander, reminding you to be decent to one another just like me. Thank you for your attention."

"Fern," Clarity confided in her plant, "how would you go about this if you were in my situation? Seems everyone has an opinion about this already. Weirdly strong... opinions. I feel like no matter what I write, someone is going to get mad at me. On the one hand, I unilaterally stopped the world in its tracks. There's no frame of reference for this. The suffering I've likely caused is making my frontal lobe throb. On the other hand, I did something I thought I'd never be able to do. I've changed the... world. All of it. Except maybe Lithuania."

If houseplants could give the stink eye, that would be what the fern was doing in that moment.

"Whatever I write next could change the course of history," Clarity blinked. "Of the... future. Daryl De Voort wants me to keep this pandemonium going on for as long as I can, but is this even sustainable? Can people be denied social interaction... denied their livelihoods for months?... Years?" Clarity's eyeballs quivered. "Is it bad that I kind of want this to last forever?"

The fern just sat there. Speechless.

"This is actually the best thing that's ever happened to me," Clarity said, trying to convince herself by wrenching her face. "I may never have to leave my apartment again. Like ever. No more humiliating encounters in elevators. No more face to face... contact. People are just so... everywhere. It's just too much, Fern. My... thing is just not compatible with life. But... but I could have a normal life after all if... if this was the new normal."

For a few painstaking moments, Clarity sat stiff at her computer, taking short, quavering breaths.

I've never lied before.

*Ever.*

*I'm Catholic.*

*Extremely. Catholic.*

*Am I going to Hell?*

*!!!*

*Ugh. I'm already in Hell.*

*Okay, Clarity.*

*You can do this.*

*You can...*

*... do this.*

Blinking her stinging eyes and snuffing emotional snot, Clarity began clacking at her computer at a speed that suggested she wanted to get this finished before she changed her mind. The voice of her journalism teacher echoed throughout the labyrinths of her muddled brain, reminding her that quoting people who don't exist is acceptable because the average person never sources information. She mentally reminded herself that it was only an article. That people can and should take it with a grain of salt. That it's not technically a lie if it's vague enough to be left open to interpretation. All she had to do was write at an eighth-grade level and use a few emotionally charged words.

*Make them feel things.*

*BIG things.*

With trembling hands, Clarity typed out the headline, "IT'S HERE" and pressed 'send.'

*And now we wait.*

Taking a deep, cleansing breath, Clarity turned her chair around and stared out the window at the night sky. Within fifteen minutes, the marquee across the street suddenly changed to the words, "IT'S HERE."

# CHAPTER FORTY
## (ONE MONTH LATER)

"It's here," Tristan said in a press conference, penetrating the camera with eyes like menacing lasers. "I've been saying this every day for the past month, and it warrants being said again. Umbravians are in peril. No one is safe. At this point, Bruce has been elusively stalking our streets for thirty-one days, so I can't emphasize this enough. *Stay home.* Bruce is waiting in ambush outside. You can't see Bruce but if you could, he would likely resemble a globular amoeba. With a face. Upon the face would be a shuddersome scowl. The amoeba would be rhinoceros-sized. Bipedal. Stealthy and ready for brunch."

Tristan turned dramatically for a different camera angle.

"The Chief Situational Officer has provided anecdotal evidence that an unknown number of Umbravians have already fallen victim to Bruce and have consequentially had their humanness slurped out of their anima. Anima," Tristan nodded somberly. "That's a word I just learned today. At the risk of repeating myself I must add that there is virtually no distinction between a normal person and a *Husk*. Since Husks have no distinguishable qualities, the experts have resolved that feeling absolutely normal is a symptom of *Huskism*. Assume everyone, including yourself is a Husk. You must avoid the Husks at all costs." Tristan triangulated an eyebrow of intrigue. "But *who are they?* The fact that Bruce has already begun his inevitable takeover of mankind can only mean one thing." Tristan squinted noxiously into the camera. "*Someone* has been flouting the rules."

*** 

When Biff Chesterfield approached the podium for a press conference, his forehead was beaded with sweat, and he was breathing like Darth Vader. Much redder than usual, his face resembled Mars.

"Friends," Biff panted, looking stunned into the camera. "Folks. Cohorts. Chums. Cronies and amigos. After thirty-one days in his *thinking room* the expert concluded which nuances of humanity must be banned. We had to make some hard decisions today but make no mistake. We have listened to the expert, and we think he's pretty darned smart. I didn't want to do this, folks. So please don't blame me come election time. Our foe plays dirty and so must we. No doubt these minor adjustments to your lifestyle will be inconvenient. And believe me. This is my least favorite part of my job. Which is why I'm making the Minister of Catastrophic Events read out the verboten items from this here list. Eva?"

"Thanks for that, Biff," Eva said, her lip curled with plastic revulsion. "The following items have been deemed conspicuously human and will therefore be banned, effective immediately. Music. Laughter. Hugs. Friendship. Pleasure. Irony. A sense of purpose. The smell of tandoori chicken. Fond memories. The notion of *vibing.* Innocuous references to pop culture. Allergies. Religion. Quiffs and pixie cuts. Facial expressions. Morning coffee. The element of surprise. Education. Grandparents. The number nine. Exercise. Forehead kisses. Neil Patrick Harris. Direct eye contact. Yarn. Throwing shade. The abbreviation OMG. Childhood. Walking in the wrong direction. And questions."

The faces of reporters appeared on a giant, Zoom screen, each pummeling Eva with overlapping questions.

"What did I say?" Eva barked at the screen. *"What did I SAY?* Questions are officially forbidden by law and phrasing a sentence interrogatively will result in severe discipline. Do I make myself clear?"

The Zoom screen suddenly fell silent, upon which were dozens of contrite and slightly startled faces.

***

"Did you see the press conference?" Otto asked Piper on the phone.

Piper peered between the slats of her Venetian blinds. Across the street, the words on the marquee suddenly changed to *Question Nothing.* "This can't be real," she quavered.

"Piper, are you okay?"

A beat.

"Piper?"

"This is obnoxious," Piper said, kicking something and then wincing. "You are literally like... right there. Behind this stupid wall. And now..."

"I know."

"Our friendship is a crime?"

"Totally random."

"Like a literal, punishable crime."

"I don't even know what to say."

"Otto, I..." Piper said, curling into the fetal position on her bed with the phone to her ear, "I was too embarrassed to tell you this before..."

"Tell me."

Piper swallowed hard. "I'm in a terrible amount of pain right now. I can barely move sometimes."

"Oh my god, are you sick?"

'No, it's nothing like that. I'm just... a lot weirder than you think I am."

"I don't think..."

"Please don't tell me I'm crazy, okay? Please don't try to rationalize..."

"You're freaking me out a little, Pipes. I'm getting worried."

"I never tell people this," Piper hesitated. "I'm not even sure if I should..."

"You can tell me anything. Pipes, you know that."

"I don't know what's going on right now," Piper breathed. "With the world? But the lies..."

"Lies?"

"I can feel something... very wrong."

"What do you mean?"

"It's just... lies hurt. Like they *really* hurt."

"This is a really confusing time for everyone."

"You're not getting me, Otto. Lies literally hurt me."

"Lies hurt your feelings?"

"Not my feelings, Otto," Piper strained. "Lies cause me actual, physical pain. In my body. Sharp, throbbing, shards-of-glass pain."

"... Oh."

"Do you even understand what I'm saying?"

"I... think so?"

"Seriously?"

"I mean, you feel things differently than other people. You have like this heightened awareness? That's been obvious to me since the day I met you."

"Are you going to freak out now?"

"Piper, no. I mean, it's hard to wrap my brain around but..."

"There's so many lies, Otto."

"What?"

"I can't take it anymore."

"Who's lying to you?"

"Not to me specifically. Just... lies," Piper said, gesturing vaguely. "Everywhere. I can sense them and it's all just too much."

"Holy crap."

"Otto, I really need you," Piper said. "Like in the room with me, not metaphorically."

"Oh Pipes..."

"There's not a lot of people I can confide in," Piper sniffled.

"Does your family know about... you know. This?"

"You *are* my family, Otto."

Otto swallowed emotionally. "You don't talk about them much."

"I love my family," Piper nodded. "I do. It's just... it's hard to explain things like this to linear thinkers. I'm not really in the mood right now to be told I'm irrational or that there's pills that can make me less annoying to insensitive people. I don't particularly feel like being told that my struggles are imagined or that other people have *real* problems. Normally I can hide my nonconformity..."

"You shouldn't have to hide."

"I was conditioned to hide," Piper said quickly.

"I'm so sorry, Piper," Otto said woefully. "I had no idea things were so complicated with... I wish I could be... like literally *be* there for you. None of this makes any sense."

"The government has no right to decide what constitutes family," Piper said breathlessly. "What constitutes a *household.* You're my only support... my only coping mechanism. I mean, music also helps me cope but that's been banned too. Why the hell would they ban music of all the fecking things?"

"To break our spirits?"

"The fact is, you're my person. And now the government just banned you like pork at an airport."

"Piper, we'll figure this out, okay?" Otto said, removing his glasses and stoically blinking tears away. "I'll find a way to be there for you. We'll just have to be creative, okay? We can adapt."

Piper buried her face in a pillow and cried.

\*\*\*

"Mom?" Lola said, squeezing a cell phone to her ear with her shoulder while changing Bobby's radioactive diaper. "... Yes, I saw the news... I don't know what they meant about childhood being banned. It doesn't make any..."

Lola swerved her head to determine whether or not Garthie's velociraptor shriek was a death cry. (All good)

"Look, I've been cooped up in the apartment with the kids for a month... No, I can't sneak them out for a walk... No, not even in the halls. There's soldiers. And a narc hotline. The kids are traumatized enough as it is. Izzy's been having night terrors and Sara-Sue can't stop crying. Enzo's been getting these spontaneous bouts of rage. Garthie's falling behind in his development. Bobby may never know what a friend is... I'm trying to pretend this is fun but I'm running out of ideas and the kids aren't stupid. They can sense my stress. I can't work. Education is banned. I can't even get support from the church now because places of worship have been closed and religion apparently doesn't exist anymore... I don't know..."

Lola barked at Enzo to stop turning the light switch on and off.

"Sorry, the kids are under stimulated."

Lola screeched at the girls to stop weaponizing their Barbies.

"I don't know, Mom... Yes, I did notice that grandparents were on the list... I doubt they'll literally vanquish you. I don't see how that's feasible."

Lola inhaled deeply as her mother hysterically fretted about how Lola could manage the kids on her own.

"Mom, listen I... Mom?... Mom?... Hello?"

Lola gasped when a robot voice on the phone unexpectedly bleeped, *'This interaction is forbidden."*

Dead air.

\*\*\*

*'Honorable Prime Minister Tristan Winnings of Umbravia:*

*I compose this letter with the most amiable intentions. As a professor of Moral Philosophy and Fellow at the prestigious Neopatmos University in Agora City, I feel qualified to offer my humble musings on the current national crisis. In the words of the esteemed Immanuel Kant, all immoral actions are irrational because they violate the Categorical Imperative. (a universal, ethical principle stating that one should always respect the humanity of others)*

*With all due respect, Mr. Prime Minister, I resolve that your national decree is, in my professional opinion, irrational and ultimately immoral, on the basis that humanity is not only an inherent right, but also instinctual. How then can one impose a universal ban on our fundamental and dare I say biological instincts? Are you not setting your citizens up for failure? And where, may I ask, is the science that has influenced your reasoning that violating the universal code of ethics will protect us from a metaphysical threat?*

*If for some reason you are not a fan of Kant, perhaps you will prefer Kierkegaard, who embraces the concepts of free will, self-expression, and the human experience. Are you not the least bit unsettled that you have deprived your citizens of all three? Am I the only one who is concerned that the entire country simply fell in line blindly and without question? Without debate? Without the reason of dissenting voices? A mere conversation? Is fearmongering an ethical tool to garner compliance?*

*Don't even get me started about Jurgen Habermas.*

*You may be familiar with the famous quote by Jean-Paul Sartre: 'Hell is other people.' Sartre is wrong. Hell is in fact, the absence of other people. If you fail to see this, simply pay attention to the existential fallout of your policies. People are unraveling. Families torn apart. Friendships smashed. People are wasting away. Humans were not designed for isolation in fact such a strategy has historically been used as a form of torture. We are not prisoners of war, nor are we a threat to the nation. We are people. YOUR people.*

*In your defense, you do echo the theories of one philosopher who stated that it is better for a political leader to be widely feared than greatly loved. He also theorized that the ends justify the means. However, this philosopher's name is Niccolo Machiavelli so interpret this as you will. My only hope is that you do not mistake this for a compliment.*

*Sir, I am not merely a distinguished academic but also a friend. Husband. Son. Brother. Mentor. I find the plight of my neighbors and loved ones to be painfully relatable. We are all in turmoil, Mr. Prime Minister, and I fear the ethical repercussions could ripple throughout history in the most catastrophic way. Please, for the sake of the nation, for the world, reconsider your short-sighted, unconscionable behavior before we experience an irreparable dismantling of society's collective moral compass.*

*I remain yours respectfully,*

*Professor Girard Gosh (PhD)*

After Girard sent the email with a heaving exhale, he noticed Flossie craning her head out the window.

"What's up, Floss?"

"It's Ezekiel," Flossie replied, poking her head back inside. "He's out on his balcony, screaming things about *Azrael,* caged gerbils and the number nine."

"This I've got to see," Girard said, joining Flossie at the window.

Outside, Ezekiel was indeed on his balcony, howling a sequence of random, unrelated Bible verses and waving a picket sign with *'NOT TODAY, SATAN!'* scrawled sloppily with a Sharpie. He bellowed something about the Antichrist at an innocent mailbox which was minding its own business in the desolate street below. There was no one else to scream at, after all.

"And I stood upon the sand of the sea!" Ezekiel screamed while slowly developing laryngitis. "And saw a beast rise up out of the sea! Having seven heads and ten horns! His name was blasphemy! Do not be deceived! For the deceiver is the Antichrist!"

"Wait," Girard stage whispered. "Is he ranting about the Antichrist?"

"Son of perdition!" Ezekiel wailed hoarsely. "Even now he is already in the world! Worshipping himself! And those who fall prey to his lies will endure eternal torture and brimstone!"

"I find this weirdly understandable," Flossie said, wide-eyed.

# CHAPTER FORTY-ONE
## (SEVERAL MONTHS LATER)

"There's a rumor circulating around the alternative news outlets suggesting that you might be the Biblical Antichrist," a reporter stated at a news conference. Reporters were physically present as the government had issued pistachios to media staff. And since questions were still illegal, the reporter was careful to phrase his comments in the form of declarative sentences. "Please offer your thoughts."

The camera panned over to Tristan Winnings who squinted thoughtfully at the reporter. His hair, which had been left un-scissored since the crisis began had now grown past his shoulders. He was wearing Birkenstocks and an era-appropriate, white, knee-length tunic. Tristan ethereally stroked his full beard as a weird, celestial light glowed from behind him. "That's hurtful," Tristan said in Aramaic. "But I forgive you."

"Prime Minister Winnings," another reporter piped up, hidden in a crowd because he was probably short, "if it hurts your feelings when people call you the Antichrist, perhaps you should stop trying to look like literal Jesus."

"What do you mean?" Tristan said, cocking his head.

"Some citizens are questioning your suggestion of rubberstamping your initials on their foreheads for no apparent reason."

"I have a reason and it's rather good," Tristan nodded. "Those who have dodged Bruce by being decent human beings should get a stamp to differentiate them from the Husks. That way, we can better protect the citizens from the humans who aren't exactly human anymore."

"But Bruce could still pursue a stamped individual," a female voice called out from somewhere.

Tristan squinted through the camera light, trying to find the smartass who said that. "It's basic human decency," Tristan tried.

"You said yourself, there's virtually no difference between…"

"Look," Tristan said, flipping his Jesus hair, "there's only one way you can become a Husk. Flouting. Obviously, some A-hole walked in the wrong direction, hugged someone or sniffed some tandoori chicken. My rules are keeping people safe. This is a small inconvenience for the greater good."

"They've been confined to their homes for months with no reprieve."

"They need to adapt," Tristan stated.

"An internet poll indicated that more people than ever are thinking about setting themselves on fire."

"They suck at adapting and are holding back the team," Tristan said.

"That was unsavory."

"There are two kinds of people in Umbravia," Tristan enunciated much too clearly. "The decent citizens. And those other guys."

"Those other guys."

"I said what I said."

"So you're moralizing..."

"Bitch, I'm saving your ass," Tristan said impulsively before catching himself and adjusting his tunic in a pathetic backpaddle. "Soul. Saving your soul."

"I've been perusing Twitter and it seems not everyone views you as a messianic figure."

"Haters."

"Balcony dissenters are on the rise."

"That's a violation of the decree."

"You can't possibly prevent people from secretly disagreeing with you within the privacy of their homes."

"Then I'll need to up my game," Tristan hissed into the microphone.

***

"Was that wedgy enough?" Tristan asked as Hector followed him onto Tristan's private jet.

"It's impossible to take you seriously when you look like you're about to heal a leper," Hector said without inflection as he hauled both his luggage and Tristan's.

"Too bad the U.N. gave the thumbs down for the rubberstamp idea," Tristan said, snarfing a seat by the window and patting the seat next to him for Hector to sit. "That would have been super-wedgy."

"Please never say *super-wedgy* ever again," Hector said flatly as he primly took a seat next to Tristan. "Shouldn't you be sitting with your wife and tots?"

"They're on a union break," Tristan said matter-of-factly, inspecting the selection of glam mags in the seat pouch ahead of him.

"Which will give us plenty of time to discuss policies."

"Hector, do you have to be such a wet noodle?" Tristan said, blowing luscious locks of hair from his face in exasperation. "I'm on vacation." Then prairie dogging his head above the seat, Tristan called out to the other passengers, consisting of government officials, his faux family and a handful of his favorite sycophants. "Who's excited for Oahu?"

Hector tugged Tristan back into his seat. "Try not to be so conspicuous," he said, looking slightly seasick after eyeballing Tristan up and down. "There's a travel ban, and the international borders are sealed shut, so we need to keep a low profile. How is it going to look if the prime minister is flouting his own rules?"

"You worry too much," Tristan said, dimpling like a frat boy. "If I can part the Red Sea, then surely I can discreetly open the borders just long enough to make an exception for myself."

"You didn't part the Red Sea. That was Moses."

"Besides," Tristan said, obliviously thumbing through a copy of *Teen Vogue*, "how will anyone catch me travelling during a travel ban when literally nobody else is allowed to travel?"

Hector abruptly snatched the magazine, startling Tristan. "You are becoming unpopular."

Tristan's eyes welled with tears. "How can that be?"

"They're hopping mad, Tristan. Consider the Antichrist rumor."

"I'm not the Antichrist, that's just daft," Tristan laughed awkwardly. "I'm not, am I?"

"Of course not," Hector said dryly. "The eschatological prophesies clearly state the Antichrist will be a highly intelligent, well-respected man."

"Awww," Tristan said, nuzzling his head gratefully against Hector's suit jacket. "Thanks, Hector. You're the sweetest."

"The country has been locked down for months," Hector said, shaking Tristan off like a burr.

"But you said that..."

"You have no exit strategy."

"You literally told me to…"

"The Umbravian economy is collapsing."

"Dammit, Hector," Tristan squeaked adolescently. "You told me to incite fear. Divisiveness. You said it would secure my power. You want a wedge issue? I gave you a wedge issue."

"But now people are questioning you."

"I specifically told them not to do that."

"Well they are. And your lack of leadership…"

"Hey!"

"… Your lack of leadership is causing a major shit show on Twitter."

"That's obnoxious," Tristan pouted. "I made a decree."

"You delegated to the largely ill-prepared premiers."

"Delegation is a leadership quality," Tristan said, raising an index finger. "And furthermore, I am leading by example. I have set the theme for this entire crisis. The theme is *panic* in case that wasn't clear."

"You are flubbing this," Hector clenched. "Denying Umbravians access to each other simply prevents critical thinking from happening in public places. But you can't control what happens within households or anonymously on the internet."

Tristan protruded his lower lip toddlerishly.

"This whole thing has blown up into something bigger than you can handle." Hector lectured. "I approve of your harsh tactics. And there are Umbravians who are clinging to you, a surprising number actually, because they are understandably scared and have lost their ability to reason... don't be smug... But you are more of a cartoon of a prime minister than a veritable leader. Now you've lost control. The only way to save face at this point is to form an exit strategy. That way you can come out looking like a hero by leading your people out of a dire crisis. Be their savior."

"Savior? I can't..."

"You already have the complex," Hector pointed out, eyeballing Tristan's new look. "I don't see why you can't..."

"Would you just...!" Tristan said, flapping his flustered hands around. "I'm mentally processing here. So you want the crisis to linger on, potentially forever. But I also need to figure out how to integrate people back into society. While polarizing them. And keeping them scared. But also making them happy. While forbidding them to question me. So they'll like me. But also flee in terror at the very sound of my name. Also science. And maybe the economy."

"Umbravians are asking too many questions," Hector droned. "The fact that you did not see this coming is quite embarrassing."

"I suppose there's only one thing I can do."

Hector said, *'Form an exit strategy'* at the exact time that Tristan said, *'Squelch the dissenters.'*

\*\*\*

"Squelch the dissenters?" B.P. said, squinting at a Zoom screen, upon which was Tristan in a garish, Hawaiian shirt. Behind him were swaying palm trees and a pretentious ocean. "Isn't that a bit dramatic?"

"Not at all," Tristan said with flourish, intentionally drawing attention to his tropical surroundings. "Umbravians are asking too many questions."

"How am I supposed to..."

"I hacked your laptop and found your dissertation," Tristan dimpled smugly.

"Crap."

"I thought you said there were no wormholes," Tristan said, crossing his arms.

B.P.'s mouth moved around wordlessly for a moment. "It's only a theory..."

"Lies."

"It was only that one time..."

"Beepy..."

"And it's not even a parallel dimension."

"What was it then?"

"Kind of a... dead end?"

"Explain."

"It's confidential."

"I have access to bioweapons."

"Why would anyone give you access to..."

"I'll tickle you."

"You're making this weird."

"You have no idea how weird I can make things."

"Okay, okay, yeeesh!" B.P. said, fanning away the weirdness. "I was doing some math and accidentally found an atypical portal. It didn't lead anywhere though. It just took me to this... I don't know... void."

"Void," Tristan nodded as though he understood but for obvious reasons, he did not.

"I found myself in a metaphysical enclosure filled with nothingness. It was just dark, empty, and meaningless. I left the void immediately."

"Because it was a traumatic, existential experience?"

"Mainly because I was bored."

"How many people could fit in this void, do you suppose?" Tristan asked, stroking his chin thoughtfully."

"Why?" B.P. said, warily taking a few steps backwards.

"I'll get my security detail to send you an encrypted message regarding the plan."

"What plan?"

"I can't tell you, it's confidential."

B.P. squinted interrogatively at the screen.

"I have to go now," Tristan apologized. "I'm about to be photographed with a mongoose."

"Why wasn't I allowed to go to Oahu?" B.P. asked.

"Obviously I need you to cover for me at press conferences. And if anyone asks," Tristan winked, "I'm otherwise occupied in a think tank alongside political and military strategists. Hatching a plan to save mankind. Definitely *not* sitting by the infinity pool with a Mai Tai. Oh, could you answer my emails while I'm gone? And feed my cat?"

B.P.'s mouth formed into a baffled letter O.

***

After a disturbing phone call with the prime minister's security detail, B.P awkwardly settled her butt into Tristan's swivel chair and perused his email as per his request. She scanned the inbox until Girard's email caught her attention. Her eyeballs doddered back and forth as she scoured each line.

*Awwwww jeeeeez….*

*A professor of moral philosophy?*

*And he referenced Kant. (wince)*

*Should I...*

*Or...*

*Frig.*

*What am I supposed to do now?*

*If I...*

*Then...*

*Mutherf...*

Before she could change her mind, B.P. quickly deleted Girard's email. "Tristan doesn't need to know," she swallowed.

# CHAPTER FORTY-TWO
## (THE NEXT DAY)

**HEADLINE: WILL BRUCE INEVITABLY DECIMATE MANKIND? EXPERTS WEIGH IN**

*In the throes of the most cataclysmic event in modern history, there is justifiable hysteria regarding BRUCE, a metaphysical predator who emerged into the human population several months ago. Since then, global citizens have been confined to their homes and a number of unprecedented but totally reasonable government mandates have been put in place to protect the global population from becoming a HUSK. Ergo, an individual whose personage has been extracted by Bruce. While there is literally no way to detect Husks, the general consensus among quantum physicists is that exactly 11 Umbravians have transitioned into a Huskular entity. This alarming number is sure to rise in the coming days.*

But are the government's slightly inconvenient rules enough to stave off Bruce?

"It's not enough," said a scientist from a nondescript university who would prefer not to be named. "We need more rules. Lots of more rules. These current rules are embarrassing as they are too few in number. I don't think Umbravians fully understand what we are up against here. Bruce is ruthless, determined and of course, invisible. We must all make personal sacrifices to save mankind. Anyone who disagrees is simply not a contributing member of society and probably eats paper. Bruce hates rules. Trust me, it's peer reviewed.'

While the overwhelming majority of Umbravians have stepped up and taken this inconvenience on the chin, a small number of radicals refuse to acknowledge the well-being of others.

'The number nine!' said a deranged lunatic named Ezekiel Mortimer from his balcony in Agora City. 'A plague on us! Beware the son of perdition! A thick darkness overwhelms the kingdom of the beast, and the wicked still do not repent! Plagues! Horsemen! Bowls! I totally told you this was going to happen!'

According to experts, Mortimer fits the profile of the average dissenter. Furthermore, experts suggest that because of this kind of resistance, the government should probably respond by dragging the state of confinement out longer than what is completely necessary.

For more information on today's hourly revision of governmental Bruce policies, please visit www.everybodypanic.gov. Or simply watch the unending loop of press conferences.

Once she finished typing, Clarity goggled at her computer screen. "How are they buying this?"

*** 

Slumped on the couch, Felix surfed the internet until he stumbled onto a government press conference, which had not started yet. But an elevatorish, instrumental version of Hotel California thrummed in the background while an empty podium stood in front of an Umbravian flag.

"I thought music was banned," Mally said as she flumped on the couch and slid closer to Felix.

"The government has pistachios," Felix said, slipping discreetly away from Mally on the couch. "So music is fine for them."

"That hardly seems fair," Mally said, wiggling closer to Felix and forming into a snuggle-shape.

"What are you doing?" Felix asked tentatively.

"I thought we could snuggle and watch the press conference together."

"Hugging is on the list," Felix said, clearly nervous.

"But we're in the same household," Mally said, taken aback.

"Bruce..."

"Felix..."

"I don't want to be a Husk."

"I won't let that happen," Mally said amorously, leaning in for a kiss.

"Mally, please!" Felix said, lifting his hands as though demonstrating how he was not going to hug her.

"Felix, what's gotten into..."

"This is serious, Mally," Felix said, his voice cracking. "Please take this seriously."

"It's just a hug, Felix. And it's just a silly rule..."

"The rules keep us safe. I... I don't want to feel unsafe. You're making me feel..."

"Felix, it's okay! I promise it's okay. I'm not a Husk. I feel totally fine."

"Feeling totally fine is a symptom."

"You feel totally fine."

Felix's eyeballs bulged. "I..." he said, swallowing hard, hoping to suddenly develop a sore throat. "I feel a little weird... Blotchy."

A beat.

"Okay," Mally nodded quietly. "Whatever you need, Felix. I'll sit on this side of the couch, and you can..."

"Thank you, Mally."

A beat.

"Maybe…" Mally hesitated. "Maybe we could open up the wall and hug in my alcove of books? Bruce would never find us in…"

"Do you eat paper?" Felix snapped a little too impulsively.

Mally looked genuinely punctured. "Why would you even say that to me?"

"Sorry," Felix stammered. "Sorry, I…"

"You know I don't eat paper."

"I know," Felix said, squeezing his eyes shut. "I shouldn't have…"

"That was the most random and hurtfully insulting thing you've ever said to me," Mally said in a drifting voice.

"It's just stress, you know?" Felix said while developing restless leg syndrome. "There's a lot going on right now. And also literally nothing going on right now."

"Felix, what's happening to…"

"Folks," Biff said in the press conference which was now in session. "Buddies. Bros. Mofos and compadres. I'm afraid I've got some disturbing news. Prime Minister Tristan Winnings just sent me a memo from his think tank. The premiers of Umbravia have been informed that we can no longer use the honor system to prevent questions from being asked. It yanks at my heartstrings to tell you guys this, but I'm afraid we need to take more metaphysical measures. I was on the phone with the Chief Situational Officer of Umbravia. Nice girl. Fan of Cold Play. You'd probably like her. She explained the science behind the aforementioned, metaphysical measures but gosh darn it, I had no clue what she was talking about. Too many big words and weird math. So we'll just trust her on this one."

Mally croaked out an inaptly timed laugh but hushed when Felix darted her a suspicious glare.

"So now I've got some good news and some bad news," Biff continued. "Let's do the bad news first. Unfortunately, we have to add a few more restrictions to keep you's safe, okay? I feel real bad about this, guys. But the expert released a hypothetical computer model, and it said if we don't do this, then the number of Umbravian Husks could increase by an alarming number, too disturbing to say out loud. I saw the graph and it didn't even have a top, guys. It just went right off the page. Terrifying."

Mally and Felix looked at each other.

"So here's the good news," Biff said, clapping his hands. "I decided to make this fun and randomly pick the new restrictions out of this here fishbowl."

Mally gaped at the screen as Eva presented Biff with a fishbowl filled up with scrap pieces of paper. Looking away, Biff swished his hand around in the bowl and pulled out an arbitrary scrap.

"Wow," Biff said, reading the strip of paper. "Books. Sorry, folks, but we'll have to confiscate all the books. It's important."

Mally slapped her hand over her mouth.

"Don't freak out, Mal," Felix advised in a calm, soothing voice.

"You can't be fecking serious!" Mally squeaked.

"Books are just things," Felix continued, burgeoning dangerously to condescension. "They don't really matter in the greater scheme of things."

"Look around you!" Mally barked, stretching her arms out like a jumping jack. "Books are my whole life! My identity! My, my, my purpose!"

"Sometimes you just have to point your toes outward and think about..." Felix tried.

Mally's look of utter shock and disbelief made Felix raise his palms in surrender.

"Next up," Biff said, picking another piece of paper. "Oh, this is awkward. It seems we have to cut off your phone services. Don't worry though, we'll still let you use the internet. Just no phone calls, okay folks?"

Mally pointed at the screen, agape.

"This is fun, right guys?" Biff said, fishing for a new restriction. "Uh-oh. We are going to have to harvest the cats."

A news ticker on the screen read: BREAKING: BOOKS, PHONE CALLS AND CATS HAVE BEEN DEEMED EXPENDABLE.

"Harvest the cats?" Mally squeaked. "What does that even mean?"

\*\*\*

"What does that even mean?" Otto asked Secret who he was smothering protectively.

Otto instinctively reached for his cell phone, but his phone service had already been deactivated. Swearing though clenched teeth, he sat on the floor with his back against the wall, burying his face emotionally in Secret's fur. He perked up a bit when he heard Piper, seemingly talking to herself. Cocking his ear, Otto followed the sound to the air vent in the corner, which seemed to be carrying the sound of Piper's voice.

"Piper?" Otto said into the vent.

Silence.

"Piper, can you hear me?"

From her apartment, Piper was curled into a ball in the corner, muttering indecipherably under her breath. She startled when she heard Otto's voice coming out of the air vent. When she looked up to see where the voice was coming from, she was disoriented, her eyes puffy, her face soaked with tears. With a small reserve of energy, she pulled herself across the floor with her flannelled elbows and spoke feebly into the air vent. "I'm here."

"Did you hear?" Otto quavered.

"About the cats?" Piper said, her voice squeaking from exhaustion.

"What does this mean, do you think?" Otto said, stroking Secret intensely.

"Dunno," Piper croaked.

"What if someone shows up for him?" Otto asked tremulously. "What do they even mean by harvest?"

"I have a really bad feeling about this," Piper said, barely audible.

\*\*\*

Pax gawked at his phone in disbelief.

"For your safety," Eva Spiderly said emotionally but also unemotionally in a press conference, "an exhaustive list of people who are deemed Imperative, and which have been deemed Expendable will be composed in the coming days and available for perusal on the provincial government website. Probably Thursday. All Imperatives will be issued pistachios and will be allowed to leave their homes for the exclusive purpose of engaging in Imperative activities. As for the Expendables... well..."

Startled, Pax heard a blood curdling scream and frantic knocking. Answering the door, he found a hysterical woman, trembling with bulging eyes and jugulars.

"Myrtle," Pax said, ushering the woman into his apartment and scoping the hallway before closing the door behind them. "What's happened? How did you get here? Out of your apartment on the thirteenth floor?"

"I evaded the military," Myrtle sobbed breathlessly. "And I stealthily maneuvered my body around the security lasers."

"Tell me what's happening," Pax said, assisting the trembling woman into a chair.

"It's Howard," Myrtle sobbed. "He's gone."

"Oh my God," Pax said, blanching. "Should I call an ambulance or..."

"No," Myrtle said, fanning away the horror of it all. "He's literally gone. He just disappeared."

"I don't understand," Pax said, shaking his head.

"We were enjoying some Earl Grey and Peek Freans," Myrtle said, trying to catch her breath. "We do that every afternoon by the artificial fireplace. We started talking about this and that. Howard offhandedly wondered if maybe the government could have handled the Bruce crisis differently. Which is fair, I think because we've never really handled a crisis this way before, so how do we even know it'll work? Anyhow, Howard got up to go pee, but he didn't return from the bathroom. I heard this sound. It's hard to explain. Like a staticky, zappy sound. I knocked on the bathroom door, but he didn't answer. I eventually shouldered the door open, but he wasn't there! The bathroom was completely empty! All that was left of him was some purple steam and a metallic smell in the air."

Pax gaped, stupefied.

"Pax?" Myrtle warbled. "What happened to Howard?"

# CHAPTER FORTY-THREE
## (THE NEXT DAY)

"How the hell should I know what happened to Howard?" Eva said, brisk walking at a rude pace with Pax following behind.

"What are these metaphysical measures you and Biff keep talking about?" Pax said, quickening his pace. "What did you do to this guy?"

"Questions are banned," Eva remarked. "This Howard person asked a question. He knew the consequences."

"You're not answering me," Pax grimaced.

"Look," Eva said, swerving around to face Pax. "The Feds..."

"Stop blaming the Feds and start taking responsibility for your policies," Pax demanded. "Did you hurt Howard? Is he ever coming back?"

"That's confidential."

"His wife is falling apart."

"It's a cautionary tale."

"What did the Chief Situational Officer tell you?" Pax persisted. "About this... this science?"

"Calm down, Pax. It was just a wormhole."

"So you're saying Howard is in a parallel dimension?"

"Don't be ridiculous. It's just a void."

"So I'm supposed to tell Myrtle that her husband is in a void?" Pax said, throwing his arms up in exasperation. "How does one go about initiating that conversation?"

"He'll be fine, Pax," Eva exhaled. "He's *probably* not dead. Don't you trust science?"

"You're manipulating science."

"That's not a thing."

"It is when you suck innocent people into an alternate dimension."

"Void."

"Does this even have anything to do with Bruce anymore?"

"Why don't you and your conscience go somewhere and play table tennis?" Eva said, rolling her eyes. "Or write each other poems?"

"You're playing games with people's lives!"

"Now you're getting it," Eva quipped, smacking Pax on the back of his suit jacket.

***

"Did you hear about Howard?" Flossie asked, offering Girard a steaming mug of black coffee.

Girard removed his spectacles and rubbed his eyes. "His face is all over social media."

"I can't believe they've taken it this far," Flossie said, shaking her head in stunned bewilderment as she took a seat across the kitchenette table from Girard.

"I wrote an email," Girard said bluntly, staring blankly.

"You did the right thing," Flossie said, placing her hand over Girard's. "The situation is highly nuanced, and they should be consulting with experts in all relevant fields. Including yours."

"But my opinion is not sanctioned," Girard blinked. "I'm an educator. Education is banned. I wrote a book. I'm a critical thinker. That makes me one of the *Expendables.*"

"You sent the email before the metaphysical interventions," Flossie said, nodding reassuringly. "You'll be fine."

"If something happens to me..."

"Girard..."

"Flossie, there's a very good chance they could make an example of me. I'm rather high profile..."

"You listen to me," Flossie choked emotionally. "I love you, Professor Girard Gosh. You are a decent man."

"Not according to..."

"A man of conscience."

"That could cost me my..."

"Conscience is incredibly sexy."

Girard involuntarily sprayed out a raspberry laugh, in spite of himself.

"Girard, I'm proud of you for standing up for what you believe in. Despite the lunacy of all this."

"I'm going to have to be very careful what I say here on in."

"The hell you are," Flossie said, startling Girard when she abruptly slammed her coffee mug on the table.

"Flossie..."

"You are not going to let the world descend into madness, or let the political elitists rewrite the universal code of ethics. You can't watch people suffer like this. I know you. I know you don't have it in you to just stand by and watch this all happen without intercepting."

"I can't leave you," Girard croaked, his eyes pinkening.

"You won't," Flossie promised. "No matter what happens, we are both going to... look at me, Girard... we are both going to do whatever we can to help."

"What if we get separated?"

"I'm not going anywhere," Flossie said, shaking her head. "We'll be together no matter what. Whether we're stuck here in this apartment or disappear somewhere in a puff of purple steam, it'll be you and me, Gosh."

Girard swallowed hard.

\*\*\*

"Greetings, and a special welcome to my nine million, twenty-seven thousand, six hundred and one new followers," Willatrix livestreamed. "I'm sure you're all worried about Howard who suddenly vaporized in his bathroom. I'm going to lend you some wisdom, and it may be a hard pill to swallow, given how you are all such benevolent sparrows of sympathy. "Willatrix leaned in very close to her laptop camera. "Forget him. He is unworthy of compassion."

Willatrix buried her face in her hands for exactly two minutes to make a point.

"That was difficult to process, wasn't it," Willatrix nodded. "Do not misunderstand, we must keep Howard in the back of our minds so as not to make the same mistakes he did. But compassion is the non-renewable resource of the soul. We must reserve our compassion for the victims of Bruce – unless it's totally their fault - because it is virtually impossible to have compassion for more than one person at a time. Thus sayeth the potato."

Willatrix paused briefly to give thanks to Celestandrea the lunar harvest monkey.

"Tangent," Willatrix continued, snapping out of her trance as though the pagan prayer did not just happen. "Our boycott of the day... and this was a challenge since almost everything has already been legally banned... is internet influencer Roxanne Tarragon. Children of the cornflowers, do not be deceived. While her vlog is alarmingly similar to mine, her motives are impure. She is misleading her unassuming lambs with performative activism and virtue signaling. Please warn your friends. Tell them to beware of this wolf in ethically sourced clothing. She is exploiting this crisis to accrue followers. Beckon her followers to join us instead, on our quest for enlightenment and bliss. For mine is a soul you can trust."

Willatrix turned on a floor fan to make it look as though her hair was being blown by an ocean wind.

"This has been Willatrix Oleander, reminding you to be decent to one another, just like me. Thank you for your attention."

# CHAPTER FORTY-FOUR
## (A FEW DAYS LATER)

Nestling his butt into a blue and white striped, canvas beach chair, Tristan basked in the sun, wriggling his toes in the powder-white sand. In front of him was an ocean, cyan in color, with foamy waves curling and crashing. A dolphin undulated through the sparkling sea swells for effect.

His laptop was balanced on his legs which were sticky with coconut-scented sunscreen as Tristan watched Willatrix's vlog through the lenses of his mirrored Ray-Bans. Swaying palms and a passing seagull reflected in said lenses.

"Furthermore, my elysian peace doves," Willatrix said with a voice that somehow mimicked the sea breeze that was currently blowing kisses through Tristan's hair, "success, power and fulfilment begin with self-love. It all starts with you. Love yourself. Deeply. Soulfully.

Unconditionally. Infatuatedly. Gaze at yourself in the mirror every day and kiss your reflection. Kiss like you mean it."

Tristan licked his lips.

"Tell yourself you are the most important person in the world," Willatrix continued. "Think of all your enviable qualities. Write them in a list. Post the list online. Inform others of your worth. Tell them you're an effing unicorn. Say it to them loudly and often."

Tristan nodded earnestly.

"You deserve attention, you beautiful, beautiful creature," Willatrix said, with her version of sincerity.

"Yes," Tristan rasped emotionally, pursing his lips to quell emotion. "I really, really do."

"Own it," Willatrix advised. "Demand it. Scream for it. You are worthy and deserving and entitled to all the universe has to offer."

Tristan nodded emotionally.

"This has been Willatrix Oleander. Reminding you to…"

"What in bloody hell are you doing?" Hector interrupted.

Tristan startled, discovering Hector looming above him, wearing a tweed suit despite the balmy sun.

"I'm taking time for my spiritual self-care," Tristan said, slapping his laptop shut.

"You are such a twat."

"Seriously, Hector. You should check out this vlogger. She'll change your life."

"I highly doubt that."

"Her words are so powerful," Tristan insisted. "I've been following her for months and she's so inspiring, I started giving her government funding."

"You are supposed to be doing a press conference now."

"Heeeectooooor…" Tristan whined, throwing a towel over his face.

"You are due to address the nation on a subject of great importance," Hector said dryly. "No more excuses."

"Beepy is supposed to do the press conferences until I get back."

"Dr. Deerlight had to take a mental health day."

"Slacker."

"You are already six minutes late," Hector droned. "Everyone is waiting."

"I'm on the flipping beach."

"Make it work," Hector said, setting up Tristan's laptop and logging him in. "And for God's sake, don't embarrass yourself."

Tristan quickly used his fingers to comb through his windblown hair, cleared his throat, fluffed his chest hair, and did something with his eyebrow that he perceived to be suavely somber.

"Citizens of Umbravia," Tristan said, suddenly serious. "This is Prime Minister Tristan Winnings, coming to you from my think tank in an undisclosed location with a grave message." He paused briefly to accept a Mai Tai from a sultry woman in a sarong. "Thank you, Leilani," Tristan said to the woman, sipping his drink before continuing. "Bruce has gotten a foothold in our nation. According to the Chief Situational Officer, the number of Umbravian Husks has increased to seventeen million and three. An exponential increase of nearly five hundred percent since an hour ago. This can only mean one thing..."

*\*\**

"You are not doing enough," Tristan said as though he was staring and pointing directly at Lola through her phone screen.

Lola felt a proverbial fist punch in the throat. Her knees buckled as she collapsed into a ball on the air mattress, leaving a pot of boiling water unattended on the stove. In her completely stunned and emotionally wounded state, she was only vaguely aware that Garthie was climbing up the curtain like a spider monkey, Bobby was wailing in his play yard while Enzo and the girls were secretly eating playdough, hiding in the bathroom cabinet.

"This is all your fault," Tristan said, pointing at Lola authoritatively through her phone screen. "The government has done everything we possibly can to protect you. We worked tirelessly to come up with creative ways to keep you all safe. All we asked you to do was make a few, personal sacrifices for the sake of..." Tristan shooed away some hula dancers. "... for the sake of the country. What will it take to get through to you people? Clearly we will have to come up with harsher..."

Lola quickly shut off her phone and tossed it aside as though it was burning her fingers. She put her hands on her ears and rocked back and forth, sobbing. Her children's shrieks, playful roaring and cries sounded very far away, and she was oblivious to the pot boiling over with foaming, scalding water on the stove.

*"It's all your fault, Lola!"* Shane's voice echoed throughout Lola's mind. *"I do everything for you! Everything!"*

Although the loud slamming, clanging and screaming was only in Lola's imagination, she winced and shuddered.

*"I'm sorry, Shane!"* Lola could hear her own voice in her mind. *"I'm sorry! Garthie's just little. He didn't know…"*

*"You have one job to do! I work my ass off and all you have to do…"*

*"It's only a Christmas tree ornament! We can get another one. Garthie was just trying to help!"*

*"I suppose you think I just pull money out of my ass for you."*

*"Of course not…"*

*"Like you've ever worked."*

*"I want to! But the babies! You wanted a big family!"*

*"Don't lie. You begged me for kids."*

*"I mean I love them more than anything but…"*

*"Yeesh! I never should have married a drop-out."*

*"You said you wanted to support…"*

*"I never said that!"*

*"You did though! You pressured me to drop out. You said you wanted to marry me right away because of the baby..."*

*"Probably not even mine."*

*"You said you wanted to handle the finances because..."*

*"Why would I say that? You're crazy."*

*"No."*

*"Crazy twat."*

*"Shane..."*

*"Why are you crying? Am I not good enough for you?"*

*"Shane, no..."*

*"You thinking of leaving? You think you can survive without me?"*

*"Please, not in front of the..."*

*"You think you can find someone better than me? An ugly, stupid cow like you?"*

*"That's not fair! I was an honor student! I could have..."*

*"Stupid cow! Stupid!"*

*"For God's sake, Shane, you're scaring the..."*

"Mummy?" Izzy asked, wide-eyed.

Catching her breath, Lola steadied her nerves by hugging her arms and tried to focus on Izzy through her dewy eyelashes. "I'm good," she quavered. "It's all good. Let's make a blanket tent."

# CHAPTER FORTY-FIVE
## (THE NEXT DAY)

The microwave dinged just as Clarity was flipping her hair into a ponytail. After hastily applying some papaya scented Chapstick and puckering in the mirror, she retrieved her breakfast rations – rubbery scrambled eggs and two strips of leathery bacon – and sat down in her compact breakfast nook. Her fingers fidgeted with her pistachio as she erected her laptop screen.

Clarity had been stewing over her dad's situation on the mushroom farm and figured now was as good a time as any to Skype him. It felt weird to have access to video calls when the rest of the province was cut off from this form of communication, but media people had pistachios. And Torrence lived in the province of Knackerton where the Bruce policies were arbitrarily different from Scatopia.

"Clare Bear?" Torrence asked, sounding genuinely surprised to see Clarity on the screen.

Clarity noticed Torrence had an identical microwavable meal in front of him. "Want to have breakfast together?" she asked, pulling the cellophane off her eggs.

"I thought video phone services were cut off in Scatopia?"

Clarity felt the blood rush to her face as she discreetly hid her pistachio under a napkin. "I... I was randomly selected for a freebie. Today. For... for good behavior. Compliance." Clarity winced at her lie.

"You have a ponytail," Torrence observed.

Clarity nodded with her mouth full of eggs.

"I've never seen you with a ponytail," Torrence said, cocking his head. "It's nice. Nice to see your face. Usually you're hiding behind a curtain of hair."

"Thought I'd try something different."

"And there's color in your cheeks."

"How are things, Da?" Clarity said, quickly changing the subject. "You doing okay with... you know. Everything?"

Torrence leaned back in his chair and ballooned his cheeks in a resigned exhale.

Clarity swallowed her eggs with a guilty gulp.

"The premier of Knackerton released the list of expendables early this morning," Torrence said in a futile attempt to cut his bacon into bite-sizes.

Clarity dropped her fork and goggled at the screen.

"Da?" Clarity croaked, watching her father slowly turn fuchsia.

"Mushrooms have been deemed expendable," Torrence rumbled despondently under his breath.

Clarity's jaw hung open like a stupid, stunned fish. In that moment she was also about as verbal as a fish. Never in her wildest delusions could she ever have imagined her rise to success would lead to her father's demise. Would he lose the farm? The house? How would he feed his Labrador retriever? Would he have to sell all his pants and sleep in his Mitsubishi? Or would he lose the Mitsubishi too? For that matter, it was essentially illegal to be homeless as one would have no home in which to be confined. Would Torrence spend the rest of his years wallowing in despair, yearning hopelessly for mushrooms? Was there any chance Torrence would find out that this was unequivocally Clarity's fault?

*He couldn't possibly know it was me.*

*He thinks the internet is witchcraft and I barely convinced him to get a computer solely for texting and Skype.*

*And they don't deliver newspapers in the middle of literal nowhere.*

*His only source of information is the 6:00 news.*

*Poor Da.*

*I hope he doesn't do something drastic.*

*Is it bad that I'm happier than I've ever been?*

*This is the first time I've ever been comfortable in my own skin.*

*Ponytails would have been a hard no for me a few months ago.*

*I'm secure in my own, little microcosm.*

*Queen of my bubble.*

*Binge watching 'Love Island' with my fern.*

*Zero awkward encounters.*

*No reason for insecurities.*

*My anxiety has essentially vanished.*

*Even my stutter is improving.*

*And my dream job... Holy frig.*

*I'm killing it.*

*But Da...*

"But that's literally all you grow," Clarity finally said.

"Don't I know it," Torrence exhaled.

"What's going to happen to you?"

"That's anyone's guess," Torrence shrugged. "I suppose it depends on how long this situation lingers on. I have some savings that'll last me two, three months maybe?"

"Da, if you need some money to keep you going…"

"Where on earth would you get the money to support me?"

"I…" Clarity stopped abruptly, remembering that as far as Torrence was concerned, Clarity was grasping to the edge of subsistence with her refrigerator blog. "… don't know."

\*\*\*

"Prairie dogs?" Mally squeaked interrogatively as she read the list of imperative items on the provincial government website. "In what way are prairie dogs imperative to our survival?"

"Bonsai trees," Felix read over Mally's shoulder, "tables, bongs, reality T.V. shows, gum, foot ointment, all fruit except grapes, yellow, thermometers, butlers, water…"

"Unscented soap," Mally continued reading, "the internet, air, cigarettes, packing bubbles, pork, scratch and sniff stickers, processed cheese, underpants, dogfood, instant gravy…"

"Pantyhose," Felix continued, "detergent, dental floss, waffle irons, staplers, chicken nuggets, false eyelashes, paper, maraschino cherries…"

"Central air conditioners," Mally sighed, "frozen dairy-free pizza, algebra, carpet, actuaries, blankets, e-commerce, Dwayne Johnson, Pho, sweater vests... mayonnaise?"

"Mayonaise?" Felix asked, squinting at the screen.

"That's what it says."

"Mayonaise," Felix repeated so he could hear the words again and make sure he wasn't hallucinating.

"Apparently mayonnaise is imperative," Mally shrugged.

Felix blinked. "So does this mean..."

"You're imperative, Felix," Mally swallowed.

"So I get to..."

"Leave the apartment and go to work," Mally said in utter disbelief. "While I stay here and atrophy."

"Wow," Felix said, stunned.

"They're going to give you a pistachio."

Felix cocked his head.

"How is mayonnaise imperative but books are expendable?" Mally blurted.

"What's that supposed to mean?"

"Felix, it's *mayonnaise*. It's a gelatinous, primordial blob of redundant calories, jarred for marketing purposes."

"You said it was your favorite garnish!"

"Garnishes have flavor, Felix! Mayonnaise is a tasteless lubricant you use to moisturize dry sandwiches. Nothing more!"

"You're jealous."

"Confused! How is mayonnaise going to save mankind, but books are dangerous and about to be confiscated?"

"You should be thankful that one of us can earn a living!"

"Why can't I work though?" Mally squeaked. "What's going to happen to the bookshop? This is so random!"

"So you think you know more than the expert?"

"Who is this expert even? And why doesn't he read?"

"You need to trust the experts! They know a whole lot more than us and..."

"Felix..."

"If we do the right thing, this will all go away. I want it to all go away!"

"Can you please just try to understand..."

"You're going to make this crisis linger on forever! Don't!"

"I thought you cared about the things that matter to me, Felix!"

"This isn't about you, Mally. This is for the benefit of humanity. Why can't you understand that?"

"Try to put yourself in my position," Mally squeaked. "The only reason you're getting your freedom back is because you sold out! If you were still playing the harpsichord..."

"You think I'm a sell-out?"

"You're a musician and you know it! Just look at your damn harpsichord fingers!"

"I'm a mayonnaise guy!"

"Only by profession! In your heart you're a harpsichord player! You were born that way and there's not a damn thing you can do about it!"

"You... you don't know me at all!"

"My point being, if you stayed true to yourself, we would be going through this together! You would understand why I'm..."

"Music is expendable. Obviously I made the right choice."

"I can't even look at your right now."

"I did nothing wrong," Felix barked in Mally's face. "I have nothing to be ashamed of! You're the one who is unclean! Books are..."

"You're not getting it, Felix! If you accept the pistachio, we will be delegated into two, separate social classes. Imperative and expendable. We couldn't be together anymore."

Felix chewed his cheek contemplatively.

"I don't want to be trapped in this apartment alone, without you. Can't you see you're all I have left? I love you, Felix!"

"I love you too but..."

"Besides, I'll be worried sick about you being out there. What if Bruce finds you?"

"That's just nonsense. I'll have a pistachio."

"You think a little, green nut is going to... Like five minutes ago you were obsessed with the notion of becoming a Husk. You said we were all in grave danger and accused me of downplaying it. You accused me of eating paper! You're not exactly acting like a person who is afraid of Bruce right now."

"Why do you have to be so selfish?"

"What?"

"Don't you want me to get my life back?"

Mally pinched the bridge of her nose. "I can't tell you what to do. If you want to take that damn pistachio and leave me alone in this apartment, stripped of my livelihood, identity, dignity, sanity and any form of a coping mechanism or emotional support... while you enjoy a normal life... I guess I can't stop you."

Felix blinked. "Okay, bye," he said casually as he hastily left the apartment.

# CHAPTER FORTY-SIX
## (THE NEXT MORNING)

Barely awake, Mally rolled over in her quilty bed with a groggy groan, instinctively stretching her arm over the spot where Felix used to sleep. She patted the mattress in various places, expecting to feel Felix. When reality sunk in, she whimpered and pulled a quilt over her head.

BOOM!

Mally suddenly sat bolt upright on her mattress when she heard an angry commotion coming from the next room. In her flannel *Winnie the Pooh* pajamas, she warily scootched to the door and peered around the corner. Slapping her hand over her mouth with a wispy gasp, Mally saw soldiers sweeping rows of books from her shelves. She winced, turning away. But as the soldiers carelessly and heartlessly tossed her beloved books into a toxic waste receptacle, Mally impulsively burst through the door.

"STOP IT!" she shrieked hysterically. "CAN YOU JUST FECKING NOT?!?!"

Mally recoiled when a soldier turned to face her, wearing a hazmat suit and a seemingly superfluous gas mask.

"Books are expendable," the soldier said, muffled behind the oxygen hose on his face. "You're lucky we don't put *you* in the receptacle."

Before she could fully process the horror, another soldier imposed on Mally's personal space and demanded to know if she had any more books. Mally's eyeballs lolled towards the secret wall that concealed her alcove of first editions, then across the room to where Felix had boarded the wall back up to separate their apartments. Her eyeballs then lolled back to the soldier. "No," she said stoically.

\*\*\*

Norman was stirring his boiling marshmallow root a little slower that day. Completed crossword books were strewn seemingly everywhere around his apartment. His television was turned on but was tuned into some arbitrary channel with back-to-back Bill Murray films, of which Norman paid very little mind. He muttered nonsensically to himself, under his breath. His eyeballs bulged when he heard rapping at his door.

"Norman?"

"Young Pax?" Norman said feebly, shuffling much slower than normal across the room, his socks making static on the carpet.

"How's it going in there?" Pax asked from the other side of the door.

"Making marshmallows," Norman whistled. "But there's no one I can give them to. I don't suppose ye'd be allowed to come inside for a visit and a cup of joe? Seeing as ye have a pistachio?"

"I'm really sorry, Norman. I'm not allowed to interact directly with people who lack pistachios."

"Figures. What time is it, do you know?"

"April," Pax replied.

Norman nodded.

Time did not make sense anymore.

"I haven't heard from you in a while," Pax observed.

"No phone," Norman shrugged. "And I don't have one of them pocket robots ye young folk communicate with."

"You don't sound like yourself, Norman."

"How's that?"

"You sound..."

"Old?"

Pax exhaled loudly through his nose.

"I don't have the energy I once had," Norman said, his voice drifting. "I just sort of walk around here in a kind of fog. No one to talk to. No way to get out and stretch me legs. Just sit in here day after day, breathing in this stagnant air. Every day another notch on the wall. I'm even getting sick of marshmallows. I can't realistically eat them all me- self. Sometimes I don't really know what the point is anymore."

"Norman, this is temporary."

"Maybe ye young folks can see it that way."

"A lot of people are thinking about you."

"A lot of good that does me when I'm sitting in here, drowning in this ear-splitting silence."

"It's really hard to hear you talk this way."

"Yeah? Well, imagine how hard it is for me to actually live in this existential cesspit."

"I'm going to do everything I can to help, okay Norman? This isn't fair. It's just not. All this collateral damage… I'm going to fight like a fricking ninja…"

"There's nothing ye can do," Norman said despondently. "The government's told us to hunker down, possibly for months or years and have offered zero beacons of hope. People who try to think positive are demonized in the news. Nothing to look forward to."

"They're starting to randomly offer pistachios to select people."

"Us centenarians are the last thing on the government's radar. They don't care what happens to us. I could instantly decompose right now in a state of filth and neglect, and Chesterfield wouldn't bat an eyelash."

"I care, Norman. I care very much," Pax insisted. "I don't care if this breaks me. I don't even care if it's futile. I'm not going to be able to sleep easy until you are okay."

Norman snuffled and his jowls quivered emotionally.

"Norman?"

"Why?" Norman gently sobbed. "Why are ye so determined to help a forgotten old soul like me?"

"You matter, Norman," Pax said, sitting and making himself comfortable with his back against Noman's door. "Community matters to me."

"Community doesn't even exist anymore," Norman said. "Why is this so important to you? Why do you refuse to give up on us, like that rabbit in the battery commercial?"

"It's a cultural thing I guess," Pax shrugged. "My parents immigrated from the Hebridean Islands of Scotland when I was twelve. Do you know anything about the culture there, Norman?"

"Can't say that I do," Norman said, pulling up a chair.

"We have this thing called the *Hebridean Code,*" Pax explained. "It's an ancient edict the Hebrideans formed to ensure the survival of our community. *Never walk past a person who needs something. Never turn a person away who has nowhere to go. Everything we have is for sharing. A true friend is a literal family member. Storytelling brings people together and is essential for survival. And most importantly, never exploit another person's kindness.* These tenets were ingrained in me since I was a small child. Community is everything, Norman. Our individual survival depends on it. At least that's what the MacLeods think."

"Ye have a good family," Norman nodded.

"My dad once told me about an ancestor of mine," Pax added. "He was the chieftain of the Clan MacLeod. A long time ago, he jumped in front of a charging bull to save a friend who was about to be executed unjustly."

"NAH," Norman joked.

"Seriously," Pax giggled. "See, the Duke of Argyle sentenced a man to death for hunting a deer on the duke's land to feed his starving family. He was to be gored to death by a bull in front of a crowd of spectators. Before the execution, in front of everyone, my ancestor confronted the duke and told him it was unfair and demanded that his friend be released. When the duke laughed his arse off, MacLeod said, *'If I can stop that bull, will you pardon my friend?'* The duke told MacLeod to go to his death."

Norman wriggled suspensefully in his chair, eager for more.

"As the bull charged," Pax continued, almost giddy at this point, "MacLeod leaped in front of his friend and grabbed the bull's horns. He held on to the horns as tight as he could, getting thrashed violently around. The crowd screamed, *'Hold fast! Hold fast!'* And he just held on."

Norman's milky eyes began to glow with wonder.

"Eventually the bull got tired," Pax continued. "And when the bull collapsed, MacLeod took out his dirk and killed it. And because there was a crowd of witnesses, the duke had no choice but to set MacLeod's friend free."

Norman dabbed the corner of his eyes with a handkerchief.

"Every Scottish clan has an emblem and a motto," Pax explained. "Our emblem is a bull, and our motto is *hold fast.*"

"Suits ye," Norman said, a bit of color restored in his cheeks. "I'll bet ye that ancestor of yours is mighty proud of ye, Son."

"Didn't I ever tell you about Hebrideans?" Pax said mischievously. "We believe… we *know* that our ancestors are not only with us but are also actively a part of our lives. They advise, guide, protect and cheer for us."

"I'm really glad ye stopped by today."

Pax noticed the winsome spark that had returned to Norman's voice. Storytelling had healing properties and he knew it. "Same."

Three fresh marshmallows suddenly plopped out of Norman's mail slot.

# CHAPTER FORTY-SEVEN
## (LATER THAT DAY)

"In what way is this not elder abuse?" Pax railed in Parliament to a very non-plussed Eva Spiderly. "Minister Spiderly, I was talking to a constituent today, one hundred and six years old, who's been completely and utterly alone since the crisis began. No phone or internet. Nobody except me checking up on him. The view out his window is a brick wall! Minister, our elders are the most cherished members of our society. Their eyes are filled with a trillion stories. They are a portal to our history. Where would we be without their wisdom? Their advice? Their perspective? They deserve better than this! We can't just essentially imprison them until the crisis is over! That's immoral! It's like my neighbor Girard said..."

"Mr. Speaker," Eva said plastically, trying to look prepared by shuffling blank papers, "for obvious reasons we can't just set them free, simply because they're bored. Consider the plight of mankind."

"Grow a conscience!" Pax hollered at Eva.

"Agora East, behave yourself," said the Speaker of the House.

"Agora East will not behave himself!" Agora East barked back. "Will the Minister of Catastrophic Events please tell us all here today, when. Will. You. Free. Norman?"

"Minister of Catastrophic Events?" said the Speaker of the House, lolling his head towards Eva.

"Thank you, Mr. Speaker," Eva said evenly. "I'm not sure who Norman is or why the member has decided to leave his decorum at home today. Chesterfield's government has provided the elderly with the same standardized microwave dinner rations as the rest of Scatopia. And we ultimately decided *against* sending the elderly away in a psychedelic camper van to a special hotel for the rest of their days. *You're welcome.* Unfortunately, we will have to confine the elderly longer than any other demographic for exactly the reasons you listed above. They have the unfair advantage of perspective. They know too much. They've seen too much. The last thing we need right now is for our efforts to be thwarted by people warning us about history repeating itself. Which obviously is not the case here because nothing like this has ever happened before."

"Answer the question!" Pax yelled. "When. Will. You. Free. Norman!"

"The short answer," Eva said, perusing her blank papers, "Is *never.* I'm not sure why the member feels the need to pound his chest so. The elderly have been given the absolute bare minimum necessities to keep them alive. Your constituent IS alive, is he not, Agora East? Life is a gift, Mr. Speaker. This is not the time for ingratitude. Clearly the

Chesterfield government has been nothing short of benevolent and altruistic while steadfastly listening to the expert during this unprecedented crisis."

"Here, here!" shouted some guy right before the Parliament erupted with applause.

"Member for Agora East?" said the Speaker of the House. "The grimace on your face implies you have something to say."

"Thank you, Mr. Speaker," Pax said, trying to compose himself. "If the Minister of Catastrophic Events refuses to acknowledge her blatant disregard for the elderly, then please. Tell me at the very least you give a flying squirrel about our children."

"Oh here we go," Eva said, rolling her eyes.

"I have a constituent," Pax said, reading from a legal pad, "who can't bring herself to watch the news anymore because the government is giving her P.T.S.D triggers as their messaging is reminiscent of her abusive ex-husband."

"Oh come ON!" Eva said, pointing a mocking finger at Pax. "That's a far stretch, don't you think?"

"She has five young children," Pax persisted. "Childhood has been banned. Education has been banned. There aren't enough rations to feed her kids. She can't even get the support she needs from her mother or from her church. What resources are available to…"

"Bullshit!" hollered a heckler.

"Give it a rest, MacLeod!" shouted another heckler.

"Ignoramus!"

"Get him out of here!"

"Agora East eats kittens!"

"Sustained," the Speaker droned.

Pax squinted interrogatively at the Speaker.

\*\*\*

"Greetings, earth angels," Willatrix said, addressing her vlog viewers with praying hands. "And namaste to my twenty-seven million new followers. I hope you have all been using this special time of isolation to reflect. To be creative and productive like me. Why not write that novel you've always thought about writing but just couldn't find the time? Paint a masterpiece in a style all your own. Secretly teach yourself to play the panpipes. Learn Japanese. Acquire an enriching hobby like candle making or riding a unicycle. Get in tune with your inner-hamster. Become a herpetologist. The possibilities are endless. Which is why I struggle to understand the negative energy I've been sensing on the internet."

Willatrix performed a sacred cleansing ritual, too weird to describe in actual words.

"So many toxic people online," Willatrix said with a swoon. "I spent most of yesterday commenting with honesty on internet threads and the volume of selfish whiners and mollycoddled grumblers made my heart hurt. Isolation is a virtue, my celestial dorpers. These people lack creativity and cannot comprehend the interconnectedness of the universe. Complaining about brain fog, fatigue and lack of motivation? Grieving for all the things they lost? That is simply foul. We are called to a higher purpose. Anyone who struggles with isolation is a selfish…"

A knock at the door caused Willatrix to triangulate an eyebrow. "Excuse me," she apologized to her viewers as she answered the door, finding a soldier.

"Here is your pistachio," the soldier said bluntly, handing Willatrix a green tree nut.

Without hesitation, Willatrix took the nut in her fingers. After marveling at it for a moment she quickly slipped on her burlap gladiator sandals and zipped out of her apartment, forgetting to turn off the camera on her computer.

***

The room was conspicuously empty as Mally sat in her wingback chair, still in her pajamas, processing the lack of books and the odious, wooden slats that now separated Felix Clover's apartment from hers. She felt hollow. Partly from emotional barrenness and partly from lack of lunch. The rations included microwavable avocado toast. The avocado had already turned brown and would have been unappetizing even if Mally's stomach was *not* twisting like a wet towel.

Felix loved avocados.

Eventually Mally found the motivation to get out of the chair and look for a clean shirt in the closet. When she opened the accordion doors, she found the closet still stockpiled with tins of tuna fish from when they thought an asteroid was about to pummel Earth, rendering it uninhabitable. Felix had taken everything with him except his damn tuna fish.

Felix loved tuna fish.

Rather than starving, Mally grabbed a fork and sat on the window ledge, eating the flaky tuna directly from the can. She looked despondently outside, noticing a small peppering of people occasionally walking past. Not nearly the city throng she once saw during the Pre-Bruce Era. But weird nonetheless since she was still confined to her apartment while a few others roamed around outdoors.

Across the street, the marquee sported the words, *"IMPERATIVES ONLY."*

Her glassy eyes widened when she spotted a shock of corduroy walking along the sidewalk below, stopping in front of a svelte woman with a floof of chestnut hair, wearing an overalls dress with deep, mismatched pockets. The corduroy cavorted with the floof.

"Felix?" Mally croaked, dropping her fork.

The pair idled for a while, with flirtatious posturing, throwing their heads back often with laughter. Mally swallowed a gasp when Felix presented the woman with a jar of mayonnaise he just happened to have on his person. After a gasp of surprise and wonder, the woman pulled what appeared to be a jar of maraschino cherries from her deep pockets and presented it to Felix, who responded with an open-mouth Muppet smile and a hand-wandering hug.

Mally bit her bottom lip until she tasted blood.

Following the condiment exchange, Felix caressed the side of the woman's face, moving her floofy chestnut hair away so he could kiss her stupid, pillowy lips. The woman flipped her hair as Felix led her away with his hand on the small of her back.

"You little bitch," Mally half seethed, half sobbed.

She was referring to Felix.

# CHAPTER FORTY-EIGHT
## (ONE WEEK LATER)

"Are you sure we should do this?" Girard asked nervously as Flossie spread birdseed onto the windowsill.

"You said yourself that this new cultural shift is morally wrong," Flossie reminded Girard as she coaxed a pigeon inside with some peanut butter speckled with birdseed on her index finger.

"But so is breaking the law."

"But the law is unethical," Flossie said, carefully attaching a small piece of paper to the pigeon's leg before setting it free.

"You're consequentializing a moral dilemma," Girard said, glowing with admiration. "I'm so proud of you."

"We're going to be okay," Flossie reassured Girard. "You know we're going to be okay?"

"Sure," Girard swallowed.

"Are you having some kind of Utilitarian crisis or..."

Girard was never one-hundred percent on board with Utilitarianism. While he believed wholeheartedly that it was wrong to sabotage tens of thousands of people to save a hypothetical few, the whole thing seemed like more of a numbers game than anything else, disregarding contextualization and a plethora of other human intricacies. Deontology wasn't a good fit either, with its concise list of ethical rules that could be conveniently memorized. While in graduate school, Girard saw the word *rules* and instantly bristled. Totally not his jam. Nothing as nuanced as morality can be as static and over-simplified as that.

Two of Girard's colleagues at the university exacerbated Girard's struggle to find his place in academia. Professor Ned Swallowsbury, a staunch Utilitarianist, often locked horns with Deontologist Anatole Hildebrand, causing Girard to be stuck in the middle. Quite literally as Girard's office was situated between the two of theirs. Ned and Anatole were both rooted fervently in their philosophies, each accusing the other of being morally bankrupt, and most arguments resulted in the two esteemed academics shouting very eloquent insults and hurling cafeteria beignets.

Again, Girard would be caught in the middle.

While Girard could appreciate the partial truths in his colleague's philosophies, he could not subscribe fully to either as they were both flawed. Being apparently wired differently from other moral philosophers, Girard Gosh was considered a controversial figure in academia. This was especially true when he penned his theory of *Goshism:* a philosophy which subscribes to the notion that...

*Rules are meaningless.*

*People cannot be trusted to make moral judgements on another's behalf.*

*The establishment is killing us.*

*One cannot find the truth by memorizing a list of arbitrary rules devised by academic elitists.*

*We know the difference between right and wrong because we FEEL the difference between right and wrong.*

Girard's theory was once considered dangerous within the realm of moral philosophy. His peers considered his anti-establishment views offensive to the academic establishment. And Girard's notion of conscience was an affront to centuries of research devoted to a field of study in which lots and lots of smart people compose elaborately structured rules about how to tell the difference between good and bad. Nonetheless, Girard stood his ground, making him somewhat of a rogue professor, but a favorite among students. Ultimately, the popularity and relatability of his theories left the faculty no choice but to grudgingly respect him.

So much had been jostling around inside Girard's brain regarding the government's emergency response strategy. The whole thing was something of a Utilitarian, Deontological, Consequential, Relativist, Welfarist, Aristotelian cluster-feck. And it most definitely violated the various tenets of Goshism. He regarded the Bruce policies to be

Machiavellian in nature, a philosophy that made Girard cringe. Throughout the Bruce crisis, whenever he heard politicians drone on about their warped perversion of Utilitarianism, Girard would almost literally hear his conscience vomit.

At any rate, to answer Flossie's question...

"No."

"Then grab a pigeon," Flossie urged.

"Flossie, in the event that we get caught..."

"Do I need to remind you of the fifth characteristic of your own mother-loving theory?"

"We are doing the right thing," Girard nodded. "There's no doubt in my mind about that. It's just that the system does not align with my philosophies. The right thing to me is not what the government defines as right. There are consequences to being ethical in an unethical society. We need to discuss the very real possibility of..."

"How could anyone possibly trace this back to us?"

"Are you sure this is going to work? They're not exactly homing pigeons."

"They don't have to be," Flossie explained. "All they have to do is carry these messages anywhere they want to fly. Eventually people will find them and read..."

"Wouldn't it have been easier just to text these messages to a bunch of people?"

"Too easy to trace," Flossie said matter-of-factly. "Besides, people are psychologically more likely to retain information brought to them by a pigeon."

***

"Cats?" a soldier asked, bluntly in a guttural tone.

"I keep telling you no," Otto said, slamming the door in the soldier's face, wincing when he heard the soldier sneeze in the hallway.

Once the bootsteps dissipated down the hall, Otto padded across the room and liberated Secret from his sock drawer. The cat's ears were flattened backwards, and he uttered an irked 'rrrrreooorrr' from deep in his throat. Otto carried his perturbed feline to the air vent.

"Piper?"

Piper wanted to reply. But she felt like a stone in her bed, feeling too heavy to move. The air vent was all the way on the other side of the room. She feebly chirped, "I'm here," hoping Otto could hear.

"This is getting ridiculous," Otto said. "The soldier shows up every day, looking for cats. He keeps sneezing so I think he might suspect something."

Piper opened her mouth but lost her words.

"I don't know if I can keep hiding him in my sock drawer," Otto sighed. "This is not sustainable. Why would they want to harvest cats anyway? What does that even mean? My heart is pounding, Piper. What would I even do without Secret?"

Piper rolled over, her blankets tangling around her as she faced the vent, staring at it. Otto needed her. He had always been there for her, listened patiently to her rants, made her feel special and safe when the world seemed so cruel. She wanted to return the favor, but her brain felt like television static.

Secret had never left his side since Otto found him as a malnourished kitten, abandoned in the laundry chute of his university residence. Otto used to dip his finger in milk and let Secret lick it off until he was strong enough to chew kitty kibble. Otto was basically the kitten's mommy. Secret was his good luck charm in veterinary school — always purring in a floofy coil on Otto's desk. He inspired Otto to open his cat café. Secret was an extension of Otto. His furry little bruh. His shadow. His soul. If Otto lost his cat...

Piper felt like the worst friend in the world. A horrible feeling buzzed through her entire body, telling her she didn't deserve Otto. He was basically St. Francis of Assisi, and Piper couldn't find the gumption to say something? To quell his ache which Piper could literally feel throbbing in her chest? His fear was screaming in her ears. His sadness felt like a pillow over her face. She cared. She felt horrible for Otto. But she also felt *nothing.*

Her very best attempt went something like this...

"It sucks."

Otto felt a little stung by Piper's seemingly aloof reply. But he pursed his lips and nodded with understanding. "I don't mean to unload on you. I'm just... I'm just really scared."

"I know," Piper said, struggling against the squeak in her throat.

"What do you think I should do if they…"

"Guys?" came the confused voice of Mally through the air vent.

"Mally?" Otto asked, utterly perplexed.

"Ugh…" Mally said with a weird awkwardness. "Yeah. It's me."

"What's going on?"

"I…" Mally stammered. "I don't mean to interrupt but I heard the two of you through the air vents and…"

"Mally," Otto said, cocking his head. "Is everything okay? You sound kind of off."

In her apartment, Mally looked utterly bewildered as twenty-three cats roamed around the flat, swirling around her ankles and climbing up her back. One cat had even nested and fallen asleep on top of her head.

"I…" Mally quavered. "I have a bit of a situation here."

# CHAPTER FORTY-NINE
## (A FEW MOMENTS LATER)

"How did twenty-three cats get into your apartment?" Otto asked Mally through the air vents.

"It just sort of happened," Mally explained. "I started hearing some of the neighbors... you know... through the air vents like how we're talking now... they were worried about their cats because of the harvest. Well, Felix left behind all this tuna and..."

"Wait," Otto said, shaking the perplexity from his head. "What happened to Felix?"

"He got a pistachio and bailed," Mally said morosely. "Then he left me for a tarty floof with maraschino cherries, but I digress. See, I figured I could hide the cats in my alcove."

"Alcove?"

"I have a fake wall. Behind it, I keep my first editions," Mally said, prying a cat off her wooly cardigan. "So I lured all the neighbor's cats..."

"How?" Otto squeaked.

"Put Secret in the air vent," Mally said matter-of-factly. "I'll lure him over by opening a can of tuna and putting it next to my vent. Secret can just crawl over to mine."

"Are you sure that'll work?"

"Let me see," Mally pondered sarcastically. "It worked for twenty-three other cats so... Fiasco! Mr. Whiskers! My hanging basket of begonias is not a toy! Stop swinging from.... So yeah."

"What do you think, Pipes?" Otto asked, squeezing Secret protectively.

"I guess," Piper offered, noncommittal.

Exhaling with a heave, Otto tearfully smushed his face into Secret's fur for an emotional goodbye kiss. "I'm sorry, Secret. This is temporary, okay? We'll be together soon. I promise."

"I put the tuna out," Mally could be heard through the air vent. "Ready?"

With trembling lips, Otto opened the grate on the air vent and placed Secret, who resisted by snagging his claws insistently to the edges of the pipe inside. After pushing Secret's stubborn cat butt into the vent, Otto listened to the sound of kitty claws scuttling behind the walls.

\*\*\*

### HEADLINE: 'BRUCE IS EVEN MORE PERNICIOUS THAN WE ONCE THOUGHT' EXPERTS SAY

Just when we thought we had cracked the Bruce enigma, our ominous foe has upped his game. The fact that the Husk count is increasing daily at a startling rate, reaching numbers equivalent to the population of small country has quantum physicists baffled.

"The hell?" said an anonymous quantum physicist from Croatia. We'll call him Bartholomew. "I have spent the entirety of my career studying heinous hellions from alternative dimensions and I find this unsettling. I have witnessed nothing of this magnitude in my years in academia. The sheer volume of Husks can only imply one thing. Facial recognition. Clearly our efforts are futile if Bruce can identify a human by virtue of his or her facial features."

This disturbing hypothesis emerging from Croatia has caused ripples of panic in the scientific community. Leading experts globally are urging world leaders to enforce policies that will protect humans from being recognized. The consensus is that global citizens must each wear a paper bag over their head with eye holes cut out of it.

"It's the only logical solution," said the resident expert in Liechtenstein. "It's just basic, common sense. Bruce can't recognize you if you have a bag over your head. I mean, obviously it's a personal choice. But if you choose not to wear a paper bag over your head, that would be the wrong choice. Don't be vain."

Whether or not Umbravian politicians choose to adopt the paper bag policy as per the recommendation of concerned experts is *anyone's guess. Regardless, the issue is sure to be polarizing and cause lots of emotionally charged arguments on the internet.*

Clarity glared at the computer screen with her twitching finger hovering above the send key. A singular flick of her pinky would cause another wave of fear to sweep the nation. Again. She could not shake the image of her father, his face contorted with worry, out of her mind. She would send him money, anonymously of course, so he probably wouldn't lose the mushroom farm. Probably.

*Da will be fine.*

*I'll take care of him.*

*These articles are giving me a steady flow of money.*

*In obscene amounts.*

*Surely, I could cover expenses for Da if...*

*Is it really wrong of me to want to feel safe?*

*Feel normal?*

*Da would want me to...*

*Ma...*

*Good grief, why am I so conflicted about this?*

*Obviously, the right thing to do is...*

A lamentable warble from outside startled Clarity, causing her finger to slip. With a gasp, Clarity realized she had accidentally sent her article. She winced. No turning back now. When the warble turned to a booming shriek, Clarity bounded to the window and craned her neck outside. She spotted Ezekiel on his balcony, wearing sackcloth, and wailing at the sky with his fist in the air.

"THE PISTACHIO WILL NOT SAVE YOU!" Ezekiel roared. "FOR THE DECEIVER IS AMONG US!"

Clarity swallowed a bulbous guilt ball.

"WAKE UP!" Ezekiel continued. "ARISE! AVOID THE ROAD TO PERDITION! THE SPIRIT OF FEAR HAS POSSESSED OUR NATION, DISFIGURING IT BEYOND RECOGNITION! WE WILL NOT LET THEM DIVIDE US WITH THEIR ACRIMONY AND THEIR EMNITY AND THEIR MEMES! QUESTION EVERYTHING! QUESTION EV…"

ZZZ ZZZZ ZZZZZZZ ZWUMP!

Clarity suddenly startled, winced, recoiled, and looked away, her entire body reverberating in horror, as she witnessed Ezekiel being swallowed by a metaphysical orifice, which sucked him into an invisible void. Then the portal closed like a pair of terrifying lips and all that was left of Ezekiel was a tuft of purple steam, swirling in the air.

# CHAPTER FIFTY
## (THE NEXT DAY)

Clarity was quivering like a traumatized glob of congealed gravy. She had been hiding under her bed all night and even as the garish morning sun squinted at her through the window, she remained paralyzed with fear, rogue box springs puncturing her back. She could not unsee the image of Ezekiel being squeezed through that menacing vortex, vaporizing into a state of nothingness. Did he cease to exist entirely?

*This is all my fault.*

*I did this.*

*ALL of this.*

*I'm so deep in this, I can't even...*

Clarity jolted when her computer alerted her of a video call. Swallowing hard, she pulled her laptop across the floor and answered the call from her protective haven, under the bed.

"Da?" Clarity said too quickly to even catch her breath. She squinted at the screen. "Where are you?"

"Mitsubishi," Torrence griped, adjusting his body uncomfortably inside his car. "Where are you?"

"Under my … bed," Clarity stuttered. "Why are you calling from…"

"I live here now."

"What… why?"

"Mushrooms being expendable," Torrence winced, finding a scrunched soda can underneath him, "I was not only shut down, but now the government seized my property and turned it into an Air B&B for vacationing diplomats. How's your day going?"

"Da, that's utterly terrifying."

"You resemble congealed gravy," Torrence pointed out. "Tell me what's going on."

"I don't want to talk about it."

"What did they do to you?"

"They?"

"Something has traumatized you, and I want to know what's going on."

"Da…"

"Talk to me, for gosh sake."

"I… can't."

"Oh you will."

"Da… please."

"Stop pretending like all this is normal!" Torrence bellowed in a way that made Clarity twitch. "Snap out of it, Clarity! In case you haven't noticed, the world has ended and you're sitting there under your bed acting like this is all just some trendy fad! Like one of those wacky internet challenges involving detergent or gorilla glue! Would you look around… look at ME? The world is unravelling like the toe of a dollar store sock while you just…"

"I'm… I'm so sorry."

"Something's up."

"What," Clarity swallowed, "do you mean?"

"I may not have a formal education," Torrence nodded gravely, "but I know when I'm being lied to. Something reeks of shitake mushrooms, and one way or another, I'm going to find out what stinks."

***

"What a glorious day to be a Moon Daughter!" Willatrix said, twirling, as she livestreamed from her cell phone in a scenic park. She was matter-of-factly wearing a paper bag over her head with eye holes cut out of it. But her beatnik personality was undeniably Willatrix. "As you can see, I have chosen to wear a paper bag over my head with eye holes cut out of it. Have you chosen to do likewise? Tell me in the comments. Remember, my glowing orbs, there is no judgement on my vlog. I am a safe place. Wearing a paper bag is a personal choice and I deeply value..."

Willatrix paused briefly to badger a passerby whose face was unbagged, asking what in the hell was wrong with him. She conspicuously dodged away from the person, trying to avoid him, repulsed. Then without missing a beat...

"For those of you joining me for the first time," Willatrix said ethereally, "I am a free spirit. An uninhibited bird in flight. I can't even help it. You see, freedom is something that bubbles from within. A state of mind, really. A beautiful, intangible feeling. Nobody can take from you what the universe has hidden deep in your soul like a precious geranium seed. Yet a distressing number of haters have been tweeting of late about a perceived oppression."

Passing a rowdy party of paper bagged revelers, Willatrix was recognized and stopped for a selfie. She graciously accepted a martini, wished them all a namaste and continued walking and livestreaming past a grove of shimmering aspens.

"I don't know what these haters are talking about," Willatrix continued, attempting with failure to take a sip of her beverage through the paper bag. "I don't feel as though my freedom has been taken away. How can it be when freedom is inherent? Tangent. My boycott of the day is size zero pants. Petite women should conform or go pantsless."

***

"Piper?" Otto said through the air vent, clearly worried.

Piper just wanted to be alone. To retreat inside herself and disappear. Otto's voice was both taunting her and awakening something deep inside her that wanted to come back to life. Being alone was both what she craved and what she feared. That terrible numbness.

"Piper?" Otto tried again. "How do you feel?"

"I don't feel anything anymore," Piper rasped through the air vent, lifeless.

"...What?"

"The whole world is disconnected," Piper said in a faraway voice. "I feel like everyone is forgetting each other. They feel so... far away."

Otto felt helpless. His eyes scoured the room as he tried to conjure something to say. Anything to keep Piper alert. Connected.

"At the cat café," Otto said, suddenly inspired. "Do you remember that customer who thought we were an item? The dude with the 'stache. He used to come in every Thursday and buy out all my pumpkin fritters. The art therapist. Bert, I think his name was. I wonder why he needed all those fritters?... He wouldn't believe us when we tried to tell him... He was like, 'obviously you two are together.' And I said, 'not *in the Biblical sense.'* It's weird, don't you think? How people used to assume… It's this weird… thing. The connection. You know, before I met you, I used to laugh at people who used the term *kindred spirit.* I was like, *'okay, Anne of Green Gables. Enjoy your raspberry cordial.'"*

Otto swallowed what felt like a large glob of mucosal hopelessness. It was excruciating talking about his precious cat café, which was more than likely gone forever. He took a leap and lost everything. His investments. His dream. His joy. His future. Otto's stomach grimaced sickly at the thought of never going back to his happy place. As painful as it was, talking about the café might be the only way to lure Piper out of her dark hole.

Empty silence.

"Piper, you're scaring me."

More silence.

"I…" Piper quavered. "I don't know if I can do this anymore."

\*\*\*

"Lola?" Pax called, tapping on Lola's door. "Everything okay in there?"

"Just cutting eyeholes into a bunch of paper bags," Lola called back from inside her apartment.

"You sound distraught," Pax noticed.

"Fine," Lola said, clearly not fine. "Everything's fine."

Pax winced when he heard a thump and then a little toddler voice wailing. "I'm here to help if there's something…"

"It's just one thing after another," Lola said breathlessly. "First they banned childhood, now the paper bags…"

"Lola, I…"

"Pax," Lola said breathlessly, "I can't wear a paper bag over my head. I'm… I'm claustrophobic."

"Oh…"

"I can't help it," Lola said, almost defensively. "I panic. Can't breathe. The feeling of having my face covered… I've had a weird few years and…"

"You don't need to explain."

"I need to talk to someone about this, Pax. Please."

Pax swallowed, followed by a wrenching silence. "I'm listening."

"My ex. Shane," Lola quavered. "Being with him was… I don't know. Isolating."

Pax stroked his chin in thoughtful attention.

"I thought it was just because my kids were little," Lola continued. "Having babies can be isolating, right? But Shane would get really mad when I tried to reach out to anyone. Even my mom. Shane could get loud sometimes, and it would scare my… It was just easier to keep him happy. Without even realizing it at first, all my personal connections just disintegrated, and I spent most of the time just… alone. With the kids. But alone, you know? Being confined to my apartment is triggering these images in my mind... It's hard. Really hard. I've been falling apart. In front of the kids."

Pax blinked several times in rapid succession, resisting tears.

"I know you're thinking that I'm stupid for staying with him for so long."

"I wasn't thinking that."

"He wasn't all bad," Lola said quickly, defensively. "He could be sweet sometimes. He brought me flowers in between his episodes. Tiger lilies. He knew they were my favorite. Occasionally he would surprise me and the kids with pizza. He loved-bombed me every Valentine's day with an insane number of love notes hidden everywhere, wine, singing telegrams, heart-wielding teddy bears galore and rose petals in the bathtub. On the good days Shane was a real charmer. And he was an epic kisser... Shit. I shouldn't have said that."

Pax pursed his lips to quell laughter.

"But he was... unpredictable," Lola said in a low voice. "His expectations... If I overcooked the rump roast, didn't vacuum quite right or I forgot to pick up his special beer, he... he locked me in the crawl space. Embarrassing. I probably shouldn't be..."

"It's okay, Lola."

"I don't like to be confined," Lola said. "I can't stand to have my face covered."

"Lola, the paper bags are optional for now," Pax reassured her, leaning against the closed door.

"Didn't you see the marquee outside?" Lola asked. "It says *'Paper Bags: The Righteous Option.'*"

"That's not exactly a legal order," Pax pointed out. "You have a legitimate reason..."

"For cripe's sake," Lola blurted. "Have you been on Twitter lately? The Gods of Popular Opinion are telling everyone to distrust people who don't wear paper bags over their heads. It's taken over the internet. People with faces are public enemy number one right now. How can I subject my children to... I'm already utterly alone, I can't exactly afford to be shunned from society... more."

"I don't want you to worry about this Lola. Let me..." Pax noticed his cellphone beeping with a text: *"Sorry, Pax. It's just not working out. It's not you, it's me... Biff."*

Pax's face contorted in perplexity. "Is Chesterfield breaking up with me?"

# CHAPTER FIFTY-ONE
## (THE NEXT DAY)

"How is this feasible?" Pax said in Parliament. "You can't possibly standardize something like that. There are some people who can't physically…"

"Out of turn," droned the Speaker of the House, with a somewhat confused expression.

"Thank you, Speaker," Eva said, emotionlessly. "I'm not sure what the member is doing here today, seeing as how we turfed him from the party…"

"I came back as an independent," Pax explained. "As per the encouragement of my neighbor Norman Lovelorn. He told me to *hold fast* and that spoke to me."

"You just can't take a hint, can you, Agora East?" Eva squinted.

"I have…" Pax began.

"… *a responsibility to your constituents,*" Eva said snarkily, mimicking Pax with sarcastic puppet hands. "Excuse me while I gag myself with a spatula."

"Claustrophobia is a subject that demands discussion," Pax added.

"Order!" boomed the Speaker of the House. "Honorable Minister of Catastrophic Events?"

"Thank you, Mr. Speaker," Eva said, rolling her eyes superiorly. "As I was saying, to avoid political liability, we are treating the paper bag issue as a personal choice. But I'm not worried because I am confident that Scatopians will do the honorable thing. In fact, a government-subsidized social media poll stated that the most educated citizens are the ones who choose to wear paper bags. Those who don't tend to disrespect the Oxford comma. And often drool."

"Let me rewrite that statement for you," Pax interjected. "You have manipulated citizens into policing each other in order to absolve yourself of any responsibility…"

"The facts state," Eva continued, "Bruce is a natural phenomenon of which we as a government have no control. It would be arrogant of us to presume we can control nature. The laws of quantum mechanics. Metaphysical anomalies. Obviously we have to control something so if it's not Bruce, it might as well be Scatopians."

"So you admit that you are manipulating the narrative?" Pax squeaked with his arms in the air.

"Settle down, Agora East," the Speaker scolded, "or I'll put you in a timeout."

"Your rules aren't even working!" Pax persisted. "So why are we still doing this?"

Eva exhaled. "To quote the expert, if something doesn't work, the next course of action is to do *more* of the thing that's not working. It's basic science. Ask around."

"And why aren't you wearing a paper bag, Eva?" Pax challenged.

"Being a prominent government official, I have to move my mouth around a lot and a paper bag would obstruct my verbiage," Eva said, rolling her eyes. "I don't see you wearing a paper bag either, Pax. Do you lack education? Are you qualified to be here? How do you feel about the Oxford comma?"

"Mr. Speaker, please!" Pax pleaded. "I have no issues with Scatopians choosing to wear paper bags over their heads! I honestly want to do everything we can to keep our citizens safe. And I do understand we need to be creative in our tactics as we are navigating blindly though an unprecedented situation. But we need to allow grace for those who can't safely wear a bag over their head! There are some valid reasons that we cannot morally ignore! We are already so polarized. The last thing we need right now is to moralize..."

"If we allow grace for one," Eva barked back, "then everyone is going to want grace. Yeesh, Pax. It's almost like you don't understand the notion of standardizing something."

"This is about public safety," Pax reminded Eva. "Is it totally necessary to turn this into a political wedge?"

"Yes."

"Okay," Pax said, using his hands to level the absurdity in the air. "Let's find some middle ground here."

"No."

"I'm assuming the data resolves that paper bags are effective."

"This is an emergency, Pax. Nobody has time to wait for data."

"If it's optional anyway, why not encourage Scatopians to have compassion for those who can't…"

"I repeat," Eva barked, "this is an emergency. This is no time for energy-expending things like compassion. Besides, compassion is not in the provincial budget."

"I'm really uncomfortable with the direction this narrative is taking," Pax continued.

"What narrative?" Eva exhaled.

"The whole notion of demonizing people who might not entirely be on board with government policies," Pax said with a liberal use of hand gestures, "pitting one citizen against the other! As long as they are in compliance, who cares if they disagree with you? I thought this was a democracy."

"Leave democracy to the ancient Greeks and get with the times, MacLeod."

"And our citizens can't ask questions?" Pax squeaked with his hands in the air. "There's been two residents in my building already who have been banished to the Void! One was just having tea with his wife and the other one… Well, that was just Ezekiel being Ezekiel, and nobody takes him seriously anyway, so what's the frigging point in making him disappear?"

"WE'RE SAVING LIVES!" Eva spat in a hissy scream, almost cross-eyed with rage.

"Evidence?" Pax said, crossing his arms.

"What is this?" Eva snarled. "A frigging courtroom? The evidence is all around you, Pax. Do you have access to the internet? All the angry people on social media are currently alive, so that means it's working. Lives saved. Everyone agrees with me, you turnip."

"You said that out loud," Pax pointed out.

"Give it up, Pax. Nobody can hear you over all the rapid-fire tweets."

\*\*\*

"I know a place," Felix said to the cherry lady as he linked his fingers in hers and yanked her by the hand, pulling her playfully down the post-apocalyptic street. Her name was Olga. Not that it matters.

Dirty smog obstructed the sun, rendering the atmosphere a dreary shade of flint. Smashed triangles of glass peppered the sidewalk. Vulgar graffiti. No birds. Silence groaned. A car alarm screamed feebly from a faraway parking lot. The boulevard trees were all dead. Tiny tufts of ash, some still aglow were wafting silently in the air. The historic church on the corner was casually engulfed in flames as people mindlessly walked by. The bank was gone – now just a pile of blackened rubble, with glowing embers accenting the debris. A school, exterior walls crumbling, windows blown out, had the word *CONDEMNED* spraypainted across in huge, black letters. Noxious, red smoke swirled up from the sewage grates. A jackal crossed the street.

"Oh my gosh!" Olga said, flushing when Felix tugged her towards the husk of what Otto's cat café used to be. The doors were boarded up and the word **NO** was spraypainted in red across the smashed window. "I've always wanted to come here. I've heard their prickly pear lemonade makes your eyeballs roll back into your head."

"My treat," Felix winked as he shooed away a few straggling looters who were retreating out the broken window with armloads of biscotti and cat merch. "Not that it'll cost anything."

"Wait," Olga hesitated just before Felix boosted her rump through the window. "You don't suppose there's still cats in there? I don't want to touch that which is unclean."

"Cats no longer exist," Felix said, lifting Olga through the window as she yipped with delight.

Once inside, Felix erected one of the many overturned bistro chairs and secured a wobbly table by the window. Shadows of past chaos loomed around them from the smashed glass pastry showcase to the toppled kitty perches, now covered in cobwebs. Rats squeaked in protest as they scuttled across the cracked, cobbles, their paws sticking like Velcro to the sticky smoothie spillage that had puddled on the floor months prior. Mangled light fixtures dangled gloomily from their exposed wires in the ceiling. The flat screen T.V. was missing, leaving behind brackets lodged stubbornly into the cracked wall.

"This is so quaint," Olga said giddily as Felix pulled out a bistro chair for her to sit. "I quite like it."

"We basically have it all to ourselves," Felix said as he sat, trying to ignore the moaning squatter who was slumped in a drunken coma across the room with a pool of urine forming beneath him. "You smell like chrysanthemums."

"I'm blushing," Olga said, flirtatiously flipping her chestnut floof.

"Can I get you something from the kitchen?" Felix asked. "Cooking isn't my thing but maybe I can toss some fruit in a blender and call it a smoothie?"

"Sorry man," belched a gangly bloke as he hopped the front counter with a bushel basket filled with pineapples, frozen dragon fruit and extremely tired plantains. "Just snarfed the last of it."

"Gosh," Felix said, running his fingers through his hair. "This is not nearly as romantic as it played out in my head."

"Felix, sit," Olga urged. "Everything is perfect. Let's just sit here and look at each other with desirous expressions."

"It's just kind of awkward, you know?" Felix laughed nervously. "I just wanted to take you somewhere nice."

"It's really okay," Olga smiled like an amorous cartoon. "I'm just happy to be here, imagining what it would be like to run my hands over all that corduroy."

"Maybe later we can go back to my place and eat tuna fish directly out of the tin."

Olga blinked.

"Like I said," Felix said as he developed restless leg syndrome. "My cooking is abysmal.  I even manage to burn my microwavable rations. I wouldn't want to subject you to that."

"Felix, I would love…"

"Dammit."

"What?"

"I left all my tuna fish at Mally's."

"… What?"

"I left quite abruptly…"

"Who's Mally?"

Felix blinked. "Didn't I tell you about…"

"No."

"She's just…"

"I hate her."

"You…"

"I don't know who she is, but I question her motives."

"Can I just go over to hers and retrieve my tuna?"

"Slut."

"Me?"

"No, Felix. You are a quintessential gentleman," Olga blurted, blowing frustrated, floofy bangs from her forehead. "It's Molly."

"Mally."

"Who the hell is she and why does she have all your tuna fish?"

"She…" Felix said smally as he watched Olga's eyes narrow into slits of ire. "We… were engaged."

Ogla's nostrils flared like a provoked bull getting ready to charge. "You can't be serious."

"Olga…"

"Was it consummated?"

Felix raised a sheepish eyebrow and feebly half-shrugged.

Olga slapped her hand over her mouth to suppress an indignant, shocked yelp.

"I ended it," Felix insisted. "She was expendable, Olga! There's no way she and I can be together now!"

"You touched a woman who was unclean?"

"You can't catch expendable-ness, I don't think."

"I am so uncomfortable right now."

"Why though? I only want you!"

"To think I shared my cherries with you."

"Your cherries are superb, Olga! You have to believe me. Mally is nothing more to me now than a next-door neighbor!... What's going on with your face right now?"

"She lives next door?"

"I put the wall back up."

"How can you make a clean break with her making beluga noises through the wall?"

"What... *what?*"

"I want to be exclusive."

"We are."

"Mally's existence is making me feel incredibly insecure."

"Olga, there is no future for Mally and I," Felix pleaded, cupping his hand over Olga's, but flinching when she quickly pulled her hand away. "Her values don't align with mine. But here you are with that chestnut floof and that kissable swan neck and those... teeth..."

"I don't want Mally to be real."

"But you are imperative, and I find that sexy."

"What if..."

"She's confined to her apartment," Felix insisted. "Possibly forever. There's no chance of me crossing paths with her ever again."

Felix suddenly fell backwards in his bistro chair as Olga lunged over the table at him. Seeing nothing by stray hands, blood-red lips and blazing eyes barreling urgently in his direction, he recoiled in horror, thinking he was about to be murdered. He shuddered in a sweat as he felt fingers snaking up his corduroyed thigh.

"Is she dead to you?"

With bulging, quivering eyeballs and perspiration beading on his forehead, Felix urgently nodded.

***

"What in chuffing hell is this?"

Clarity winced as the shrill octave of Daryl De Voort's voice pierced her eardrum through the phone. "I... I just thought..."

*"We Are All Going to Die,"* De Voort choked out the headline. "Good start. Frightening headline. Great hook. But this article..."

"I'm sorry."

*"It's all a lie,"* De Voort read through clenched teeth. *"Well, not a lie so much as a misunderstanding. I sent a poorly worded text and then it all went pear-shaped. Please, just carry on as per usual. The guilt is eating me alive day and night, I have to come clean. Please don't hate me.  I don't want to go to Hell. And for the love of God, please eat mushrooms. Lots of mushrooms."*

Clarity flared a contrite nostril.

"Why did you do this, Clarity Trout?"

"I... I've been carrying on with this for so long..."

"You can't just punch the world in the face with the truth like this! Consider the ramifications!"

"But it's fine!" Clarity implored. "It's totally okay! People only read the headlines anyway! Nobody reads the actual article!"

"Which is why this infernal article was sent to print without being proofread!"

"If... if you would just listen..."

"We could lose our funding over this," De Voort croaked. And while Clarity could not physically see him, he sounded as though he was yanking fistfuls of his sparse hair. "If you don't fix this..."

"I... I don't think I want to..."

"What do you mean you don't *want* to?" De Voort squeaked. "Are you saying you've grown tired of security and acclaim? That you want to revert to being a cowering mouse, pathetically groping for cheese? Did you enjoy being a failure, Clarity Trout?"

"I... I just don't want to hurt..."

"Click bait is like heroin," De Voort lectured. "Everyone's desperate for the next hit! If you don't give it to them, there'll be a veritable lynch mob!"

"I feel bad," Clarity stuttered. "I've... I've never lied like this. What... what if they don't let me into Heaven?"

"Of course they'll let you in. Just bring your media pass."

"But people are... Like, all these people... My da..."

"Squeak, squeak, little mouse."

"Can't you just..."

"Squeak, squeak."

Clarity blinked hard. "Wh... what do you want from me?"

# CHAPTER FIFTY-TWO
## (THREE WEEKS LATER)

Lowering his Ray-Bans seductively down his sunburned nose, Tristan narrowed his eyes as a bikini-clad, suntan-oiled, windblown version of Gloria walked womanishly down the beach in his direction. Wobbling his head lecherously, Tristan licked his smirky lips and sauntered towards her.

"Gloria," Tristan said sensuously," in ecxelsis deo."

"Tristan, we need to talk," Gloria said flatly.

"Want to do a little *improv?*" Tristan breathed into her left ear.

Gloria winced and squirmed from the blowy sensation in her tympanic cavity. "You're off-script."

"I thought you were method," Tristan said, undulating his arms around all of Gloria's special parts. "There's a candlelit tiki hut with our names on it. Coconuts with straws. Pork on a spit. Come on, Doll. I want to see your character *arc*..."

"Tristan..."

"Let's get jiggy."

"Tristan, ew," Gloria said, squirming stealthily from Tristan's octopus-arms. "I need to talk to you about something important."

Tristan pouted.

"Tristan, I no longer find this role fulfilling."

"You don't mean that."

"I do."

After gaping for a nanosecond, Tristan pretentiously jibed, "You're drunk. It was that pineapple drink with the little umbrella..."

"I want out of the contract," Gloria said matter-of-factly.

"What?" Tristan laughed nervously. "You can't just..."

"I'm a professional," Gloria said professionally. "This role is demoralizing and not nearly feminist enough. At this point of my career, I should be playing strong, female leads. Not reducing myself to..."

"Your role is nuanced," Tristan implored. "But if you want your character to arc more..."

"Please stop saying that."

"I can do something to make your character more dimensional," Tristan grasped. "I could give you a disease!"

"That's unhygienic."

"What if I..."

"No."

"Or I could..."

"No."

"But Gloria, we have such good onscreen chemistry!"

"It's over, Tristan."

"You can't do this to me," Tristan whined. "You owe me a favor."

"Tristan, this whole thing was a mistake."

"What if I..."

"I've already booked a private flight out tomorrow."

"What am I supposed to tell people?" Tristan squeaked.

"Just tell them I was swallowed by a whale shark or something. I really don't care at this point."

"What about the kids?"

"Simon is on the phone with his agent."

"And my little princess?"

"Angelica was cast as Young Cosette in the Lithuanian touring production of *Les Mis.* She's been gone for two weeks; you just haven't noticed."

"Damn Lithuanians," Tristan grumbled.

"It's normal in Lithuania," Gloria reminded Tristan. "You can't expect Anjelica to stay here when there's opportunities somewhere else."

"Gloria," Tristan said a little too emotionally. "Gloria please. We were so adorable together. You can't break up the family like this."

"You realize we weren't really married, right?"

"Gloria, I need you," Tristan implored. "Without you, I could lose everything. Quite literally everything."

"Good-bye, Tristan," Gloria said, waving Tristan away and walking down the beach in a non-Tristanish direction.

"Canker blossom!" Tristan screeched emotionally at Gloria's nonplussed backside as it disappeared into a distant silhouette. "You'll regret this! I am a snack, Gloria! *A snack!*"

Tristan's tirade was suddenly interrupted when a glob of pigeon poop splattered onto his forehead. Repulsed, he searched for the feathered culprit, using his hand to shield his eyes from the blazing sun. Squinting, he spotted a pigeon with something tied to its foot. Clenching with revenge, Tristan lunged at the bird, missing it, falling face-first into the sand.

"You little..." Tristan seethed, spluttering sand from his mouth.

When the pigeon landed, pecking at something on the beach, Tristan ungracefully pounced on the bird, groping it with both hands while it flapped and warbled in protest. After stubbornly tussling with the pigeon in a frenzy of flying feathers and talons, Tristan managed to yank a piece of paper which had been carefully tied to the bird's foot, getting farcically pigeon-scratched in the face.

"The hell?" Tristan said, reading a message written on the paper while the pigeon vindictively swooped and assaulted Tristan's tangled mess of hair.

The message read, *"EVERYTHING IS GOING TO BE OKAY."*

\*\*\*

"Who is this?" B.P. asked, confirming that the phone call was coming from an undisclosed number.

"A friend," Flossie said on the phone, using a voice-altering device. She sounded like Barry White. "There's something you need to know. About the Husks."

B.P. gulped with her eyeballs quivering.

"Do you know what isolation can do to the human mind?" asked the basso profundo version of Flossie.

"I'm more of an expert of *the physical properties of nature at the scale of atoms and subatomic particles*," B.P. swallowed nervously. "But go on."

"Isolation can cause you to descend into madness," Flossie said. "It can make you forget how to be human. Turn you into a shell of your former self. Sound familiar?"

"That sounds like a Husk?" B.P. quavered.

"That sounds like a Husk," Flossie repeated somberly. "So how do we know whether the sudden rise of dehumanization of late has been caused by Br…"

"Okay, bye," B.P. said quickly, dropping the phone as though it was biting her fingers.

Trying to shake the oddity from her traumatized head, B.P. whimpered as she perused Tristan's emails, shooing away some pigeons that had flown into the room through an open window. When one pigeon landed on the computer keyboard and another did a beak-dive into the side of her head, B.P. could ignore the pigeons no longer.

"Where did all these pigeons come from?" B.P. mewled, dodging an uncoordinated bird.

Noticing a message that had slipped from a pigeon's foot, she read. *"OPTIMISM IS A FORM OF COURAGE."* Another message said, *"THIS IS NOT NORMAL."* Others said, *"WE WILL ALL BE TOGETHER SOON," "YOU ARE STRONGER THAN YOU KNOW," "YOU'VE GOT THIS," "THE WORLD IS BETTER WITH YOU IN IT,"* and *"YOU ARE LOVED."*

When the computer suddenly came to life with Tristan's face on the screen, B.P. yelped and scrambled to hide the pigeons in desk drawers.

"Beepy?" Tristan said in the unplanned video call.

"All good," B.P said, unsuccessfully trying to hide a frantic pigeon down her shirt.

"I'm afraid I have some somber news," Tristan continued.

"Oh?" B.P. said innocently, resting her chin on her hands as though the room was not filled with clandestine birds.

"Gloria has been swallowed by a whale shark and my children have chosen to grieve in Tenerife with their Aunt Minerva."

"So they quit?"

"Don't be cheeky," Tristan grumbled. "I need you to deploy the military..."

"Haven't they already been deployed?"

"... to investigate the origin of a propaganda pigeon," Tristan said, displaying the incriminating message harvested from the pigeon's foot.

B.P. gaped. "It flew all the way to Oahu?" she muttered.

"What is that supposed to mean?"

B.P. tightened her lips until they numbed.

A flappy, cooing noise emerged from a desk drawer.

"What's in the drawer, Beepy?" Tristan challenged authoritatively.

"... Pens."

A seemingly possessed pigeon flew mindlessly into window glass while a cooing, upside-down ramen bowl walked across the desk with pigeon feet.

"Are there propaganda pigeons in my office right now?"

"I don't know."

"Don't lie to me, Beepy. This is a matter of national security."

"The window was open."

"We've been infiltrated."

"By pigeons?"

"This is an affront to everything I stand for."

"Okay."

"Treason."

B.P. squinted bewildered at the screen.

"This is terrible for my image," complained Tristan. "First I lose my wholesome family and now these damn pigeons are attempting some kind of warped uprising. My whole world is falling apart."

"Maybe this is a good time to leave Oahu and return to your responsibilities?"

"Don't be daft. Tweet something for me, will you, Beepy?" Tristan said, snapping his fingers at the screen. "Say that the government will not tolerate pigeons who hold unacceptable views and anyone who heeds the pigeons will be on the receiving end of an intense, character assassination campaign."

"I don't think the pigeons wrote the…"

"Tweet it, Beepy."

## CHAPTER FIFTY-THREE
## (LATE THAT NIGHT)

Little Izzy squirmed restlessly in her sleep, whimpering. Lola's eyes sprung open from a deep slumber, and she instinctively felt her way through the dark until she found her little girl who was sweating and tangled in her *Sponge Bob* blanket.

"Izzy?" Lola whispered, sliding between all the sleeping kids who were piled onto the air mattress. "Izzy, Mummy's here."

When Izzy blinked her eyes open and deciphered the outline of her mother's face in the darkness, her bottom lip quavered vulnerably.

"Baby, what's wrong?" Lola asked, caressing Izzy's sweaty hair. "Did you have another bad dream?"

"Mummy?" Izzy squeaked. "Is the monster going to eat me?"

"There's no monsters, Izzy. You don't have to be afraid."

"Then what are we hiding from?"

"What makes you think we're hiding?" Lola asked. Her heart was thrumming wildly as she suddenly realized her child was clearly not buying what she said about this being the world's most epic staycation.

"Why are there soldiers in the hall?" Izzy breathed. "Is there a war?"

"They're protecting us."

"What from?"

"Izzy, I know this is hard to understand but…"

"I can hear the news on your phone."

"… Oh."

"That's why I know about the monster."

"You don't have anything to worry about," Lola said, caressing the sweat from Izzy's forehead. "There is something going on, but…"

"Bruce," Izzy said bluntly.

"So far, Bruce hasn't hurt any children," Lola assured her trembling first-born. "You really don't have to be scared of…"

"Then why can't I go outside and play?"

"Uh…"

"Why does the prime minister of Umbravia hate kids?"

"Oh, Honeybear. I don't think Prime Minster Winnings hates kids. He has two of his own."

"Then why are children against the law?" Izzy said, her eyes glossed with tears.

Lola gaped but was suddenly distracted when she heard the jiggling of a door handle. She emerged from the air mattress and caught Enzo in the process of trying to make a break for it.

"Enzo!" Lola whispered loudly enough to rouse the other children. "What do you think you're doing?"

"Escaping," Enzo said, looking up innocently at Lola.

"You can't just go out there," Lola said, pulling Enzo by the arm.

"How come?" Enzo shrugged. "Garthie did."

"Garthie d..." Lola said, her heart momentarily stopping when she did a headcount and found that one child was missing. "GARTHIE!"

"What's happening?" Sara-Sue asked, rubbing her eyes with her little fists.

"Where is he?" Lola cried, frantically checking the bathroom and kitchen cabinets.

"He wanted to see what's outside," Enzo said guiltily.

"And you let him?" Lola shrieked.

"I'm only three," Enzo said with a protruding lower lip.

"Oh God, I..." Lola quavered, spinning around in a panic, and pulling at her hair. "I have to go out there."

"But there's monsters," Sara-Sue said, looking vulnerable in her little, heart-speckled nightgown.

"Izzy," Lola panted, "I need you to mind the little ones."

"But I'm little too!" Izzy whimpered, curling herself into a ball.

"Garthie's out there," Lola sobbed. "I'm sorry, Izzy but I have to do this."

"What if you don't come back?" Izzy said stoically, trying to swallow back an impending sob. "I thought you said there was nothing to be scared of!"

"I..." Lola stammered. "I promise. I... I'll come back. You're safe here. Please don't go anywhere. Please!"

With a deep breath, Lola stealthily darted out of her apartment, edging her way down the hall with her back to the wall. She rapped on Pax's door. "Pax?" she whisper-hissed. "Pax, are you up?"

Silence.

After muttering a hasty swear, Lola skulked around, constantly watching her back. She flinched when she heard the thud of soldier boots but exhaled when she realized they were coming from upstairs.

"Garthie?" Lola stage whispered, taking long, silent strides in the dark. "Garthie, Mummy's here. You're not in trouble, Boo Boo. Please just..."

"HEY!"

Startled, Lola spun around and saw Willatrix, standing in her doorway wearing a silk kimono patterned with Dalai Lama faces.

"Where is your pistachio?" Willatrix demanded. "And your paper bag?"

"I..." Lola quavered. "I... lost my son."

"And they let you have babies?" Willatrix scorned.

"Can... can you help me?"

Suddenly, Garthie swerved around a corner, flailing down the hall screaming, *"I'm free, I'm free, I'm free, I'm free!"*

"Get that thing under control!" Willatrix screeched. "It has no business being out here in plain sight!"

"Garthie!" Lola implored, trying to snag her rogue toddler.

"It's going to lure Bruce right into our tower block!"

"He's only two," Lola apologized. "And he's been confined to the apartment for so long..."

"I'm calling the narc hotline."

"Please, no!" Lola begged, finally grasping the seat of Garthie's fuzzy feet-pajamas. "They're all I have! Please don't..."

"What's going on out here?" yawned Pax as he emerged from his apartment.

Lola, looking like a wide-eyed, scolded schoolgirl, held Garthie close to her chest while Willatrix curled her lip.

"Ever heard of birth control?" Willatrix grumbled as she slammed the door behind her.

"Lola?" Pax said, somewhat confused.

Lola bit her lip as she carried a squirmy Garthie in her arms, back to her apartment.

# CHAPTER FIFTY-FOUR
## (THE NEXT MORNING)

"Kisses, my immaculate lotus flowers," Willatrix livestreamed from her apartment, still in her silk kimono. "You may have noticed my aura is slightly less vibrant this morning, as is the case when my sleep is disturbed. I don't ask for your pity. Only your ears. Something occurred last night that demands discussion. A poorly supervised child was running loose in the halls like a feral ocelot. Putting us all at risk."

Willatrix briefly played the theme song from *Psycho.*

"I've kept my opinion about this to myself throughout the duration of this crisis, but it is time to speak my mind. For all of our sakes. Children will be our undoing. Not just because they are impulsive, selfish, and sticky. Not just because they spread their adenoviruses everywhere and spill on themselves. Clearly none of that is their fault.

They can't help it if their skulls haven't yet hardened. So who is at fault?"

Willatrix narrowed her eyes.

"Parents of young children are the real fly in the ointment. Complaining that for *once* in their lives they have to spend some quality time with their kids during this sacred period of isolation. Blaming government policies for their children's social and developmental delays. Blathering on about how isolation is causing children, and I use air quotes, *irreparable, psychological damage.* Children are resilient and a little trauma never hurt anyone. Get over yourself, Mama."

Willatrix made bird noises for reasons that were only apparent to her.

"If parents didn't have such a blatant lack of creativity, they could do the obvious thing and teach their brats how to churn butter or how to spay a Maltese. Would it kill them to think up activities that the whole family can enjoy? Like insider trading or dancing naked around a maypole? Breeders who fail to discipline must themselves be disciplined!"

Willatrix swooned.

"Forgive me," Willatrix continued. "For I am sleep deprived. Please know that my vitriol is coming from a place of extreme love. That being said, I must now inform you of a miscreant neighbor by the name of Lola Brunt. Lacking self-control as most parents do, she produced more offspring than she can realistically control. Last night, an unsupervised pestilence in footy jammies emerged into the halls and..."

*"Who the hell do you think you are?"* a comment appeared on Willatrix's screen.

With her left nostril flaring and her corresponding eyebrow twitching with shock, Willatrix seethed. "Well then, my ambrosial grapes. Look who's commenting. It's my dear neighbor, Lola Brunt."

Thousands of angry emojis instantly started floating up the screen.

*"Stay out of my business, you froth-mouthed Neo-Puritan."*

With widening eyes, Willatrix remained stoic. "Lola, Love Dumpling. We are all one. This is not the place for salty language."

*"You have no idea what I've been through."*

"This is no time to be self-absorbed," Willatrix said, unflappable. "You need to understand something about children, Lola. Their uninhibited nature will put us all in harm's way. They just blurt out their human instincts like an unwanted tuba. Your little snot faucets will lure Bruce directly into our building. Now here's what you can do to be a better parent..."

*"How can you sit there and criticize me? You've never deeply loved anything but yourself."*

"I love community..."

*"Seriously? You were literally the only person in the building who didn't drop everything to help me when I first arrived."*

"So now you expect everyone to just *drop everything* for you?" Willatrix scoffed. "Simply because you can't control your reproductive impulses? Typical. The whole world revolves around your little whelps, am I right, Lola?"

*"You don't GET an opinion about this, Willatrix."*

"Because the universe did not gift my innards with fetal tissue?" Willatrix said with faux ache in her voice. "Had the universe germinated my seed, I would have made vastly different choices than you. I will now provide you with a list..."

*"I just LOVE virtue signalers. They are so helpful and inspiring."*

"No judgment," Willatrix said ethereally. "But my infants would feed exclusively on quinoa and vegan beef puree to ensure proper cognitive development. And Lola, again no judgement, but had you taught your tots the art of baby puja as I did with my hypothetical children, perhaps yours wouldn't be quite so..."

*"Feck you!"*

\*\*\*

"Go Lola!" Otto cheered with a fervent clap as he watched Willatrix's vlog on his laptop. "Piper, are you seeing this?" Otto called through the air vents. "Did you see Lola's comments just now?"

From her apartment, Piper was lying, practically catatonic on the floor next to her laptop screen, upon which was Willatrix railing about Lola and a blizzard of angry emojis floating around. Piper uttered a faint chirp which Otto perceived to be a reply.

"Piper?"

Piper replied nonverbally with a facial twitch and an apathetic shrug.

"Stay with me, Pipes," Otto coaxed. "I need to know you're still there."

"I don't want to do this anymore," Piper said hoarsely.

"Are you watching the vlog?" Otto tried, his eyes reddening with worry. "Did you see? Someone finally called Willatrix on her bullshit."

Piper whimpered.

"You were right about her," Otto prompted.

"Erm?"

"You knew there was something wrong with Willatrix."

Piper blinked.

"Remember?" Otto tried again. "You said I should be careful about trying to see the best in everybody."

"Not now, Otto. I just can't."

Excruciating silence.

"Write a song," Otto blurted.

"I can't..."

"You have to do this, Pipes. You're decomposing."

"It's illegal."

"It's who you are."

"I'm illegal."

"I want my girl back," Otto said, throwing a shoe hard against the wall. "You're unravelling. I get it, Pipes, I do. But you're losing yourself and if you're lost then... I'm lost."

Piper squeezed her eyes shut, trying futilely to stave off the horrible, misfiring thoughts that were pummeling her brain.

*Otto just doesn't get it.*

*Maybe he never really understood me the way I thought he did.*

*Can't he sense that I need time alone?*

*I don't want to be alone.*

*I just don't want people around.*

*I feel so alone.*

*Why do I have to feel...*

*Everything.*

*Nothing.*

*Everything and nothing at the same time.*

*What's going on?*

*Otto needs me.*

*I can't give him what he needs.*

*I can't.*

*I'm not the person he thinks I am.*

*I'm useless.*

*I don't deserve him.*

*Maybe he'd be better off without me.*

*I serve no purpose anymore.*

*I'm never going to sing again.*

*Why am I here even?*

*I don't belong in this world.*

*There's no place for me here.*

*There never was.*

*I was lying to myself.*

*It's all a lie.*

*Trapped.*

*Numb.*

*I'm slipping away.*

*Fading.*

*... Fading.*

# CHAPTER FIFTY-FIVE
## (LATER THAT DAY)

"So when folks on the mainland got word of the Hebridean's hospitality," Pax recounted the story from outside Norman's apartment door, "a gaggle of freeloading outlanders figured they could exploit the decent villagers in Kneep."

"Kneep," Norman giggled from inside his apartment. "That's kind of fun to say, idn't it?"

"I hadn't really thought about that, Norman," Pax chuckled. 'But I suppose it is. You'd like Kneep, Norman. Imagine mountains in the distance. Mysterious moors. Powder-white sand beaches. An ocean with impossible colors. Purple. Azure. Turquoise. Ballet slipper pink. Shimmering silver. The seawater is a different spectrum of colors every day."

"I feel like I'm there right now," Norman sighed with wonder.

"Remember what I said about it being against the law to exploit Hebridean hospitality?"

"The offense was punishable by banishment."

"That's right, Norman. But remember, this happened long before that law was established. At this time, it was only the ancient code that protected them. But that meant nothing to outlanders. So when the freeloaders arrived in Kneep, the locals welcomed them and embraced them as family. But these were poor folks, so when they had nothing more to give, the freeloaders simply moved on to the next household and exhausted all their resources as well."

"Well dang!"

"See, the Hebridean code forbade them to turn weary travelers away. So they had to hatch an elaborate plan to make them want to leave out of their own free will."

"I'm on the edge of my seat here, Son..."

"They invited the freeloaders for a party on the beach," Pax said, his voice dripping with suspense. "All the women in Kneep seductively urged the freeloaders to join them for a swim in the ocean. These were quite alluring ladies, Norman. So it didn't take much convincing. Keep in mind, they were in the shallows, but the outlanders had no way of knowing that. Anyhow, once they were in the ocean, the women of Kneep all faked insanity and pretended to drown them."

"But it was shallow!" Norman cackled, slapping his knee.

"Exactly!" Pax laughed. "So the freeloaders left that island so fast and when they returned to the mainland..."

"Hey!" barked a soldier, thumping down the hall towards Pax.

"I'm from the government," Pax explained, rummaging for his pistachio.

"No storytelling," the soldier said, nonplussed.

"I thought it was books that were banned," Pax said, cocking his head. "The decree doesn't say anything about the oral storytelling tradition."

"Loophole," the soldier said. "You are not embracing the spirit of the rules."

"The what?"

"You're done here," the soldier said, pulling Pax away. "Go do something imperative."

"What about Norman?" Pax said, wriggling his arm from the soldier's clutches.

"NO!" Norman wailed, pounding on his door. "You can't do this to me! I look forward to the stories every day! It's all I have! PLEASE! No!"

\*\*\*

Cheerios were everywhere. Quite literally everywhere. The kids found the emergency stash Lola hid when the world first ended – but Enzo found the secret Cheerio box at the bottom of the underpants bin. Lola could vaguely hear the crunch of squashed Cheerios beneath the feet of her children who were thumping around the apartment while she attempted to focus murkily on her computer screen. Her eyes were glassy as she gaped, zombified.

"I don't know where all these pigeons came from," Willatrix said from the safety of the screen, "but you must not fall under their narcotic influence. Please do not believe everything you read, my vulnerable sandpipers. While the pigeons may seem well-intentioned, the messages they carry are potentially lethal. Tangent. My boycott of the day is Lola Brunt."

Seemingly thousands of angry emojis suddenly floated up the screen at the mere mention of Lola's name. Lola felt the blood rush to her head like a barometer of shame. She steadied, physically willing herself not to faint from a tsunami of dizziness that unexpectedly whooshed over her.

"Lovers, I urge you," Willatrix said with praying hands. "If you see or hear anything indecent coming from Lola's general vicinity, do not hesitate to alert the military. Even if it's a rumor, do not await confirmation. We must not take any chances."

Lola scrunched her face with perplexity at the screen.

"And she has *children*," Willatrix swooned. "It's not my place to specifically *say* that she is unfit to parent. But if you are of this opinion, leave your comments on my..."

An imposing rap on the door caused Lola to gasp and drop her coffee mug which smashed dramatically on the floor. Shaking her burnt fingers, she stepped on several Legos and matchbox cars on her way across the room. When she opened the door, a soldier loomed above her, wearing a gas mask.

"Oh my God," Lola quavered, hiding Garthie behind her body. "Please, I'm doing my best. Please don't... please..."

Lola held her breath when the soldier removed the gas mask, revealing the face of Flossie, who shook her hair free from her helmet.

"Flossie?" Lola hyperventilated, holding her chest.

Flossie wiped the sweat from her brow with a sleeve. "I thought you could use a nap."

# CHAPTER FIFTY-SIX
## (A FEW MOMENTS LATER)

"Does Girard know you're here?" Lola asked after scoping the hallway and discreetly closing the door.

"He loaned me the costume," Flossie replied. "He was a post-apocalyptic soldier a few years ago at the faculty Halloween gala... What are you..." Flossie continued, making a beeline towards Lola's laptop.

"I will not be remembered as being a woman who kept her mouth shut," said the face of Willatrix on the screen.

Flossie abruptly shut off the computer. "At least we can agree on one thing," she muttered. "Lola, don't watch that garbage."

"I have to defend myself. She's turning the whole world against..."

"You've already been in one toxic relationship," Flossie said, taking the liberty to collect the shattered pieces of Lola's coffee mug. "You don't need to let the internet suck you into another one."

"What if you get caught?"

"Tell me what to do," Flossie said, reaching for Bobby who was screaming in his play yard. "I'm going to have to insist that you take it easy for the day."

"I'm already in so much trouble..."

"You mean Willatrix?"

"Have you seen how many followers she has? She's urging people to narc on me for... having toddlers."

"It's an illusion."

"You don't understand," Lola said on the brink of tears. "Everyone is in attack mode right now. How did I become public enemy number one? I'm trying so hard..."

"Lola, what you see on the internet does not necessarily reflect reality."

"Why is everyone..."

"Not *everyone*."

"... being like this? The virtue signaling is... it's just too much."

"These people are scared and traumatized," Flossie said rationally. "Demoralized. They've lost control of every aspect of their lives. They think they'll feel better if they fluff themselves up and control the way others perceive themselves. They want to find someone to blame for their grief. They are desperate to find meaning in all this insanity, so they try to turn everything into a cause."

"But why me?" Lola begged. "What did I do to deserve being treated like a steaming dog turd on the sidewalk? I haven't put anyone in danger. All I want is to protect my kids."

"Lola, please. For the sake of your own mental health, stop watching that vlog."

"Shouldn't I at least keep my eye on her to see what she's plotting against me? I should be prepared..."

"You're only making her more powerful by indulging her. Go lie down. I'll fix a snack for the kids. Do you have anything in the pantry?"

Defeated, Lola flopped on her cot and fumbled around with her phone, stumbling on a press conference.

"Turn that off, Lola," Flossie's voice wafted from the kitchen as she inspected the contents of the cabinets. "What did I say about..."

"Propaganda pigeons," Tristan somberly droned.

Flossie suddenly spilled what was left of the emergency Cheerios all over the floor. "What did he just say?" she asked as she quickly scootched in next to Lola on the cot.

"They've been arriving in droves," Tristan said, suspiciously eyeballing a bird flying overhead. Predictably, he was still on the beach. "Nobody has any idea where these pigeons came from, but their arrival is giving me suspicion that something ominous is afoot. The Chief Situational Officer has advised that the scandalous messages attached to the incriminating bird feet were likely not written by the pigeons themselves. Rather, the pigeons are likely shills for an unknown enemy who is bent on brainwashing people into subscribing to their unacceptable views."

"Unacceptable views?" Flossie said, unsure if she should chortle, retch, or punch her fist through the wall. *"Propaganda pigeons?"*

"What is he even talking about?" Lola yawned.

"Should we tolerate those who hold these views?" Tristan asked with a triangulated eyebrow. "Should we allow them to take up space?"

Flossie grabbed Lola's phone and yelled at it. "It's called hope, you parsnip!"

"Poor, innocent pigeons," Tristan said, pronouncing the letter P much too moistly. "Being exploited by these perverted pariahs for political purposes. I assure you these pigeons had no say in the matter. We are investigating the issue and will sniff out these warped propagandists. And be assured that justice will be served."

"What does he mean by..." Flossie spat.

"These pigeon-exploiters will be prosecuted, persecuted, potentially imprisoned and have their food rations cut off. This is a promise." Tristan finished with a nod.

"He has taken this too far," Flossie snarled.

"Why are you so upset about..."

"I need to get Girard on the phone... Dammit! Phone calls aren't a thing anymore!"

"Flossie, what..."

"Winnings is on to us," Flossie choked.

"Are you saying..."

"Girard and I..."

"YOU sent the propaganda pigeons?"

"They're not propaganda pigeons," Flossie said, looking much like a pigeon herself with her hands flapping around frantically. "They're just regular pigeons. We sent them out weeks ago, hoping we could intercept this escalating state of trauma the world is collectively experiencing. This whole thing has been so demoralizing, we thought if people could feel better about themselves, maybe we could undo some of the..."

"What's going to happen to you?"

"Hell if I know!" Flossie shrieked. "Tristan Winnings is out of control!"

\*\*\*

Mally was watering her begonias when her door was violently kicked down by five soldiers who surrounded Mally offensively with their weapons poised in her direction. Mally's mouth formed into a stunned oval.

"WHERE ARE THE CATS!" one soldier roared from beneath his turtle-like helmet.

"W… what do you mean?" Mally whimpered feebly, tentatively raising her hands in surrender.

"SEARCH THE FLAT!" the soldier ordered with a jerk of his head. His imposing weapon followed Mally's every move.

"I…" Mally whimpered, "I didn't do anything…"

"SHUT UP!" the soldier barked, making Mally jolt and recoil. He pursed his lips when Mally turned away to blink back tears. "WHAT'S THAT THING?"

Mally followed the soldier's weapon which was pointing to a remote control that had fallen on the floor during the military kerfuffle. She shrugged but dashed to pick it up when the soldier guided her with his rifle.

"You don't seem to own a T.V," the soldier said through clenched teeth. "What's that for then?"

Mally shook her head helplessly.

"WHAT'S IT FOR!"

Ugly crying, Mally used the remote to open the alcove, revealing scads of cats, mewling and lurking elegantly around the bookshelves."

The soldier's eyes narrowed. "SHE'S COMING WITH US!" he bellowed as the other soldiers clamped Mally's arms and dragged her out of the apartment.

"W... where are you taking me?" Mally sobbed.

"NO QUESTIONS!" barked the soldier as they ungracefully escorted Mally into the hall.

Felix's door creaked open, and he stood stupidly, watching Mally being manhandled.

"Felix?" Mally squeaked as she turned her head towards him.

"I'm so sorry, Mally," Felix said hoarsely. "I had to. I... She..."

A woman's hand grabbed Felix by the shirt and yanked him back inside the apartment.

# CHAPTER FIFTY-SEVEN
## (LATER THAT DAY)

Flossie stroked Bobby's back as he drifted off to sleep in his play yard. The other children had finally collapsed in an exhausted pile on the air mattress while a whispery lullaby vibrated in a lulling hum from behind Flossie's pursed lips. As long as the soothing melody was not heard by the soldiers skulking in the halls, an abrupt military ambush could be avoided.

Hugging her knees on the cot, Lola wiped her nose indiscreetly with her sleeve, doing whatever it is that's the opposite of relaxing. A protruding, blue neck vein was throbbing, and her left leg was restless. Flossie noticed Lola's eyes reddening and her breath quickening.

"It's going to be okay," Flossie said, recycling her lullaby voice.

"People keep saying that," Lola quavered. "When Shane was messing with me. When I left everything to start completely over. When the world ended..."

"You're stronger than you know."

"I know," Lola said, rolling her eyes. "A pigeon told me."

"Lola, I know it's hard, but we have to stay optimistic. Otherwise..."

"Do you have kids?" Lola hissed, instantly regretting her volume when Flossie's face suddenly melted into a punctured expression. "Are you claustrophobic? Has an internet influencer put a cyber bounty on your head? Your migraine-addled head?"

"Lola," Flossie breathed remorsefully. "I didn't mean..."

"I get that this is hard for everybody," Lola said, trying to steady her voice. "But this whole goat rodeo is affecting some people WAY more than others. In fact, there's people out there actually benefiting from this nightmare. While I'm being consistently set up for failure, demonized, harassed, locked up with no reprieve. They told me to adapt. But when I adapted, they banned everything that I was using to help me adapt!"

"I really didn't mean to trivialize... It's just that we have to believe things will get better or we'll all descend into madness."

"Optimism is a crime now."

"Maybe you'll get a pistachio."

"No."

"They are starting to give pistachios out to more people," Flossie said, her eyes glistening earnestly. "I know the selection process is random, but maybe you and the kids…"

"I have anaphylactoid allergies," Lola said with stiff lips. "Tree nuts."

"You can't even…"

"It's bad," Lola said. "Even if I touch a pistachio, it could do me in."

"And the children?"

"It's hereditary."

"Surely you could get an exemption…"

"Checked already. Nope."

Flossie bit her lower lip contemplatively. "This isn't fair," Flossie said hoarsely.

"Fair?" Lola cackled facetiously, reducing her volume when the children wriggled in their sleep. "Since when was anything fair? Nobody's cut me a break my whole life. The universe feckin' hates me and everything that matters to me, the system snarfs. I'm just waiting for some emotionless suit to show up and take my kids, and they're all I have left."

"You are doing such a good job," Flossie said, her voice trembling.

"None of that matters," Lola snuffed. "It doesn't matter how hard I try, how much I bust my ass… I sometimes feel like whoever's in charge pulled my name out of a fishbowl and randomly chose to sabotage my life. This Bruce snafu is just continuing the trend."

"Lola…"

"Meanwhile, I have to pretend that life smells like Japanese cherry blossoms, so my kids don't lose their faith in humanity. So they can have delusions of a bright future. So I can distract them from being traumatized." She snuffed again. "I have to lie to my kids. I'm not okay. And it's not okay to not be okay."

"It's okay to…"

"People who are struggling with the restrictions are being harassed into silence," Lola blasted in a stage whisper. "Why is nobody allowed to struggle?"

"It's complicated," Flossie said. "Girard wrote a book about what he calls *Tribunal Compassion*…"

"Do I look like a person who has time to read?" Lola asked, pointing to her disheveled hair that had not been washed in six days."

Flossie put a reassuring hand on Lola's arm. "I'm thinking… I'm thinking maybe it's time we did something about this."

"What do you mean?"

"I…" Flossie said, lifting the corner of a sheer curtain, peering discreetly outside. "I think we should get out."

"Out?"

"Out."

"Like outside?"

"I don't know how much longer I can go along with this," Flossie swallowed. "You've had enough. We've all had enough."

"What about Bruce?" Lola squeaked. "Bruce is out there. I can't... I have kids. Bruce..."

"This isn't about Bruce anymore," Flossie said breathlessly. "This hasn't been about Bruce for a very long time. Tristan Winnings is exploiting a crisis. He's exploiting our suffering. Our fear."

"There's nothing we can do," Lola insisted. "Didn't you hear Winnings? If anyone disagrees with him, he'll make their lives a living Hell."

"We're already in Hell," Flossie said. "And if we don't do something now, this hellscape is only going to get more sulfuric."

"What would we even do?"

"I... don't know."

"Floss?" came a voice from the air vent.

"Girard?" Flossie said, following the sound of Girard's voice to the air vent.

"Be careful, Love, okay?" Girard's voice said. "I can hear everything you're saying through the air vents."

"Me too," Otto's voice came from the air vent.

"Same," came Pax's voice through the air vent.

"The soldiers are in the hall," Girard warned. "If we can all hear you then..."

"Dammit!" Flossie hissed. "Do you think they heard what I said about the pigeons?"

"I don't know," Girard said. "But you're right. We need to do something, or this nightmare is never going to end."

"Based on what's going on in Parliament," Pax said, "we won't be able to rely on the current government to resolve anything. I'm trying but..."

"What should we do?" Otto asked.

A heavy silence lingered in the air.

"We have to go out there," Girard swallowed.

"Outside the block?" Otto squeaked. "Like on the literal outside of this building?"

"Philosophically speaking," Girard said, "doing nothing in the face of immorality is itself immoral. Even more so, in fact."

"That's adorably moral of you, Girard," Otto interjected sarcastically. "But have you even thought this through? It's not just one politician who is locking us in here. It's an entire system."

"The system lacks moral integrity," Girard pointed out.

"Girard," Otto persisted, "Aren't you the least bit concerned that if we stand up for ourselves, we'll all be rejected by society?"

"I already have," Lola said, raising her hand.

"Society can't reject me," Girard stated. "Because I have already rejected *it.*"

"You've rejected society?" Otto said nasally. "You don't seem antisocial or anything."

"Oh, I'm a big believer in community," Girard said earnestly.

"What's the difference?"

"In a community," Girard explained, "everyone looks out for each other. There's a sense of fellowship and each person contributes differently and according to their unique abilities. Everyone matters. Everyone is embraced. No one is left behind."

"And society?"

"Society does not exist," Girard said flatly.

"Wha?"

"Society," Girard exhaled, "consists of arbitrary constructs, devised to control, divide, and ultimately sell us things. Nobody matters. Each of us is just a standardized cog in a big machine. We constantly have to prove ourselves, usually by purchasing something or buying into a concept. *Follow this elaborate set of completely made-up rules to prove you are a good person.* We are expected to conform and contribute in identical ways, otherwise the machine will not function. If someone is atypical, or they figure out that society is manufactured and nothing more than a fallacy, that individual is considered a threat to the system. And treated accordingly. Destroyed. People who stand out are more likely to change the world, and believe me, the system does not want to be changed. Once you rationalize that it's a trap, the establishment holds no power over you."

"He's so hot," Flossie smiled.

"So to answer your question, Otto," Girard concluded. "No, I am not afraid of being rejected by society. It's an illusion."

"That's deep, dude," Otto nodded. "But that doesn't change the fact that *we could end up in the fricking Void if we leave this building!*"

"I have babies to think about," Lola quavered. "What if…"

"Is Mally hearing this?… Mally?… Mally, are you here?"

"Where's Mally?"

"Dunno."

"What about Piper?"

"She's… not herself right now," Otto said dolefully.

"Can you get her attention, Otto?"

"I'll try."

"Norman?"

"Norman, can you hear us?"

"Where's Norman?"

***

Forlorn in his empty apartment, wearing a conical party hat, Norman morosely placed a marshmallow-adorned cake on his coffee table. The icing spelled, *'HAPPY 107$^{TH}$ TO ME.'* Shuffling across the carpet, Norman took a seat on the sofa between some throw cushions with faces drawn on them. Each of the pillows was topped with identical party hats, and each wielded a tiny parcel, wrapped festively with reused paper and ribbon. Empty martini glasses were placed strategically on the coffee table in front of each pillow while ridiculous streamers were taped to the wall behind them.

"Thank ye all for coming," Norman exhaled despondently to the pillows. "Let's party."

He half-heartedly breathed into a party blower, which made a feeble, farty kazoo noise.

The door was suddenly shouldered open. Norman jolted as a soldier screamed, "NO MUSIC!" from behind a gas mask.

"It was just a party blower!" Norman squeaked while having his arms pinned behind his back by an unnecessarily aggressive soldier.

"IS THIS A GATHERING?" thundered a soldier, pointing to the anthropomorphized throw cushions. "I'M GENUINELY CURIOUS BECAUSE I CAN'T SEE A DAMN THING FROM BEHIND THIS MOTHER-LOVING GAS MASK!"

"Those are just pillows!" Norman insisted with trembling jowls. "Can't ye do the decent thing and give me some wiggle room? It's me birthday!"

"Birthdays aren't on the list, Gramps," grunted a deadpan soldier as he dragged Norman mercilessly from the apartment.

\*\*\*

"Norman's a little hard of hearing." Otto said into the air vent. "He might not be listening in."

"So here's what we need to do," Girard stated. "We need to recruit as many people as we can, otherwise this is never going to work. Not everyone will be on board, so we can't just blindly..."

"Is he serious?" Lola quavered, clutching Flossie's arm.

"What other choice do we have?" Flossie shrugged hopelessly.

"Pax has a pistachio," Girard pointed out. "Maybe he could contact all his supporters? Send encrypted messages? Slip flyers under their doors?"

"On it," Pax said definitively.

"Myrtle will be game."

"After what happened to Howard, I wouldn't doubt it."

"Maurice and his family? Betty Agnew? The Brothers McIntosh? Mrs. Flannery from downstairs? I've heard her crying a lot lately from under the floorboards."

"How are we going to pull this off even? We're basically vacuum-sealed inside the tower block."

"And once we're outside, we're vulnerable to all the Willatrixes scoping for sinners with their binoculars.

"Anyone have any ideas? Strategies?"

"Yeah, man. How do we get out of here?"

"Should we paint ourselves blue and charge outside while screaming obscenities in Gaelic?... Sorry, I'll let myself out."

"*How?* Let yourself out *how?*"

Time stood still for a split moment when someone banged violently on Lola's door, waking the children from their nap. Flossie and Lola looked at each other, bug-eyed for a moment before Flossie nudged her head towards the door. Lola clutched Flossie's arm as they answered together. Lola stifled a scream when five soldiers loomed over them in the hallway, one of whom was yanking Mally by the wrist. Another was ushering a very perplexed Norman who was still wearing a party hat.

Flossie squeezed Lola's hand as they both swallowed hard, their eyes brimming with tears.

"We heard you through the air vents," a gruff soldier said in a sandpapery voice.

"This is it then," Flossie's voice cracked. She squeezed her eyes shut, anticipating the inevitable.

Horrible silence.

"Count us in," the soldier nodded.

# CHAPTER FIFTY-EIGHT
## (A FEW MOMENTS LATER)

Standing stunned in Lola's apartment, Flossie, Girard, Lola, Otto, Mally, Pax and Norman found themselves in a rather surreal situation, with five soldiers in the room, dropping their weapons with a thud on the floor. Their name badges absolved them of awkward introductions. *Beaumont, Hopkins, Mulligan, Emerson and Featherpillow.*

"John is fine," Featherpillow muttered preemptively. "Just call me John.

"How do we know this isn't a trick?" Lola said, squinting at Featherpillow. I mean John.

The soldiers liberated their sweaty heads from their intimidating gas masks. Revealed were their surprisingly humanish faces, eyes drenched in remorse. One of them guiltily chewed the inside of his cheek.

"We took an oath to protect you," Emerson said in a voice that sounded much less like a desensitized thug than it did when it was previously wheezing through a gas mask. "All we can offer you is our word."

"We've never been on board with this," Hopkins said with his eyes bulging in earnest. "We were following orders, we had to. But we never wanted…"

"I see you have Mally," Otto said with his arms crossed, nodding in Mally's direction. "What did you do with the cats?"

"The cats are okay," Beaumont said, raising his hands in surrender. "Me and the guys rented a storage unit and we're keeping all the confiscated items hidden until… well. Until whatever happens next."

"I get it guys, I do," Featherpillow chimed in. "You've been scared shitless of us for months and you rightfully thought we were the enemy."

"You have weapons," Lola reminded them. "Shame on you. I have children and…"

"Check the chambers," Emerson said. "They're empty. They've been empty the whole time."

The neighbors looked at each other, searching for non-verbal signals. Anything.

"We're on your side," Mulligan insisted. "We heard everything you've been saying through the air vents."

"So you've been spying…" Otto challenged.

"Otto," Flossie said, gently touching his sleeve.

"I'm sorry, Flossie," Otto grudged, "I'm just struggling with the fact that these creeps have been stalking the halls for God-remembers-how-long, and now they're offering us some kind of ambiguous olive branch? Are we really that gullible?"

"We can't in good conscience continue follow orders when they are blatantly hurting the people we promised to protect," Beaumont insisted. "It's plain unethical."

"Good lad," Girard nodded in approval.

"Prove it," Otto spat.

"How do you want us to..."

"Give me back my cat, you son of a bitch," Otto said with surprising volume.  "Apologize to Norman for ruining his birthday! And did you do something nefarious to Piper? I can't fecking find her. If you've hurt Piper..."

"You can't possibly leave the building without our help," Beaumont declared.

"Are you blackmailing us?" Otto squinted.

"You need help," Emerson nodded affirmatively. "Strategic help."

"We are very stealthy," Featherpillow nodded with farcical seriousness.

"So you're saying you can help us organize..."

"There's a lot of military personnel who are strongly opposed to what's going on here," Mulligan said confidentially. "We're not the only ones."

"We have been rigorously trained to carry out covert operations," added Hopkins.

"You'll need to keep things peaceful," added Emerson. "And legal. We can help you with all that."

"Does your chief or whatever he's called know what you're up to?" Otto asked, triangulating an eyebrow.

The soldiers swallowed hard and looked sheepishly at one another.

"He *doesn't?*" Otto said with widening eyes.

"I think we should take the leap," Norman said with a watery warble. "They could've made me disappear for drawing faces on pillows and blowing the blowy-blower..."

"Wait, what?"

"But instead, they brought us all together," Norman cooed emotionally. "For me birthday."

"And I'm basically the devil's concubine," Mally added, raising an index finger. "Because Cats. And Books. They could have held me as a political prisoner or discarded me in a toxic waste receptacle. Yet here I am. Featherpillow even gave me a can of Dr. Pepper he was saving for later."

"John," Featherpillow said through a stiff smile. "Just John."

"Look at these," Mulligan said, rummaging for his phone.

The others craned their necks to get a glimpse of the screen, upon which were the faces of three ginger-haired, freckled tots. One had a cartoonishly toothy camera smile, and the littlest was sucking her thumb.

"Teddy, Heidi and little Casey," Mulligan dimpled proudly.

"Aww," Lola melted into a maternal puddle of butterscotch pudding. "Casey has a pink faux fur bunny just like Izzy's."

"I haven't seen them in months," Mulligan said with a snuff, blinking rapidly. "They've been all I could think about this whole time."

"So you have cute offspring and plenty of storage on your phone for pictures," Otto said abruptly. "So we're just supposed to, what? Pretend the past several months never happened?"

Mulligan's breath hitched, snagging him into a crying spell. Emerson rubbed Mulligan's back, whispering reassurances in his ear while the other soldiers lowered their heads.

"Well shit," Otto said, gobsmacked.

"I know this is hard on the kids," Mulligan nodded, sniffling.

Lola squeezed little Enzo's shoulders protectively.

"I can't stop thinking," Mulligan continued, "what must they think of me? I can't possibly be making them proud by terrorizing people. MY people. What's going to happen to them if I keep doing this?"

Sara-Sue perked up from her hiding place behind Lola when she noticed Mulligan fighting back tears. She wordlessly ambled across the room and unexpectedly squeezed Mulligan in a fervid hug while everyone in the room gasped. As Sara-Sue clamped him with the grip of a compassionate reticulated python, Mulligan's trembling arms tentatively embraced the little girl.

"Screw it," Mulligan said, resting his cheek lovingly atop Sara-Sue's head. "When you're right, you're right, kid."

"He's good," Lola nodded, biting her lip. "We're good. It's all good."

The soldiers each crouched down and gently reassured Sara-Sue that they were friends and that they were there to help. Hopkins cackled good-naturedly when Sara-Sue grabbed his nose with her tiny hand. Beaumont let her try on his helmet, which covered the little girl's entire face.

"So are we really doing this?" Lola asked after a suffocating moment of silence.

Everyone in the room swerved around to look at Otto, whose shoulders were slowly relaxing. Finally, he nodded.

# CHAPTER FIFTY-NINE
## (THREE WEEKS LATER)

The abrupt knock on Biff's door occurred while Biff was binge watching *Lust Triangle* reruns on his ridiculous, floral couch with a ginormous vat of popcorn and a box of tissues. He was wearing a terrycloth bathrobe and his wife's feathery house slippers.

"Gimme a sec!" Biff called, hoisting his body from the couch, leaving behind a lingering dent in the cushion.

Licking the butter-like topping from his fingers, Biff lumbered towards the front door of his modest, suburban bungalow and answered, finding Tristan outside, quivering vulnerably.

"Tristan," Biff stated the obvious.

"Hold me," Tristan whimpered, wilting like a fragile daisy into Biff's meaty arms.

"There, there," Biff consoled, his hands discreetly wandering down to the small of Tristan's back. "I'm here now. You're okay. Tell Biff what's going on."

"Is that popcorn?" Tristan sniffled, wasting no time inviting himself in, hopping the coffee table and landing stealthily on the couch, helping himself to a stress snack. "My life is a total dumpster fire," Tristan sobbed with his mouth full of popcorn. "It's all falling apart, Biff. I can't *even* right now."

"Tell me," Biff said solemnly, taking a seat next to Tristan with bulgingly sincere eyeballs.

"My wife left me," Tristan squeaked unintelligibly. "With the kids. The *kids,* Biff. They resembled me. It was so cute."

"Tristan, jeez," Biff said, shaking his head with doleful disbelief.

"They were so good for my image, you know?" Tristan sobbed breathlessly. "Now they're all gone."

"You are completely undeserving of this pain," Biff said, discreetly turning off the T.V.

"Then my advisor quit," Tristan said, his face wrenching with emotional agony.

"Hector Morosely?" Biff squeaked with surprise. "Why on earth..."

"He called me a name, Biff. It was so hurtful. Borderline abusive."

"That doesn't seem like Hector. What did he call you?"

"Unelectable," Tristan wailed.

"Being a Christian man, I must apologize in advance for my salty language. But that Morosely character is a doofus."

"Just because I didn't take his advice about an *exit strategy*," Tristan said, using sarcastic air quotes. "He said my policies are abhorrent but not in a good way. He thinks I've pushed people too far."

"How so?" Biff asked, tilting his head sympathetically.

"By lying."

"About what?"

"Jaysus, Biff. Don't make me explain," Tristan snorted emotionally. "He said that lying is dishonest. But like, obviously I have to lie. If I don't lie about how I've been lying this whole time... you know. About my basic knowledge of what's going on..."

"Nobody's perfect," Biff nudged gently.

"If I tell the truth now, nobody will trust me."

"Indeed, it's a delicate matter," Biff said, rubbing gentle circles on Tristan's back.  "The last thing you need is for your approval ratings..."

"It's too late, Biff," Tristan said, flopping hopelessly on the couch. "My approval ratings are tanking. And Hector thinks it's my fault. Can you believe that?"

"I've got nothing," Biff said, pulling his pockets inside out and shrugging.

"I'd be on a sandy beach in Oahu right now if the resort management hadn't been so oversensitive about the explicit compliment I paid that lounge waitress."

"I'm sure she looked real pretty, Tristan."

"So here I am, Biff," Tristan exhaled in defeat. "No wife. No family. No advisor. My mom legally disowned me. Half my cabinet up and quit. My cat ran away, but not before he pissed on my favorite Giorgio Armani viscose popeline shirt. I'm losing my popularity which was previously my finest attribute, second perhaps to my tremendous hair."

"Truly tremendous."

"My reputation is swirling down the drain of a proverbial urinal. My sycophants are dwindling. My ego is numb and tingling as though someone sat on it. My special prime minister mansion is being gutted due to asbestos. And the network has no intentions of ever taking me back, I checked."

"So here you are..."

"Devoid of dignity. Temporarily homeless and totally alone."

"You will always have me," Biff said, pointing at himself for effect. "And you can stay here as long as you need."

"You mean that?" Tristan asked hopefully.

"Sure I do," Biff said, raising his right hand in an oath-like way. "The wife's visiting her mother indefinitely. You can sleep in my bed."

"Where will you sleep, Biff?"

"Now you just let me worry about that," Biff winked. "You have enough on your plate. We can make this fun! How's about I go make some more popcorn and then we can stay up late and watch a Nora Ephron marathon together."

"Hold that thought, Biff," Tristan said, answering his cell phone. "Tristan Winnings here, please love me."

"Tristan?" B.P's bewildered voice came from Tristan's phone.

"What is it, Beepy? I'm in the middle of something here."

"I think you should turn on the news," B.P said, stunned and monotonic.

"It's not time for the…"

"I really think you should turn on the news."

"Why?"

"Turn on the news."

"What channel?"

"Every channel."

After fishing the remote from between the couch cushions, Tristan flicked on the television. On the screen was what appeared to be the once-desolate streets of Agora City, now clogged with hundreds of people. Each person was running down the street in giant, individual hamster balls. Tristan's jaw and the remote dropped simultaneously.

"Uh… Biff?" Tristan called.

"Making popcorn!" Biff called back cheerily from the kitchen, making himself heard over the din of the hot air popper.

"I... I think you should see this!"

Biff waddled back into the room, beaming like an imbecile with his arms wrapped around a vat of popcorn that was the size of a large bushel basket. When he saw the television screen, he dropped the vat, causing popcorn to fly and tumble everywhere.

"What in Sam Hill..." Biff gasped, his face whitening like a crisp hotel sheet.

Tristan could do nothing but sputter and point at the screen.

"Are those hamster balls?" Biff said in befuddlement, popcorn crunching under his feet as he walked towards the screen.

"Yes, those are hamster balls," said the news anchor on the screen, holding a microphone and pointing to the streets where an endless stream of hamster balls spilled out from around every corner in the sprawling city. "Nobody knows where they came from or where they are going. But it seems they have a pretty clear message for the Prime Minister of Umbravia."

"I don't want a message!" Tristan squeaked in protest. "They can't do this! I didn't sanction it! Isn't that sort of like cheating?"

"Technically they have the right to protest," Biff pointed out.

"Put a cork in it, Biff!" Tristan spat. "This is totally illegal. And if it's not, it will be after I make a brief phone call."

"It is quite difficult to make any arrests for a number of reasons," the reporter continued. "This atypical procession appears to be somewhat unoffensive – unless of course, you happen to be offended by it. The hamster balls are seemingly impenetrable, so neither Bruce nor the authorities have access to the dissenters. And the whole protest is surprisingly legal, respectful, Bruce-safe and peaceful save for one guy who screamed, but as it turned out, there was a bee in his ball."

"I'll deploy the military," Tristan grasped.

"There appears to be a substantial military presence at this event," the news anchor continued.

"Who deployed them?" Tristan yelled at the screen.

"The hamster-ballers appear to have a military escort," the news anchor added. "Apparently, civilians are not the only ones who have had enough."

"They can't have enough!" Tristan whined. "I haven't said it's enough yet! That's my job!"

"It's quite astonishing, really," the news anchor said, looking directly at Tristan through the screen. "I suppose there are limitations to what the government can get away with. The message is loud and clear. Umbravians want out. Will Tristan Winnings listen to them? How this will pan out politically is anyone's..."

"SHUT UP!" Tristan shouted desperately at the television, causing Biff to wince. "Do you see what's happening here, Biff?"

"I'm not sure I can ever unsee..."

"This is blatantly disrespectful!"

"I mean as far as protests go, this one seems kind of innocuous and creative."

"I specifically told them they weren't allowed to disagree with me! And now this?"

"Listen, Tristan, I know the whole hamster ball thing is a little unsettling but…"

"I'm totally losing control," Tristan hollered. "I've lost every damn thing that matters to me and now control? The thing that matters most?"

"It does seem that way, doesn't it."

"I can't lose control," Tristan shrieked, pulling his hair. "Not now. Then everything I've done will be for nothing."

"Let's sleep on it," Biff urged.

"There's no time for sleeping or other frivolities!"

"Just let them get this out of their system and then just forget it happened."

"Forget about like a trillion people running around in hamster balls?"

"That does leave an impression, doesn't it."

"This isn't over, Biff."

"It's not?"

"You still there, Beepy?" Tristan seethed into his phone.

"I don't know," B.P. sighed. "I guess?"

Tristan squinted ferociously at the television screen. *"Release Augustine."*

# CHAPTER SIXTY
## (LATER)

"You realize that Augustine is a lion, right?" said a bewildered zookeeper whose name was most likely George, based on his nametag.

B.P. Deerlight blinked.

"You sure you heard the prime minister correctly?" George probed with a sideways glance. "Augustine here is an apex predator. Not even I am allowed in his enclosure. You expect me to just set him loose to lurk around the city?"

"It's for the greater good of society," B.P. said even more deadpan than usual.

"Is this a prank?"

"I'm very serious right now," B.P. said without inflection.

George lolled his eyeballs towards Augustine who was in his enclosure, licking a graphic slab of mutilated, raw meat with his sandpapery tongue. B.P. startled when the lion belched out a loud snarl and abruptly swatted with his commanding paw.

"He's no pussy cat," George warned with a steepled eyebrow.

B.P. waved at Augustine with fluttery fingers while she remained stiffened with fear.

"This could pose a serious threat to the community," added George.

"The prime minister insisted," B.P. blinked.

"Did he."

"He said it's an official order."

"To release a carnivore?"

"Just to control people's behavior. Not to hurt anyone."

"I'm going to say this again and this time I'll enunciate. *Augustine is a lion.*"

"Tristan says it's probably safe. Ish."

"I disagree."

"You can't do that. There's rules."

"What about you?"

"Me?"

"What do you think of all this?"

B.P. moved her mouth around wordlessly for a moment. "This?"

"Do you think this is a good idea?"

"The prime minister..."

"I'm not asking the prime minister. I'm asking you."

"I..." B.P. said, her eyeballs scoping around for a means of escape. "I just do what I'm told."

"Aren't you the advisor?"

"Chief Situational Officer," B.P. swallowed.

"You seem like a smart lady."

"Tested at genius levels. Quantum mechanics is really hard so..."

"Do you agree with the prime minister?"

"There are consequences for not..."

"In your professional opinion..."

"See, he's kind of unhinged. He kidnapped me from the lab? I'm not really sure what else he's capable of."

"Why on earth are you going along with this, Dr. Deerlight?"

"I just told you, I..."

"He's an unemployed soap actor. You don't even need talent to do that."

"He confiscated my math. The Void? I really don't want to go back there..."

"Fine," George grunted. "If it's a legal order, I suppose I can't deny you the lion."

B.P. exhaled.

"But you have to sign a waiver stating that the zoo will not be held responsible if Augustine decides to make lunch of an unassuming Umbravian."

\*\*\*

"Felix?" Olga chirped as she pulled the cellophane off two, identical microwavable meatloaf dinners. "Rations are ready, Lover. Come here and feed me bites of meatloaf from a fork. It'll be super-erotic."

Felix did not reply. He was staring, mouth agape, out the window. "Hamster balls," he breathed.

"What's that?" Olga asked, blowing on the swirling steam wafting from the plastic tray.

Felix's eyebrows rose nearly to his hairline. A ridiculous parade of hamster balls, each containing a scampering Umbravian flailing their arms for balance, cascaded through the streets in an unyielding current. When he squinted, Felix could decipher recognizable faces inside some of the giant, plastic orbs: Otto, Norman, Pax, Lola, Flossie, Girard..."

"Mally?" Felix accidentally said out loud.

Olga dropped a serving spoon, which clattered more loudly than it needed to when it hit the linoleum. "What did you just say?"

Felix's lips parted. Just as Olga was about to launch into a vitriolic Ted Talk regarding Mally's likening unto the Eighth Abomination, a press conference began playing on Olga's tablet.

"I thought Umbravians were smarter than this," Tristan said on the screen with a lisp that always became more prominent when he was lying. "This, this, this fringy revolt with these, these hamster balls. It's a punch in the face to all the Umbravians who have been behaving themselves for the past several months. Don't give them the attention they seek. Should we tolerate these arachnophobic Presbyterians who abuse the use of staplers and despise the Irish?"

"I told you!" Olga spat, pointing smugly at the screen.

"They are not your friends," Tristan continued. "While they appear to be protesting peacefully, these ruffians are clearly a threat to society. State-run media outlets have pre-emptively leaked that *those people* in the hamster balls have intentions of overthrowing the government in disturbing and terrifying ways. They are secretly armed with staplers. They will steal your socks and teach your puppies not to love you."

"I knew it!" Olga said, pounding her fist on the table with satisfaction. "I totally called it! Felix, remember what I said to you last night after we made love seven times consecutively, wearing nothing but Converse sneakers?"

"I..."

"I told you *those people...*"

"Olga, she's out there."

"Don't say her name! If you say her name..."

"Mally is..."

Olga swallowed a scream, her face purpling. "Say her name again, and I'll take back the axolotl and the special cheese, I swear to God!"

"I was engaged to her, Olga."

"No!"

"Can't I be a little worried about her out there in that hamster ball?"

"She was an indiscretion."

"She's not a bad person," Felix muttered.

"Excuse me?" Olga squeaked at an octave that only a Norwegian elkhound could hear. "What about the books? And the cats? And her fondness of Simon & Garfunkel?"

"Simon & Garfunkel?"

"Yes, Simon & Garfunkel!" Olga shouted with her hands raised in exasperation. "Whenever she's alone, she twirls around her apartment in her Snoopy lounge shorts and sings *I am a Rock* into an eggbeater which she pretends is a microphone. Scandalous!"

"How did you know..."

"Oh calm down," Olga snorted. "I was stalking her."

"You were…"

"Are you going to make a big deal about this?"

"Why would you…"

"It was the respectable thing to do," Olga said, waving Felix off. "What, do you expect me *not* to creep out on the ledge and watch her through her window while she sleeps? Give her the death stare? Wait for her to do something immoral?"

"I can't believe you would actually…"

"You heard the prime minister," Olga persisted. "She's an arachnophobic Presbyterian with a thing for staplers. She cannot be trusted. And as a conscientious citizen I must defend the Irish at all co…"

"She's not though," Felix said, shaking his head urgently. "I spoke to her every day in the elevator… I lived with her. She's Anglican and she thinks spiders are misunderstood and adorable!"

"And you believed her?" Olga said, crossing her arms.

"You stalked her," Felix moaned, nursing his head. "This is seriously creepy and probably illegal!"

"And what, singing a beloved folk song *ISN'T* illegal? Hoarding books? Smuggling domestic shorthairs into a secret niche? Running around in a ginormous hamster ball, trying to overthrow democracy? That woman is an extremist and must be dealt with!"

"You're scaring me."

"What, why... I'm not the one you should be afraid of."

"I thought it was cute how jealous you were before. But now..."

"Oh Honey. I have cherries."

"I don't know about this."

"Sit. Feed me meatloaf."

"I should go."

"Where? This is your place."

"I never should of..."

"You're safe here. With me."

"I..."

"I thought you wanted to feel safe."

Felix swallowed hard, reddening as his eyeballs lolled towards the window, hearing cheers of protest outside.

"Look at me," Olga said sharply.

Felix's eyeballs obeyed.

"You are not one of them," Olga said sternly.

"I know but I..." Felix swallowed harder. "I'm also not one of... you."

Olga's eyes widened to the point of nearly bursting. "Do you want to leave me? Do you really think that would be a good idea?" she continued, impaling her meatloaf maniacally with a fork, uttering a guttural, shuddersome bark. Then reverting to her formerly demure self, she chewed gingerly and gave Felix's hand a loving squeeze. "Choose your enemies wisely, Love."


***


The only signs of life were the shallow nose breathing and the migraine that was slowly creeping into Piper's ocular cavities. She lay limp on her bed, too exhausted to cry, too unmotivated to blink and too numb to move from the sprawling position of her body on the bed. A thick brain fog oozed into her head, rendering her thought process stagnant.

*I'm never going to sing again.*

*It's never going to end.*

*This is it for me.*

*Alone.*

*Uninspired.*

*Nothing to look forward to.*

*No music.*

*Ever.*

*I guess it's... over.*

*I can't try to force myself to fit like a square in the circle hole.*

*No more.*

*But if I...*

*Then...*

*What about Otto?*

*...*

*I'm just weighing him down.*

*I'm toxic.*

*I want to get better but...*

*What if I don't find my way back this time?*

*Things aren't going back to normal.*

*I'll always be like this.*

*Everything.*

*Nothing.*

*He won't feel obligated to me anymore if I...*

*He'll be so much happier... without... me.*

*Without me.*

*...*

*...What's that sound?*

Piper thought she heard muffled cheers of freedom outside but discounted it as an isolation-induced delusion. She'd had several of them, ranging from phantom guitar riffs to a lifelike Otto mirage wafting through the wall.

When something thudded hard against her window, Piper slowly turned her head, her hair crispy from tears that dried hours ago. Or maybe days. It took all the energy she had to haul her body from the mattress and lumber across the room. Opening the window, a disoriented pigeon flapped around, shaking something free from his little foot.

A scrap of paper.

Blinking the sting of daylight from her eyes, Piper read…

**THIS IS YOUR MOMENT.**

Scrunching her nose, Piper craned her neck to look outside.

"Oh my God…"

Hamster balls were everywhere. Containing people. Containing…

"Otto?" Piper squeaked when she recognized her bespectacled friend, flailing around inside a hamster ball with hundreds of others, face beaming, shouting what sounded like, *"Woo Hoo! Freedom, Motherf…"*

"Otto!" Piper screamed out the window, waving frantically. "Up here!"

Otto turned a corner and was out of sight. With her heart suddenly pounding like a funk base guitar, Piper scoured the room, which seemed to be whirring around like a salad spinner. Piper zeroed in on her guitar and urgently grabbed its neck.

# CHAPTER SIXTY-ONE
## (LATER THAT NIGHT)

"They're still at it," Clarity said in disbelief to her speechless fern as she stared out the window at the relentless dissenters in the street. "Is it me or is this whole situation becoming more and more like a freaky mushroom trip?"

A curser blinked menacingly at Clarity from her glowing computer screen, nagging her about the unfinished article. She moaned as she sat and gawked at the blank screen.

*'HAMSTER BALLS: A SIGN OF THE TIMES?'*

*No. (backspace)*

*'SELFISH BASTARDS DISRUPTING OUR LIVES!'*

*No. (backspace) How do you even compare this to the disruption of our lives the past several months? They'd never go for that.*

*'SOCIETY DECLARES COMPASSION FATIGUE FOR ARACHNOPHOBIC PRESBYT...'*

*Uh... (backspace)*

*'STAPLERS, GLUE GUNS AND EXTREMELY SHARP PENCILS DISCOVERED IN THE HAMSTER BALLS: YOU CALL THAT PEACEFUL?... CONTINUE ON PAGE 13 — OFFICE -SUPPLIES: A NEW KIND OF WARFARE.'*

Clarity mused for a moment. Defeated.

*At least it's weird enough that people probably won't believe it. Probably.*

Clarity's fingers stopped clacking abruptly when she heard a spectral groan wafting from the wall.

The ghost.

Clarity tried to type again, but the eerie sounds sent a wave of horror directly through her body. Her frightened whimper hitched when a loud belch echoed through the air vent. Clarity scrunched her nose and tentatively tip-toed into the hall, peering around. With her heart pounding, she swallowed hard and tried the door handle of the next-door flat. Predictably, the door creaked open.

Eerie vapor swirled around the room, filling Clarity's lungs, making her cough and wave away the noxious fumes. As it dissipated, Clarity noticed that the vapor was actually cigar smoke pluming from a well-used ashtray.

Her eyes widened when the dissipating haze revealed a rotund man in a powder blue, velour tracksuit, wearing a whistle around his neck. He lounged on a saggy couch, watching a classic horror movie starring Vincent Price, taking a loud swig of beer, and shoving his hand into a crinkly bag of Fritos. As he noisily crunched his snack, Clarity noticed the room littered with empty beer cans and identical, empty Frito bags, strewn literally everywhere.

"Hey!" the man barked when he discovered Clarity standing stiffly in the doorway with bulging eyes.

"Sorry," Clarity said quickly, covering her eyes and ramming into a wall while trying to leave.

"Who are you?" the man said, thumping towards Clarity with squinting eyes and orange crumbs in his beard.

"Clarity, from... from next door. I... I thought..."

"Oh..." the man reconsidered for a moment but then leaned challengingly into Clarity's personal space. "You're not supposed to be here."

"I... thought this flat was haunted."

The man shut the door loudly, making Clarity feel trapped inside. "That's why they put me here. Everyone thinks it's haunted. People stay clear of this place, usually. Nobody's supposed to know... Bumbee. Joe," the man said, discreetly offering his hand for Clarity to shake.

"Joe Bumbee?" Clarity repeated.

"Seeing as how you're from next door, I suppose you were bound to find out sooner or later," Joe said, running his finger through his greasy hair. "I'm the expert."

"The…"

"The expert," Joe said, scratching the furry stomach under his zip-up top. "Premier Chesterfield consults with me on matters of great importance."

"You…" Clarity stammered. "Are the expert?"

"Technically, I'm a junior-intermediate volleyball coach," Joe nodded "But I know everything so…"

"Oh my God…" Clarity quavered.

"Lookit," Joe said, wagging his index finger in Clarity's face, "As far as you're concerned, this flat is haunted, get me?"

"Excuse me…" Clarity said, trying to leave.

Joe held the door closed with his palm. "You can't tell anybody about this," he warned. "It's highly confidential."

"Can I just…"

"You can't go to the media or anything…"

Feeling as though she might throw up, Clarity scrambled out the door.

\*\*\*

"Comfy?" Biff asked, snuggling into the bottom bunk, nestling into his cushy, Star Wars quilt.

"I do enjoy being on top," Tristan said aloofly from the top bunk, slithering into a comfortable position in his designer silk nightshirt. He discreetly pulled out a cosmetic compact, and after examining his under-eye gels, Tristan winked at his reflection and slapped the flip-top shut.

"This is fun, right?" Biff bubbled. "We can watch T.V. or just stay up all night and talk."

"T.V. is good," Tristan said quickly, snatching a remote control and aiming it towards the plasma screen on the bedroom wall.

Flipping through channel after channel, Tristan winced as every single station was presenting non-stop coverage of the hamster ball uprising. "They're depraved," Tristan moped resentfully. "They've completely taken over the airwaves. Stupid Presbyterians."

Biff burbled his lips and mused for a moment. "Maybe... you should hear them out."

"What brand of acid are you dropping and where can I get some?"

"I'm just saying, Tristan," Biff said, propping himself up with an elbow. "you've been throwing a lot of policies around, but have you considered how these policies are affecting your people?  Protests happen when folks don't feel heard. Have you been listening..."

"I don't have to listen to you," Tristan said, hiding his head under a pillow.

"Turn it up," Biff said pointing at the screen. "They're interviewing…"

"No," Tristan said, muffled under his pillow.

Biff tussled briefly with Tristan for the remote, then turned up the volume.

A reporter whose ponytail was swinging, ran alongside Pax's hamster ball, pointing a microphone in Pax's direction while he took long, exaggerated strides. "Tell us why you are here tonight," she said to him. "Wait a minute… You're Pax MacLeod the rogue M.P.P…"

"Everyone's story deserves to be told," Pax huffed as he sweated profusely in his hamster ball. "A lot of people are hurting, but they haven't been allowed to be part of the conversation."

"A lot of people hate you," the reporter pointed out.

"Thanks for that," Pax smirked, still running. "See, the thing about democracy, is that in order to enjoy its benefits, you have to be okay with people you hate having the same rights as you."

"We'll pretend we didn't hear that," the reporter said as she swerved towards Norman's hamster ball, running alongside. "Over here we have a surprisingly spry centenarian doing a kind of free style run inside his ginormous rodent orb. Excuse me, Misinformed Codger. Perhaps you are confused and have no idea where you are or how you got here. Assistance is available."

"No thanks!" Norman said gleefully, shuffling with finesse inside his hamster ball. "Isn't this grand? I feel like I'm eighty-eight again!"

"Explain your participation in this… well, *this.*"

"I've lived through a lot of warped guff," Norman panted, still running. "Wars. Depression. Bigotry. Civil unrest. Corruption. Segregation. One thing's clear as mud. Regardless of what side you're on, segregation always puts you on the wrong side of history. I've seen it with me own eyes!"

The reporter *accidentally* rolled Norman's hamster ball off the road. "What about you?" the reporter said, catching up with Girard's hamster ball. "I take it you're an uneducated radical, devoid of conscience."

"Professor of moral philosophy," Girard chuffed as he jogged in the ball.

"Come out from under your pillow and see this, Tristan," Biff urged as he goggled at the television screen while Otto was being interviewed.

"You can't make me," Tristan moaned from under the pillow.

"This lad says he lost his café business," Biff continued. "On account of everything being illegal. Poor guy."

"No Biff," Tristan scolded. "He's the bad guy. Get it straight."

"Is he though?" Biff asked, cocking his head. "He seems pretty hip and formally educated."

"You're taking their *side?*"

"I don't know if I want to take a side," Biff said, shrugging one shoulder.

"You have to take a side, Biff," Tristan hissed. "This is a wedge issue."

"Buddy, come on, you know?" Biff said, flicking the top bunk from his quilty nest below. "These guys just want to talk to you. It wouldn't hurt to..."

"You're one of them."

"I've got your back, okay? I've always had your back."

"Traitor."

"Come on now, that's not fair. I let you have the top bunk."

"This wasn't supposed to happen," Tristan said, the tears in his eyes glossing from the light of the television screen.

"I mean, culturally Umbravians are decent people, so if you tell them to hate each other, you have to expect that sooner or later they're going to push back. I mean..."

"Oh... my... Godlike ass..."

Biff sat up stiffly in the lower bunk as Tristan gaped in shock from up top. On the screen, was the indisputable figure of a woman, adorned with a bucket hat and faded thrift shop Nirvana tee, layered under a flannel shirt that was flapping and fluttering in the wind. She was wielding a guitar and doing a sound test on the roof of a Brutalist residential tower.

"Sweet Baby Jesus in a manger," Biff shook his head in disbelief.

"What in bloody hell is she doing?" Tristan screeched, clutching white-knuckled to the side of his bunk.

# CHAPTER SIXTY-TWO
## (A FEW MOMENTS LATER)

"Can everyone hear me?" Piper said bashfully, wincing and stepping back, startled by the shrill feedback and reverberation from the microphone. She took a deep breath when she looked down from the roof of the tower block, feeling woozy from the height. She gripped her guitar for comfort. "I'm... I'm not supposed to do this but..."

"That's Piper!" Otto screamed from inside his hamster ball, pressing his palms against the concave plastic around him. "Up there! You guys, it's Piper!"

Hundreds of hamster balls instantly stopped in the streets.

"I do alt rock..." Piper said, clearing her throat, tuning her guitar. "Punk. Neo-grunge type stuff." She cleared her throat again. "I've had this melody clanging around in my head for the past several months, but I wasn't allowed… It's going to haunt me forever if I don't get it out."

The boisterous noise from the hamster ball hubbub depleted into a thick silence as everyone in the street gawked up at Piper.

"Anyone feel like screaming?" Piper asked awkwardly. "I mean… we're all going to the Void anyway, am I right?"

A din of chortles echoed through the dense darkness of the night.

"I've never played in front of people before," Piper admitted nervously, turning up the distortion. Way up. "So be nice, okay? I call this, *Don't Wall Me In*."

Piper exhaled and blew air out of her cheeks.

Otto gaped up at Piper with awe glazing his eyeballs.

Piper steadied her shaking hand before strumming in an urgent, arpeggiated picking pattern.

*"The world ended today, but that's okay they say,"* Piper sang, apprehensively scoping the street beneath her. *"You're safe another day, they say. Keep doing what we say, you'll be okay, okay? But you feel so far away, and this is not okay…"*

"My girl," Otto said, his teary eyes glowing in the streetlamp light as Piper played a meteoric dirty power chord that launched her into an entirely different realm of sound.

*"You're behind this wall!"* Piper belted. *"And I feel so small! Got nothing left at all, at all, at all! I need you here with me, feel your energy! Why can't they let us be? Why can't they just let me be me?"*

Piper's angry Fender Mustang meowed in a defiant, sustained scream.

*"I feel everything, nothing! I feel everything, nothing! All for nothing, it's all or nothing! Here goes nothing!"*

Another screamy meow from the guitar.

"YES!" Otto screamed, followed by uproarious cheers from everyone in the street. "SHE'S DOING IT! THIS IS HAPPENING RIGHT NOW! SHE JUST JOPLIN-ED THE HELL OUT OF THIS SONG! I KNOW HER!"

*"Don't wall me in!"* Piper burst into the chorus, her voice shredding, shattering the sky. *"This is me and I am real! And I'm allowed to feel! You take and take and take from me - still have my integrity! You can't break me, you can't break me, there's no more you can take from me! Don't wall me in! Don't wall me in! Don't wall me in!"*

\*\*\*

*"Don't wall me in! Don't wall me in!"* Biff sang off-key, dancing around the bedroom in his blinding yellow onsie with the butt-flap, wiggling his derriere in time to Piper's driving rhythm.

"For God's sake, Biff," Tristan grimaced. "Would you cut that out?"

"I like this song," Biff beamed stupidly. "It's groovy."

"You're supposed to be my guy."

"Dance with me, Tristan."

"This song isn't just offensive to me," Tristan pointed out. "It's an affront to your authority as well. Didn't you pick music out of a fishbowl?"

"Hey man that was Joe Bumbee," Biff said, catching his breath. "Music is the cat's pajamas, in my humble opinion."

"Music is neither the cat's nor any other domesticated animal's nightwear, Biff. How are we supposed to demoralize people into compliance with music going around, lightening people's moods? Besides, this sounds alarmingly similar to a protest song."

"I love Bob Dylan," Biff said, shaking his head fondly.

"I was feeling a bit guilty about my counteraction plan," Tristan said, pointing at Piper screaming herself hoarse and totally shredding it on the plasma screen. "But this song's overwhelmingly positive reception consolidates my strategy."

"What do you mean?" Biff asked innocently right before jolting and wincing at what he saw next on television.

The song abruptly stopped.

Piper recoiled in horror when she heard a loud, throaty roar, scraping through silence like a jagged razor blade. Within nanoseconds, the hysterical crowd disbanded, dispersing like termites in every direction. Hamster balls were scattering everywhere. Piper impulsively abandoned her music equipment and darted for the stairs leading back inside the block tower.

A red fug spread like a vapor into the sky.

A civil defense siren pierced every eardrum within a fifty-mile radius.

The lion stalked through the fug, his tail swishing back and forth in a predatory way.

"Tristan," Biff quavered, watching the plasma screen in utter terror. "What have you done?"

"I told you I was going to release Augustine," Tristan shrugged.

"Augustine is a *lion?*" Biff squeaked adolescently. "I figured Augustine was the name of a conflict resolution facilitator."

Tristan mused pensively. "That could have worked too."

"What's all that red stuff!" Biff warbled, pointing again at the screen.

"Oh, I just did that for dramatic effect."

"Tristan, why!"

"Why?" Tristan laughed nervously. "Biff, what if the foreign press taps into this hamster ball thing? I'll look like an idiot in front of the whole world."

"A lion, Tristan? A *lion?*"

"I had to get them to go back inside, didn't I?"

"But now there's a lion!" Biff reiterated by pointing at the screen. "Why did you think this was a good idea?"

"This is what people wanted!" Tristan said, raising his arms in exasperation. "Popular opinion pressured me into taking drastic measures! I want to be popular!"

"But you influenced popular opinion in the first place!"

"But social media influenced *me* in the first place!"

"But you influenced social media to influence *you* in the first place!"

"But mainstream media influenced me to influence social media, which influenced me to influence *them* to influence *me* to give people what they want in the first place! Although I subsidize mainstream media and they basically do whatever I tell them so I essentially influenced *them* first! Jaysus, this is hard!"

"Wouldn't it be easier just to listen to them?" Biff pleaded. "They just want to talk to you! The whole world is watching, Tristan. Wouldn't it look good on you to be an attentive leader?"

"It's a little late for that, I'd say," Tristan exhaled.

***

Once everyone retreated to their homes, save for a few stragglers flailing down the street and a stray hamster ball rolling down the road like a ridiculous tumbleweed, Tristan's face appeared on the marquee.

"Citizens of Umbravia, this is your leader," said a pixilated version of Tristan. "I renounce the deplorable actions witnessed today in the city of Agora. I advise anyone who watched this national embarrassment unfold to immediately splash your eyes with holy water. I'm afraid these cads have ruined it for the rest of you. The lion and this spooky, red fug will ensure that nobody – and I mean *nobody* will leave their place of residence until further notice. Fun fact: Hamster balls are a symbol of toxic masculinity in some cultures. I have deemed them illegal. It sickens me to see the military supporting such roguery. I have therefore fired the military. They will be replaced by Vikings whom I have commissioned from Scandinavia. Their longships should be arriving on Tuesday. Have a pleasant evening."

# CHAPTER SIXTY-THREE
## (THE NEXT MORNING)

Her strawberry blond eyelashes fluttered. Clarity Trout blinked the dreamy delirium from her eyes, pulling herself out of a dark, sinking sleep. A weird feeling suddenly clamped her ribcage, causing a flutter of panic. Out slipped a mousy gasp.

*Am I awake?*

*What a weird dream.*

With her head still sunk into her pillow, Clarity's eyeballs lolled around the room. The concrete walls of her oppressively geometric bedroom intimidated her. The tiny, rectangular window offered little hope – in fact, it seemed to be squinting at her. Judgmentally.

"Fern?" Clarity said scratchily in an early morning octave. "Fern, I had a trippy dream."

With a weary groan, Clarity turned her foggy head to face a potted fern placed meticulously on a mismatched bedside table. She blinked hard, as she was prone to do, bungling on her notable stutter. "Of course, it wasn't real," she said to the plant. "How could it be? How could it... be?"

Another mousy gasp.

Scrambling from her squeaky mattress, fumbling, entwined in her threadbare, floral sheet, Clarity dashed to her rectangular window. Standing on her tippy toes she peered outside. Her eyeballs quivered.

A desolate, deserted street.

Not a single soul.

No one.

Anywhere.

A hauntingly red fug lingered in the sky.

A brownstone husk stood where the theatre used to be.

Outside, a flashing marquee was blinking the word *'NO'* largely and boldly.

The billboard across the street sported the same message. *'NO.'*

Spraypainted across the windows of random, vacated shops, *'NO.'*

Searchlights scoured the streets from seemingly nowhere. Possibly the sky.

An eerie silence loomed thickly in the air like a terrifying margarine.

Except…

*What's that sound?*

The throaty snarl of a… lion.

*Wait, lion?*

From the elusiveness of a dark alley, the indisputable figure of a sleek lion lurked around the corner and stalked the empty street. Each pad of his terrible paws composed the rhythm of a foreboding dirge. His ribs protruded hungrily, undulating through his amber fur with each step. Guttural threats emerged from deep in his throat as he lolled his mighty head back and forth as though patrolling the streets. For a split moment Clarity thought she saw the ironic predator flash his unforgiving eyes in her direction.

"Fern?" Clarity quavered with a hard blink. "It… it wasn't a dream."

***

"What did I just see?" Willatrix vlogged, giving her computer screen the stink eye and curling her lip in revulsion. "I barely slept last night, my fluffy love chickens. Images of that revolting revolt will remain embossed in my conscience forevermore. This morning I read online that those terrible Presbyterians were concealing staplers in their hamster balls, not to mention glue guns and extremely sharp pencils. Simply loathsome. While the weaponized stationary has not been recovered by the authorities, my clairvoyant gift is telling me that the news article is accurate. Allow me to express my moral outrage. I urge you all to be extremely acerbic and terrified for your safety."

Willatrix launched further into her diatribe, accentuating her wrath with superficial hand gestures, using the potato as a prop.

"I'm embarrassed to admit it, but I noticed multiple neighbors of mine threshing around in those horrible hamster balls. I will provide a list of names in the comments so you can bombard their personal social media accounts with vitriol. I fear I am the only virtuous one in this tower block. Have mercy on me, *Madam Universe.*"

Willatrix said a prayer in a language she made up on the fly.

"Tangent," Willatrix said, boinging her eyes open. "My boycott of the day is office supplies. I do not condone this bizarre new fad of weaponizing pencils and normalizing toxic masculinity. If glue guns can be used nefariously, God only knows what these radical lunatics will do with paperclips, or God-forbid, sticky post-its. It's best we eliminate all stationary and those who use it, in the name of national security, and of course, righteousness."

Willatrix winked at the screen.

"This has been Willatrix Oleander, and I fully endorse the use of punitive lions. Thank you for your attention."

***

*"This has been Willatrix Oleander,"* the vlogger said on Otto's laptop screen, *"and I fully endorse the use of punitive lions. Thank you for your attention."*

"Asinine!" Otto said, sweeping the laptop off his desk. "The world is mad!"

***

*"I fully endorse the use of punitive lions."*

"I fecking did it," Piper said faintly. "For nothing."

***

*"Punitive lions."*

"Why won't you just leave me alone!" Lola screamed at Willatrix's face on the computer screen.

***

*"Thank you for your attention."*

"We were so close," Flossie said, hoarse from emotion as Willatrix's vlog phased out on her phone.

Girard groaned with empathy as he wrapped his arms around Flossie from behind, inhuming his face in her hair. "I've got you."

*\*\**

"It wasn't a dream," Clarity said to her fern for the thirty-seventh consecutive time. Her head was battering with worrisome, intermittent flutters. "There's a lion out there, Fern. A li... literal lion. I wanted to stay in my apartment forever, but I never meant to..."

Clarity jolted when her cell phone rang.

"H... hello?" she said, answering.

"Clarity Trout!" Daryl De Voort chimed with annoying enthusiasm on the phone. "Did you hear about the lion?"

"Everybody... has."

"Get this," Daryl practically sang. "The lion has made international news! I could kiss you!"

"I... I didn't..."

"Don't be so modest," laughed Daryl who was high on avarice and lack of sleep. "This is all because of YOU!"

"M... me? I didn't sic a lion on my own p... people."

"No, that was the inspired craft of our elected leader," De Voort said with a smile in his voice. "But you set the ball rolling. You manufactured fear. Hate. Hunger for revenge! I thought this concept would fizzle out after a few weeks, but you've managed to let this thing go barreling towards a veritable apocalypse! You are the best thing that's ever happened to me, Clarity Trout!"

"I... didn't mean to..." Clarity stammered, noticing another call beeping in from her dad. "Can... we wrap this up? My da..."

"How's this for a hook?" Daryl said obliviously. *"Four Horsemen Sighted Among the Hamster Balls: Could the Arachnophobic Presbyterians Be Responsible for the End of Days?"*

"My da..."

"Horsemen. Ha! I astonish myself sometimes."

"I need to take another call."

"And while we're riding this wave, fortune has favored us once again!"

"Oh no."

"Tristan Winnings is calling a flash election."

"Crap."

"Can you cover the election too? Winnings said if we convince the majority of Umbravia to pledge their loyalty to him, he'll quintuple our funding. You up for it?"

"Why is he..."

"Winnings wants to cash in on resentment people feel towards the Presbyterians, since the lion is all their fault. Also, he figures if he waits out his term, way too many people will be mad at him, which is fair."

"I should go."

"I'm not finished talking to you."

"My da…"

"…can wait. I, on the other hand, have been known to become impatient on occasion."

Clarity's head swam in nauseated loops. "Give me a minute," she said hastily before hanging up.

"Clarity Tr…"

Clarity noticed that her father was no longer on the other line, but he did leave a message.

"Clare Bear?" Torrence's staticky voice said. "Didn't want to do this in a phone message but here goes. I guess um… I guess I've hit the end of the road. I just wanted to say that I love you and that what happens next is not your fault."

"DA!"

The message continued. "They took everything, Clare Bear. I lost the Mitsubishi. Couldn't make payments. I've been squatting in an abandoned ticket booth outside the old, boarded up cinema. It's so cold. Been burning my socks just to keep warm. Had to surrender the dog. I can't eat moss forever. So I guess this is it…"

"DA, NO!"

"Goodbye, Clare Bear," the message continued. "I didn't want it to end this way. I love you so much, and I don't want to hurt you, but… I just can't anymore, baby girl. Please try to understand. I will always love you more than anything. So… Goodbye."

"NO! DA! PLEASE NO!"

Clarity breathlessly tried to call Torrence but kept getting a busy signal. She tried again and again, but to no avail. She groped clumps of hair in her fist, screeching hysterically. Torrence was the only person on the planet who understood her, who loved her, who she fully and unconditionally adored in return. Maybe it was too late, but there's always hope, right? There just had to be.

There was only one thing Clarity could do.

# CHAPTER SIXTY-FOUR
## (SHORTLY AFTER)

By the time Clarity panted breathlessly to the roof of the block tower, her windpipe tasted bloody, and her knees were buckling in surrender. She scanned her surroundings and found the music equipment Piper left behind in her haste. She fidgeted with the microphone, tapping it with her palm, hoping she could bring it to life. Clarity squeezed her eyes shut when she heard the lion snarl from the street below.

Gasping for breath, she cranked up the amp and tried the microphone.

"H...hello," Clarity said, startled by her reverberating voice, the sound rippling through the air. "Clarity. Me. I'm Clarity."

One by one, windows and balcony doors began to open. Eyes, some curious, some apprehensive, some critical and some baffled, goggled at Clarity from the safety of their flats.

"P...please don't hate me," Clarity swallowed, waiting for the echo of her voice to dissipate before she continued. "I wrote the article. The one that said, *"It's Coming."*"

Confused murmurings emerged from the apartments.

"I didn't mean it," Clarity said, her bulging eyeballs pleading for mercy. "I just wanted... it doesn't really m... matter what I wanted. I broke the world. And I'm... sorry."

Commotion stirred. One voice bellowed something threatening while Clarity cowered.

"The good news is," Clarity said in a strangled voice. "everything is going to be okay. You're safe. You don't have to hide anymore."

"Liar!" someone screamed.

"I am," Clarity said, her voice cracking with remorse. "I lied. But you've got to believe me. It's okay now..."

"It's a trap!" bellowed another person who angrily threw a glass bottle from their balcony, causing it to smash earsplittingly on the pavement. "Don't listen to her! She's one of them!"

"I never meant for this to get so out of control!" Clarity said, squeezing her eyes shut. "I just wanted what most of you want. To... to feel normal. To feel safe. Useful. Respected. I wanted to fit in somehow, you know? Make a difference? But also never leave my apartment... it's complicated.    So    when    there    was    a    big misunderstanding with my editor... and I was too scared to say no... I sort of..."

More people appeared on balconies, crossing their arms. A staccato of swears, threats, accusations and confused barbs echoed into the air.

"I'm not a bad person!" Clarity insisted urgently. "I made a mistake. I got sucked in so fast and before I knew it, everything just... just exploded. I felt like I had no choice, but I should have pushed back months ago before it got this bad."

"Is that the quiet girl from upstairs?" Flossie asked Girard, pulling her cable knit sweater more tightly around herself on the balcony.

"I've hurt my friends," Clarity gulped. "I mean, I don't really have friends, but there's plenty of people in my tower block who I respect and admire. They were nice to me, even though... My da. I hurt my da real bad. His name is Torrence Trout. He's having some dark thoughts right now, but I know he's still alive. I can feel it somehow. Please, if you know anyone in Cornish, Knackerton, Da is squatting in the ticket booth at *The Roxy*. At the corner of Douglas and Lackluster. He needs a blanket and food, so he doesn't have to eat moss."

"She's mad!" someone screamed. "Clearly there's something wrong with her!"

"Please!" Clarity pleaded. "I know this is hard to wrap your brain around, g... given everything that's h... happened... But please..."

"Is this thing on?" said B.P. Deerlight as her stunned face suddenly appeared on the marquee.

The confused stirrings of the people lulled to a perplexed silence.

Clarity let out a gaspy whimper as she beheld Dr. Deerlight on the giant screen.

Staring blankly ahead on the marquee, B.P. continued. "This is Dr. B.P. Deerlight, Chief Situational Officer of Umbravia."

Groans oozed through the city.

"I would like to shed some perspective on the current situation." B.P. continued monotonically. "In my professional opinion and based on over a decade of research, heinous hellions from alternate dimensions are quite relentless and disagreeable when they first breach the metaphysical barrier, mainly because they are confused and disoriented. Thus, the hellion will go into survival mode, exhibiting acute, defensive behavior to protect itself and maintain dominance. This phase is intense, but short-lived."

Several people stopped paying attention, while others heckled B.P. from the safety of their balconies.

"Over time," B.P. continued without inflection, "the hellion learns to co-exist with beings in our dimension, and we learn to co-exist with it. The hellion may linger in the air indefinitely, but once it's used to us, it gets more comfortable and less aggressive. Through the lens of science, if there were a heinous hellion among us, it would no longer be in self-preservation mode. The hellion has had more than enough time to acclimate. There is currently no reason to freak out. Please carry on as per usual."

Confused and bitter mutterings lingered in the air.

"Based on the number of satirical cartoons donning my likeness," B.P. sighed, "I'm thinking you all regard me as an imbecile. My messaging has been mixed and confusing. I've yacked on my own words, made no sense. I've talked in circles, regurgitated political talking points, and droned on about things that not even I understand. In my defense, I have more degrees than a balmy summer in Tampa. I'm arguably the smartest person in this country, regardless of what you all might think of me. I wanted to offer you my perspective months ago, but I was muzzled, at times literally. I decided to come clean, at the risk of sabotaging my own career and reputation because... Well, *because.*"

Clarity swallowed hard, watching in utter shock from the roof.

"You can formally quote me," B.P. said awkwardly. 'I do not endorse the use of punitive lions. Okay, bye," she said quickly, scrambling to shut off the camera and disappearing from the marquee.

From the roof of the tower block, Clarity recoiled when a deafening buzzer blasted from seemingly nowhere. While everyone covered their ears from their balconies, the door of a large cage in the street spontaneously slid open, luring Augustine inside with a slab of raw venison. The cage door slammed closed, trapping the lion inside.

***

Tristan's eyes were sleek with tears as he watched the television screen, dumbfounded, as B.P. renounced her endorsement of punitive lions. He shuddered at the sound of the buzzer and subsequent slam of the cage. He yipped when he felt the hand of Biff on his shoulder.

"I'm so sorry, Tristan," Biff gurgled breathily.

"It's all just…" Tristan sniffed. "… slipping away."

"If it means anything," Biff offered, "I still hold you in very high regard. I mean, the whole lion thing nearly made me pee my pants, but who among us is without fault? I think you're pretty stinking swell."

"No," Tristan said, almost inaudibly.

"Aw don't say things like that," Biff said, chummily slapping Tristan on the back.

"I guess it's time," Tristan squeaked vulnerably.

"Time?"

"To press the orange button," Tristan nodded.

"What…" Biff asked, his eyes widening with apprehension when Tristan pulled a compact electronic device from his pants, upon which was a conspicuous, orange button, "… is the orange button for, Tristan?"

"Trust me," Tristan said, biting his lip with uncertainty.

Biff blanched. "Tristan," he said in a voice that sounded like a petrified soprano," what is the orange button f…"

Tristan pressed the orange button.

# CHAPTER SIXTY-FIVE
## (AND THEN...)

Immediately after Tristan pressed the orange button, a blaring buzzer sounded, followed by an omnipotent Tristan voice amplifying through the air, seemingly disembodied.

*"It's over. Be normal again. You're welcome. It's over. Be normal again. You're welcome. It's over. Be normal again. You're welcome."*

The words on the marquee suddenly changed to, ***Please carry on.***

\*\*\*

Girard and Flossie looked at each other, mouths agape.

"Are we…"

"I think so."

\*\*\*

Norman did a somersault of joy. He pranced around the room, punching the air in an ecstatic victory dance, kissing each of his pillow friends and caterwauling boisterously out the window.

*"Yee haw!"*

\*\*\*

"Motherf…" Willatrix swore as she smashed her computer against the wall.

\*\*\*

Pax joyfully ran up and down the halls of the block, pounding on everyone's door, urging each of them to come out. Some people hugged him emotionally, some uttered freedom cries as they made a break for it, while others slammed the door in his face.

\*\*\*

"What's happening, Mummy?"

"The monster's gone," Lola sobbed with uninhibited joy as she collected her confused children in her arms. "He's all gone."

\*\*\*

Yowling with angst and dread, Ezekiel was violently regurgitated out of the metaphysical portal.

\*\*\*

Otto and Piper's doors opened at the same time.

They stood for a moment.

Gawking.

Unsure what to do.

After a pause that dripped with syrupy emotion...

"Come at me, Bruh," Otto said scratchily, feebly lifting his arms.

Piper suddenly burst from her flat and ambushed Otto with a hug that was visceral, potent, electric, squeezing him as though letting go would cause her to stop breathing. Otto's hands clamped desperately to Piper's back as she sobbed breathlessly into his chest. He smothered his face into her hair and cackled something that couldn't decide if it was a laugh or a cry.

\*\*\*

"Felix," Mally said awkwardly when Felix suddenly appeared at her door.

"Can I come in?" Felix asked sheepishly.

Mally half-shrugged.

"I just wanted to say…" Felix tried.

"You don't have to."

"I told Olga to leave. For good."

Mally forgot to exhale.

"I was scared, Mal," Felix persisted. "I never should have…"

"Felix…"

"I was such an idiot."

Mally looked away.

"I miss you so much, Mally."

"I…"

"The room feels wrong without you in it," Felix pleaded. "Nothing excites me anymore. Without you, life is just… mayonnaise."

Mally bit her lip.

"I…" Felix said hopefully. "I just thought now that things are back to normal…"

"Back to normal?"

"I know a lot has happened," Felix said, reddening. "I was such a basket case, I basically lost my ability to reason. What I'm trying to say is that you didn't deserve…"

Mally scuffed the toe of her shoe.

"I was just hoping that maybe… I don't know."

Mally raised an eyebrow.

"Do you think we can take the wall down?" Felix said bashfully. "Can I come… home?"

Mally wrenched her face. "I love you, Felix."

"Me too! I love you too!"

"I guess I'll always love you. But…"

"But?" Felix deflated.

"Things have happened."

"Yes, I know. I referenced that."

"Do you really think things would ever be the same between us? After everything you…"

"I think so?"

"Felix, I don't think you realize how much you… See, there's been a major breach of trust. There will always be this *thing* between us now. Wall or no wall we can't…"

"Like, I can make it up to you. I'll try so hard…"

"Felix, this feels weird."

"Could we just agree on some kind of amnesty or…"

"What?"

"I thought you were a forgiving person."

"That's not fair."

"I've apologized like a million times! What more do you want me to do? Just tell me what I need to do. What do you want?"

"I want things to be like they were before."

"Me too!"

"But that's just not possible."

"Mally, I'm literally begging…"

"All I'm saying is," Mally swallowed, "a lot's been broken this past year. And some of those things… just can't be fixed. Do you understand?"

Felix nodded, somewhat like an agitated bearded dragon as he chewed his cheek. "So this is it."

"This is it," Mally repeated smally.

Disgraced, Felix bowed away, retreating to his flat.

Mally closed her door, slid her back down the wall until she was curled into a nugget of grief on the floor. She cried.

\*\*\*

This could have plausibly been the most awkward Skype call in the history of technology. Clarity sat sullenly by the screen, unable to make eye contact. Torrence was warming by a fireplace in an unfamiliar living room. While Clarity was relieved that her father was alive and recovering, her stomach still knotted and contorted with guilt. Torrence knew everything now. He lost everything that mattered to him because of her stupid delusions of being a journalist. It all seemed so frivolous now.

"I'm proud of you, ya know," Torrence finally said.

Clarity burst into tears.

"Hey now," Torrence urged, touching the screen. "I know how much gumption it took to get up there on that roof."

"I ruined your life," Clarity sobbed, her face soaked with tears and snot. "You nearly…"

"I didn't," Torrence interrupted, holding up a hand of finality. "You did the right thing sending out a distress signal. An old friend found me at *The Roxy.*"

A pair of hands brought Torrence a tray of peppermint tea. The hands were attached to a female whose eyes crinkled with kindness. Torrence mouthed *thank you* to the lady and squeezed her hand affectionately.

"But I'm..." Clarity sniffled, "the reason you lost everything."

"Not *everything.*"

"This is all my fault."

"It could have happened to anyone."

Clarity tilted her head in disbelief.

"Clarity, don't you ever feel bad about following your dreams."

"But..."

"None of this was your fault," Torrence reiterated. "You didn't do any of this."

"But I wrote..."

"As far as I'm concerned, they took advantage of my little girl," Torrence said, pointing at the screen. "They didn't have to react the way they did. They just used you."

"But I could have stopped it."

"How?"

"I could have said something. I could have gone public…"

"Would they have believed you?" Torrence said with rising eyebrows. "There's a system out there that's a whole lot bigger than you, Clare Bear. That's why I never liked the idea of you going to that big, heartless city. But then, maybe I should have tried a little harder to prepare you. I guess I just hoped you'd never leave me."

"Oh Da…"

"I love you, Clare Bear."

"What about the farm? And the house? And the mushrooms and the dog and the car…"

"You listen to me," Torrence said, leaning into the screen. "They can suck you dry and take everything, but they don't have access to what's *in here.*" He pounded his chest with his palm.

Clarity swallowed. "I think I might come to visit. Would that be okay with you, Da?"

"Nothing would make me happier," Torrence beamed with his pinkish face, winking at his lady companion who was knitting blissfully beside him. "But maybe give me a few days to settle in first."

Clarity face morphed into an awkward contortion. It might have been a smile.

# EPILOGUE

"I can't look," Tristan said, covering his face with his hands. "Give it to me straight, Biff."

Clacking the keys of his computer, Biff conjured the results of the flash election. "Well then," he said. "What's important is that you did your best."

"Biff," Tristan moaned. "Just rip off the Band-Aid. What's the number?"

Biff swallowed. "Three."

"I only got three seats?"

"Three votes."

"Three v... *What?*"

"That's what it says."

"How did this happen?"

"Everyone liked the other guy?"

"That's impossible!" Tristan squeaked. "I told them not to do that!"

"Unfortunately, your opponent has a sharp sense of irony."

"Irony," Tristan winced. "That's not even fair."

"To boot, he's whip smart and very good at debates."

"That's enough, Biff."

"And he's..."

*"That's enough, Biff."*

"You asked me how this could happen, so I was just..."

"What, do you like him better?"

"No! I was one of the three votes!"

"So was I."

"I wonder who the other guy was?" Biff pondered dreamily.

"This is demoralizing," Tristan groaned.

"Please don't feel bad," Biff pleaded.

Tristan tilted his head. "Three people voted for me."

"That doesn't mean you're..."

"I'm a terrible person."

"You're not."

"In case you haven't noticed Biff, a whole lot of people hate me right now."

"I don't," Biff said, protruding his lower lip.

"Why not?" Tristan said, shoving Biff aside. "According to a poll in GQ, I was voted *The Biggest Disappointment in Modern History.* Why do you insist on liking me, regardless of how many times I screw up?"

"Because I know you're better than this!" Biff said, practically in tears. "I know you're a decent fella underneath all that hair product. I know this because you lisp whenever you lie, and you always look a little sad when nobody compliments your outfit."

Tristan pursed his lips.

"I think you're just a guy who wants to be loved," Biff shrugged. "You want it so bad, you go to desperate lengths to make people love you, even if it means making them hate you."

Tristan blinked hard.

"I believe in you, Tristan," Biff said evenly. "You may not take that seriously, but it is what it is."

"You do?" Tristan asked, reddening bashfully.

"I truly do," Biff smiled. "You've made some mistakes, but you can learn from them. Start a new chapter. Take your career in a much... *much* different direction."

"Really," Tristan said thoughtfully.

"I will support whatever path... whatever *vastly* different path you choose to take Tristan, so long as you follow your heart."

Tristan mused. "The Squirmish Isles. That's the nation that's held on to their ancient traditions, no? A little behind with the times?"

"Progress isn't their favorite. I hear the beaches are nice though. There's porpoises."

"Right, right," Tristan pondered. "Are they considered a kingdom or a principality?"

"There's an interim king, I think?"

"Interim."

"There's no rightful heir at the moment, so they picked a placeholder until they figure things out. I read an article."

"So there's no actual king yet."

Biff paused warily. "Not at this precise moment... why?"

"Come on Biff," Tristan said, yanking Biff by the arm. "We're going to the Squirmish Isles!"

# ACKNOWLEDGMENTS

They say it takes a village to write a book... Okay, I made that up. But this novel was a beast to write, and I could not have pulled this off without the help, encouragement, and inspiration from this impossibly long laundry list of people.

Roman, I never would have found the courage to tell this story had it not been for your compassion, integrity, perseverance, gallantry, and unwavering support for those who have no voice. Thank you for making sure that everyone's story has a platform. You are an inspiration.

Thanks to Annelid Press and the literary services of Bright Lemon Life. Thanks also to the brilliant graphic artist Graham Kennedy for the stunning cover art.

Special thanks to Dan for supporting all my eccentricities, Rosie for making hugs cool again, AFM for the enthusiastic publicity, Danielle for being the unofficial *Patron Saint of Feral Kittens,* Jeff Barkley for being a creative genius I can look up to, Joey Ramone for being *against it,* and Bono for reminding us that *'everything we know is wrong.'*

Eternal gratitude to K for giving me perspective, insight, inspiration, comfort, gentle guidance, friendship, and trust. I hope I have made you proud.

Thanks be to George Orwell, Christopher Marlowe, Rene Girard, George Feydeau, PG Wodehouse, Professor Derek Cohen, Professor Deanne Williams, Dali, Kerrie, Tammy, Lisa, Zoe, Norman, all of my cats, all of the cats who are not mine, Freddie Mercury for liking cats, the entire cast of Monty Python, Dad, Pierre, Pierre and the other Pierre. (I know a lot of Pierres)

Last and certainly... last, I would like to thank mainstream media for your dodgy morals, and political elitists everywhere for being idiots. Thanks to you, this book basically wrote itself and would not be nearly as hilarious had you practiced basic, human decency. You are an inspiration to me and satirists around the globe. Please accept my humble and heartfelt thanks.

# LOGGED IN

## A Laugh Out Loud Romantic Comedy!

**Allison McWood**

# LOVESICK LAKE

## A Darkish Romantic Farce

## Allison McWood

**Allison McWood** is an acclaimed, multi-published Canadian author, playwright and lyricist. Specializing in comedy, farce and satire, Allison's novels, plays, musicals and children's books all feature her signature quirkiness. Her writing has not only charmed readers and audiences across Canada, but her works have also been taught at Universities around the world from Vancouver to Lucknow, India. Holding a specialized Literature/Renaissance Drama degree from Toronto's York University, Allison is also a Shakespearean dramaturge, and Marlovian scholar.

When she is not writing, you can either find Allison in her red canoe, reading way too many books, playing air guitar, petting all the dogs or sipping cappuccino in a cute cafe.

www.instagram.com/annelidpress/

www.ingramcontent.com/pod-product-compliance
Lightning Source LLC
Chambersburg PA
CBHW021127260626
47169CB00005B/1483